After

Elias

After
Elias

a novel

Eddy
Boudel
Tan

DUNDURN
TORONTO

All characters in this work are fictitious. Any resemblance to real persons, living or dead, is purely coincidental.

Publisher: Scott Fraser | Acquiring editor: Rachel Spence | Editor: Allison Hirst
Cover designer: Sophie Paas-Lang
Cover image: unsplash.com/Coral Ouellette

Printer: Marquis Book Printing Inc.

Library and Archives Canada Cataloguing in Publication
Title: After Elias / Eddy Boudel Tan.
Names: Boudel Tan, Eddy, 1983- author.
Identifiers: Canadiana (print) 20190227370 | Canadiana (ebook) 20190227389 | ISBN
    9781459746428 (softcover) | ISBN 9781459746435 (PDF) | ISBN 9781459746442 (EPUB)
Classification: LCC PS8603.O9324 A64 2020 | DDC C813/.6—dc23

We acknowledge the support of the Canada Council for the Arts and the Ontario Arts Council for our publishing program. We also acknowledge the financial support of the Government of Ontario, through the Ontario Book Publishing Tax Credit and Ontario Creates, and the Government of Canada.

Care has been taken to trace the ownership of copyright material used in this book. The author and the publisher welcome any information enabling them to rectify any references or credits in subsequent editions.

The publisher is not responsible for websites or their content unless they are owned by the publisher.

Printed and bound in Canada.

VISIT US AT

 dundurn.com | @dundurnpress |  dundurnpress | dundurnpress

Dundurn
3 Church Street, Suite 500
Toronto, Ontario, Canada
M5E 1M2

To Thomas,
for proving to me that love is real and courageous and ours

I used to call the shadow my old friend. It seemed less frightening that way. I would say it with a wry smile, but nobody else would find it funny.

It has been such a long time since the shadow last came around. "I think I've been defriended," I once said to Elias. He just looked at me, unamused.

I suppose I've been too busy with the wedding arrangements to think much about the shadow. It doesn't like to be forgotten though. It always lingers nearby. As I arrived at the hotel yesterday, I should have predicted that the shadow would make an appearance. After all, it is an old friend.

The Terrace Bar is different today. I feel it as soon as I step inside. Something foreign in the air greets me like a scent I can't quite place. It's darker here than in the rest of the hotel. It struck me as odd when I first saw it yesterday, this gloomy cavern hidden within a palace of light.

My eyes adjust and all I see are flowers. They're an unnatural shade of yellow, worn by a woman softened with age, her skin like an overripe plum. She's seated alone at a table and stares straight ahead, motionless. The sadness on her face is even more unnerving against the yellow flowers of the dress hanging limply on her.

A few other guests sit at tables scattered throughout the room. Like the woman in the floral dress, their stares are fixed on something in front of them.

The bartender stands behind the long countertop to my left, framed by a wall of glass bottles. He greeted me with such warmth yesterday. Every smile he gave felt earned, inviting my confidence whenever he leaned forward or held eye contact longer than what I'd usually find comfortable. Now his arms are crossed over his chest, his eyes narrowed. A dishtowel lies forgotten over one shoulder. He's staring in the same direction as everyone else in the dim room, his head tilted upward as though listening to god.

Following their gaze, I see it's something ordinary: a television set mounted on the wall behind the bar's counter. I can't quite tell what they're watching, but it looks like the ocean. The waves are more grey than blue, churning across the screen with lashes of foam.

Why is everyone so interested in this?

Several jagged objects come into view. They rock along with the rhythm of the waves, the red paint bold against the coldness of the sea. Their shapes lack symmetry.

Are they little boats?

A woman appears on the screen. She's dressed inoffensively in neutral tones and crisp lines. Her delicate hands are placed on the surface of a lacquered desk. I hear her voice but don't hear the words.

My body begins to shiver like a taut wire as my phone vibrates in my pocket. I don't reach for it, like I normally would. It goes off again. And again. I just let it continue its inaudible cry, a silent alarm bell. But I don't need to read the messages or answer the calls. I know what has happened, why everyone at home suddenly feels the need to get hold of me. I know what everyone in the room is seeing on the television, what those floating objects are. I know, because I've always known this would happen one day. Today is that day.

The shadow comes to me.

I recognize it immediately, even though it has been so long.

It cloaks itself around my body. I feel its touch, a sickening static. A familiar numbness washes over me.

It seeps into my skin. The pricking begins softly before it gets sharper, quicker. A thousand stabbing needles.

It whispers in my ears. A deadening hum surrounds me.

Hello, old friend.

Invisible hands wrap around my throat.

I can't breathe.

I can't move.

If I had been paying closer attention earlier, I might have seen it in the periphery of my vision, felt its touch against the tips of my fingers. It was so close.

I don't know how long I stand there before my legs can move again. They march me out of the dim room, and I stumble through the hall. The light sears my retinas. The sound of my shoes on the cold floor becomes louder with every step as the hum subsides. I find my suite, the door emblazoned with numbers polished so well I can see my reflection in them. My hand shakes as it fumbles in my pocket for the key.

I throw myself into the room and slam the door shut behind me. I pull the curtains closed and switch on the television above the dresser.

This must be a mistake.

The unholy messenger in the neutral tones stares back at me, though she seems less benign. There is an emptiness in her eyes as her lips move. I can understand her words now.

Flight XI260 was on its way to Vancouver from Berlin when it crashed into the Arctic Ocean one hour ago. There were 314 passengers on board, including fifteen crew members, one relief pilot, one captain, and one co-pilot.

A face appears, and I know it so well. The square chin and uneven lips that make him look more arrogant than he is. The arrowhead slope of his nose, something he's always been self-conscious of.

Most striking of all, the darkness of his irises. Almost black, they reflect the light as tiny white orbs — two satellites in the night sky.

He's the man I'm supposed to marry in seven days, this co-pilot.

His name is Elias.

Part One

The Pilot and
the Botanist

SUITE 319

Nine hours after the crash

I was nine years old when I discovered that I wasn't afraid of death.

The heat of the sun on my bare shoulders and the chill of the wet concrete under my feet was a troubling combination for me that day.

The other children, all wild eyes and unpredictable limbs, howled like apes around a watering hole. They bared their teeth as they chased each other. They banded together to lay claim to their territories. I was careful to stay out of the path of the other boys, my eyes averted from theirs and my fists clenched by my side.

It was a relief to pull my head beneath the surface of the water. The noise from above became a muffled hum. The sting of the sun softened. I felt the grip on my mind loosen as I submerged myself in stillness.

My senses awoke as another body collided into mine. My feet stretched down toward the bottom, expecting to feel the reassurance of its tiles. There was only empty space.

My hands reached up and grabbed fistfuls of water. I managed to reach the surface for a gasp of air before I was pulled underneath again by an invisible hand. Every kick of my legs and stroke of my arms reeled me farther down. I held my breath for as long as I could, then let it all out in a swarm of bubbles. My limbs went still as I closed my eyes.

I didn't feel fear. I felt a deep and wonderful calm. *I wonder what happens now*, I remember thinking.

My breath returned in violent coughs and purged chlorine as I lay on the wet concrete of the pool's edge. There was a look of wonder in the eyes that stared down at me, as though I had risen from the dead. The first thought that came to me was I must have been Aztec.

Come to think of it now, I'd always been a different kind of boy.

You see, the Aztecs didn't fear death. They believed it was glorious. Death perpetuated creation. Without it, there would be no life. Their bones were the seeds from which new life grew. Their blood watered the dry earth. Both humans and gods sacrificed their lives so this wheel of conclusion and creation would spin on and on.

After the final breath, Aztecs travelled to one of three places. Those with honourable endings, like warriors dying in battle, would transform into hummingbirds to follow the sun. Those who met their end by water would find themselves in a paradise of eternal spring. The majority would not be so lucky. Their journey would take them to the underworld of Mictlan, a hellish place guarded by jaguars in a river of blood.

Reading about this as a boy, it seemed unfair to me how the most terrible human beings could so easily escape an eternity of bloody jaguars. Had things ended differently that summer day at the pool, I would have found myself in paradise by simply drifting too far into the deep end. However flawed it may be, it's a beguiling idea. Your life is irrelevant. Your death is what counts.

. . . . .

A falling sensation grips me before my eyelids whip open, my chest heaving. The sheets stick to my skin. I'm slick with sweat.

It was just a dream.

Everything that happened over the last twenty-four hours was only a terrible, cruel dream.

I'm in my bedroom at home. Elias is asleep beside me. I can smell him on the sheets, hear the gentle sway of his breath.

The dull pain in my chest tells me this isn't true. This isn't my bed. I'm alone.

The clock on the bedside table claims it has been nine hours since I learned Elias had flown into the sea.

I often felt detached from him. He spent his days soaring through the sky from destination to destination while I remained fixed like a bolt in the ground. I would lie alone in bed and wonder where he was in the world. I found comfort imagining his heart beating in the cockpit of a plane, a red light blinking as it travelled across a map. I don't have to wonder anymore. I know where he is, despite the light being out.

Sitting up, I notice how tidy my room is. One might expect I would have torn it apart in grief — overturned the furniture, perhaps punched the mirror until the floor was covered in a thousand shards and my fist was bloody. But even in the soft light, I can see the room is in perfect order. No thrown chairs. No broken glass. My suitcase sits neatly at the foot of the bed. A few articles of clothing hang in the armoire. There is no evidence of grief in this room.

The curtains are tightly closed. The only light and sound come from the television set above the dresser. Instead of the news, a soccer match is in progress. The world outside this room has already moved on.

What happened nine hours earlier seems distant. I recall the yellow flowers and the fragments of red that clung to the surface of the sea. I can see the grim look on the bartender's face and the glare of the hallway lamps. I picture myself paralyzed in the middle of the Terrace Bar as eyes begin to turn toward me. My unsteady feet trace an erratic path through the hall, hands outstretched as I careen from wall to wall. I remember calling Elias's phone while pacing across the carpeted floor of my suite — our suite — desperate for an answer I knew wouldn't come, leaving messages I knew would never be heard. All of this seems cloudy now, as though they are memories that have had years to fade.

Elias's face is the one thing that pierces the fog, the white orbs in his dark eyes sending signals to me from the other side of the screen.

"Authorities have now confirmed that the pilots of flight XI260 were Captain Daniel Jervis and First Officer Elias Santos, both from Canada." The messenger delivered these words.

My body's defence was to sleep. I didn't cry or collapse. The shadow remained in hiding. There was nothing I could do. I crawled into bed as if it were an ordinary night. I let myself shut down.

Now, the soccer match plays on. Someone has just scored a goal. He runs into the open arms of his teammates. The crowd cheers rabidly.

The pain in my chest moans. I scan my memory to identify what it could be, but I know it is guilt. I chose the date of the wedding. I chose the venue. Here I am, safe on this island shielded from the rest of the world, while Elias lies adrift in the frigid waters of the Arctic. The Mexican sun burned forcefully earlier today, removing all doubt of who is to blame.

Death must be a spiteful witch. Perhaps this is my punishment for revoking our deal so many years ago at the swimming pool — one life in exchange for another. Death was patient. She waited until the moment was right.

My eyes are dry and unseeing as I turn away from the television. With a deep breath, I pick up my phone. Ninety-three unread messages. Forty-nine missed phone calls. The messages I scroll through are near-identical expressions of shock and disbelief and concern, more frantic in tone the more recent they are. My parents sent a single text message: "Call us now."

"You are a bad son," I can hear Elias say in his matter-of-fact way. "You are simply the worst, letting your parents worry about you like this. If I were your father, I would have disowned you long ago."

I smile. He's right. I am a bad son. I should probably respond to them and everyone else. Even the idea of doing so tires me profoundly.

"Did I ever tell you about the time my parents left me alone at home while they vacationed in the south of France?" I ask. "I was probably only ten years old."

"How dare they?" he says with exaggerated outrage.

"They were supposed to be away for a week but decided to extend their trip. They didn't even think to tell me. I panicked for days thinking that something awful had happened. I thought maybe they had been kidnapped. I pictured them being tortured by scary Frenchmen with terrible moustaches. I had no way of reaching them. My brother wouldn't let me call the police. Do you know what happened?"

"Please tell me," imaginary Elias says with an imaginary smirk.

"They came home, finally, three whole days after I was expecting them and just sauntered through the door without a care in the world. Do you know what they told me?"

"'You worry too much,'" Elias says. "Yes, dear, you've told me this one. Many times, in fact."

"I may not be son of the century, but they're not exactly a shining paradigm of parenthood."

"You do have a point." Elias was never particularly fond of my family. The feeling was mutual. "If I recall correctly, you're forgetting to mention that they told your brother their change in plans."

"Sure, but they didn't tell me. They might as well have been in on the joke. I wanted to hurt Clark so badly then. He couldn't stop laughing. There is no uglier sound in the world."

"You're too hard on him. He was just a young boy playing a joke on his little brother like any other boy would do."

"You really need to stop standing up for him."

There's a pause. "What are you going to do now?" he asks.

"I don't have a clue," I respond. It's true. I don't know what I'm supposed to do.

"You go home."

"I can't," I say more decisively than I expect. "I'm not ready to go back. Plus, there's no way I'm getting on a plane."

"So you're going to stay in Mexico and do what? Live off the land? Swim with the turtles?" He says this in that taunting tone I used to love but grew to hate.

"That actually doesn't sound like a bad idea. Anything is better than going home and dealing with this mess you've left."

I rub my temples in circular motions with the palms of my hands. "We're supposed to be married in a week. Everything is ready. Maria is a master. I couldn't have asked for a better wedding planner. She's managed to make it all happen. Seven-course dinner with seafood caught right here on this island. Custom mescal cocktails. Wines from Baja. She was even able to book that band from Mexico City. And the trees! The trees are in bloom. Just like she predicted they'd be. This event was going to be unforgettable."

I stare at the ceiling and imagine his face. I can't quite read the expression.

"Why did you have to work that last flight?" I say into the air. "I wanted us to come down here together. Why did you let me go alone?"

"It was only going to be a few days." His voice is gentler now. "You weren't going to be alone for long."

"You were wrong."

I feel the spite rise up my throat. I want to say something hurtful, but I swallow hard. "I'm going to stay right here. This island is paradise, don't you think? Besides, we've already paid for the wedding. I may as well enjoy it."

I push myself up from the bed and walk past the vanity mirror mounted above the desk. My bags have only been partially unpacked, but I had taken the time to wedge our wedding invitation where the mirror meets its frame. *Join us in paradise to celebrate the love of Coen Caraway & Elias Santos.* The text sits above an image of us holding each other, laughing, with the city shimmering in the distance. The photo was taken on the rooftop of our apartment building. We must have taken hundreds of variations of the same basic pose. Most of them were contrived, but I think we were genuinely laughing in this one that we chose. I can tell because of Elias's eyes. They're sparkling.

Then it comes to me. I have an idea. I wait for imaginary Elias to say something, to object.

Silence.

. . . . .

Vivian Lo was born into a distinguished family from Hong Kong. Her father owned some kind of business related to international trade. The "importing and exporting of capitalist greed" is how Vivi often put it. They immigrated to Vancouver in the 1990s, right before Hong Kong's future was handed over to China. I didn't understand what her father did for work, but I did know that he was rarely seen wearing anything but an impeccably tailored suit.

I met Vivi in high school when she was a peculiar girl who seemed to have no interest in people. We hit it off because I was equally awkward and we were both obsessed with photography at the time. We would spend hours in the dark room together, talking about the books we were reading while developing our negatives. Sometimes people would make jokes about the obscene things they imagined us doing in there until someone would remind them I was obviously queer.

At our high school reunion three years ago, everyone did a poor job of hiding their resentment for us and how we turned out. We circulated through the room with such ease, such confidence. We had evolved into everything we weren't as teenagers: attractive, charming, successful, while everyone else became so dull and suburban.

Now, Vivi looks tired and pale. I can tell she's been crying even through the grainy resolution of the video-chat window on my tablet's screen.

"I can't believe this is happening," she says for the fifth time. "It's a nightmare. This only happens in really shitty movies."

"Yeah," I agree. "This would be a really shitty movie."

"Come home," she pleads. "Get your skinny ass on a plane and come home right now."

"I've already told you I can't do that." I look at her as she looks at me. Her eyes are conspicuously free of eyeliner, and I remember how I'm the only person who gets the privilege of seeing her without it. "Even thinking about home makes me nauseous. I need to be here for a while."

"In Mexico? On a deserted island, all by yourself? You don't need to be there. You need to be here with me, with Decker, with everyone who loves you. We've been worried sick."

"This island is far from deserted. You don't have to worry about me. Besides, I'm going to see all of you soon." There's silence as I pause for a long inhale. "I have an idea."

She shoots me a strange look, her eyes locked on mine.

"I was thinking," I say more tentatively than I intend. "The wedding was supposed to be in a week, right? We've already paid for everything, and we're not getting the money back. The hotel is booked, as is the catering, the band, the staff ... Guests are supposed to start arriving in five days, and none of you will be able to refund your flights and rooms. Everything is set. Plus, I'm already here."

"No," she interrupts, shaking her head. "No, no, no, no, Coen. I don't like where this is going."

"I want everyone to come here as planned," I forge ahead, "except it won't be a wedding. It will be for Elias — a celebration of his life. Everyone who should be there is already confirmed to attend the wedding. And he's originally from Mexico. Imagine how beautiful that would be. It's perfect."

"It's not perfect, Coen. None of this is perfect. This is all the furthest fucking thing from perfect!" Vivi looks angry and almost ill. Her expression softens. She chooses her words carefully, alerting my defences. That's unlike her.

"Babe," she says gently. "I'm sorry. I'm just concerned. You have received some devastating news." Her slender fingers run through her hair, an angular helmet as black as carbon that ends just above her shoulders. She glances to the side before leaning forward. "You need to come home. You shouldn't be alone. Forget about the money. That's not important. What's important is for you to be here, with us, so we can figure this out together."

"I'm not going anywhere," I say in a tone I hope sounds immovable. "I'm not cancelling the wedding. You are all going to come to this beautiful island in five days, and we are going to celebrate Elias's life together. That's what he would want."

"Is it? Is that what he would want? They haven't even found him yet, Coen!" I can almost see Vivi's softness evaporate like steam. "He might still be alive for all we know. Elias would want you to be here with the rest of us, not alone on an island."

"I am not going anywhere," I say again, believing myself this time. "You can stay at home, or you can meet me here. That's your decision. If everyone thinks I'm crazy and nobody shows up, that's fine. But this celebration is happening, even if it's just me and my wedding planner and the jazz band."

"Fine," she says in surrender. "Then I'm heading to the airport. I'll be on the next flight out."

Her bloodshot eyes follow mine, and I can't remember the last time I saw her like this. She is usually so poised. Her face appears simultaneously younger and older than usual, something vulnerable and resigned settled within the lines of her skin.

I smile. "As much as I would love for you to be here with me right now, it's going to burn a hole through your wallet to change your flight at such short notice. Besides, I know you have that gig tomorrow. I'm not letting you cancel it on my account."

"Coen ..." she says, trailing off.

"I will see you in five days. You'll be here before you know it. Until then, I'll be fine. Don't worry about me, please. I'm a big boy."

I flash her the most masculine, grown-up expression I can muster, and I'm relieved to see her laugh.

"Take care of yourself, okay?" she says. "If you need anything, call me. It doesn't matter what time, day or night."

"I promise."

She strains a smile, her lips pulled tightly at the sides, but her eyes look like they're studying me, searching for something.

IONA BEACH
Two days before the crash

"I wish you could stay." I gave him a rueful look, as though I could change his mind with the power of my eyes.

It had been a warm afternoon in Vancouver, but the warmth seemed to vanish with the light. Now that the moonlight flickered along the waves that lapped at our feet, we shivered back into our jackets. Mexico felt so far away.

"I wish I could stay too," Elias said, his eyes lingering on the wool blanket we sat on as his hand traced circles in the sand. It seemed like he meant it, though I could never really tell with him. "But there's nothing I can do about it now. Just another few flights. Then it will be over."

"It feels wrong to be flying down to our wedding alone."

"You won't be alone for long."

"Maybe I should just wait for you to return from Germany." I winced, hearing how my voice brightened with hope. "We could fly down together."

He ran his palm along the surface of the sand, smoothing over the circles he'd drawn, and shifted closer to me. The calmness on his face was undisturbed, no trace of the impatience I had braced myself for.

"You said yourself that you want to be there early to make sure everything is set. You can help Maria with the preparations; enjoy some peace and quiet before the circus arrives. You could even work on tanning that milky body of yours."

He flashed me a mischievous grin before I wrestled him to the ground, playfully jabbing him in the ribs. He laughed as he counterattacked, pinning me to the beach with ease. We were more or less the same size, but there was never a contest when it came to strength. My legs started to ache, but I didn't care.

We stayed like that for a while, hearts beating and breath panting, covered in sand with the blanket twisted around us. The bottles of beer we'd brought were now scattered along the beach. I looked up at his silhouette, the moonlit sky behind him, and he kissed me gently. I noticed something different in his eyes, an unfamiliar expression. Then it was gone, and he collapsed on his back beside me.

"I'll get a tan as long as you get your hair cut before the wedding," I said. His heavy black mane was almost silver in the light, spilling from the edges of his forehead.

"Have I ever broken a promise?"

"I'm serious. Cut your hair."

"Don't worry," he said, his voice tinged with that patronizing tone he liked to use. "I'll be more handsome than I've ever been in my life. The women will faint at the sight of me. Some of the men will too. You will be blinded by my beauty."

"Don't disappoint me," I said, my lips curled up slightly at the sides.

A deep laugh rang quietly from his throat. "I wouldn't dare. I'm more concerned about this hotel of yours. Good luck to them, living up to your expectations."

"It'll be perfect."

"Nothing is ever perfect, dear."

The sound of the waves was closer as I turned to him. "The hotel, the event, you — it will all be perfect."

A soft smile broke through his uneven lips, but he didn't respond. He simply looked at me, like he often did, as I stared into the shining orbs in his dark eyes, waiting.

With an inhale, Elias turned his head to face the night. "What's it called again?"

"The Ōmeyōcān Hotel," I answered. His lips moved, silently repeating the name to himself. "There are thirteen heavens in Aztec mythology. Ōmeyōcān is the highest one. They're setting some pretty high expectations themselves with a name like that."

"I wonder what the Aztec gods think about a fancy resort branding itself as heaven."

"This place is flawless," I said. "I accept the risk of angering the gods."

I knew I'd be married at the Ōmeyōcān Hotel the moment I spotted it in a travel magazine last year. Surrounded by elaborate gardens, it resembles a Spanish conquistador's palace standing watch over an immaculate stretch of sand on the northern coast of Isla de Espejos, a remote island in the Gulf of Mexico. The curious combination of colonialism and indigenous mythology didn't strike me as troubling at the time.

The arches and columns that line the grand halls of the hotel surround a vast courtyard. One side opens to the beach and ocean beyond through an arched gateway framed by a cascade of bougainvillea. The opposite end of the courtyard sits beneath two sweeping baroque staircases that curve toward each other as they climb upward, meeting at a terrace that overlooks the shamelessly dramatic setting.

What had really caught my eye were the trees. The glossy pages of the magazine revealed large magnolia trees arranged evenly throughout the open-air space. Their sprawling branches were covered in flowers shaped like teacups, creating a canopy of pale pink and creamy white. Maria confessed it was an impractical choice considering they bloom for only a handful of weeks each year, but that was part of the allure. Beauty is more beautiful when it's fleeting.

"If I were a god, I'd know better than to mess with Coen Caraway on his perfect day." He nudged my ribs with his elbow, his lips pulled into a teasing smile.

"It doesn't seem real, does it?" I asked, trying to spot the stars hidden behind the haze from the city lights. "Marriage, in just a few days from now."

He chuckled. "I still wonder how we got here. I never imagined myself being married, especially so young."

"Thirty-three isn't that young," I said, returning his teasing smile.

"You're right," he admitted. "This never used to be part of the plan though, to be domesticated like a dog. I guess life happens quickly and people change. Now we're just like everyone else. Normal."

"That is so romantic," I replied with Elias-style sarcasm.

"You used to agree!"

"Sure, but I've never compared married people to dogs. Although Decker and Samantha do resemble a pair of well-groomed golden retrievers most of the time." We laughed at the visual. "So loyal and codependent and stupidly content."

"That will never be us," he said with conviction.

"No," I agreed. "But maybe it wouldn't be so bad."

"To be trained like a dog?" He looked at me with an incredulous grin.

"To be stupidly content. Perhaps people would be better off enjoying the good things and ignoring the rest."

"Sure," he said. "That's fine for you. I'm from Mexico. I'm not wired to think that way."

"It has nothing to do with where you come from."

"Of course it does," he said before I could go on, his tone more serious. "You're telling me that a girl from the slums has the same chance at happiness as someone like you? To be happy and oblivious is a privilege available to a very exclusive set of people."

I knew it was a path to avoid. I wasn't going to win this debate.

"I'm just trying to comment on the human race as a whole."

"There is no human race," he responded darkly. "The two people I described — the girl from the slums and you — might as well be different species."

"Does that make the two of us different species then?"

"Perhaps."

I took a deep breath. "Even so, look at us. We've managed to build a life together. In a few days, we'll be married. Why do it if not for a chance at happiness?"

"Because it's practical, and because we can." He turned his face away from mine and looked up at the darkness. "The concept of happiness is ambiguous. It has no meaning."

"That's the point. It's different for everyone. It gives people something to define for themselves, something to strive for. What's the point of living if not to be happy?"

He responded without hesitation. "To be free."

I suppose I knew this would be his answer, but it wasn't the answer I cared to hear. There were more questions I wanted to ask him then. They flashed through my mind but didn't make it out of my mouth.

I wondered how the mood had shifted so suddenly, as I often did. Elias was a prairie sky, switching from sunshine to storm clouds without warning. When the clouds arrived, there wasn't much to be done but wait for them to dissipate.

"I guess if we're going to succumb to the shackles of domestic life, at least we'll be doing it in style," I said as I felt my body stiffen.

He sensed the displeasure in my tone. "Come here," he said, placing his arm around my neck. "The only reason I want to be married is because I want you."

I relaxed into him. "I want you too."

"And you're right. We are going to do this in style. It will be unforgettable."

Elias always knew the right things to say, though he wouldn't always say them. His words were deliberate. They had intention. Even so, I loved him more when he told me what I wanted to hear.

"How does it feel to return to Mexico after all these years?" I asked, trying to sound nonchalant as I held my breath for his answer.

There was a pause. "I feel nothing," he said.

"What does that mean?"

"I feel nothing about it. It's been thirteen years since I left. I have no desire to go back, but there's no use avoiding it forever."

It had come as a surprise when Elias agreed to choosing Isla de Espejos for the wedding. I had been nervous about suggesting it. I gathered as much courage as I could before making my pitch, preparing myself for an argument. He just shrugged and complied. No objections. Nothing. It was so easy.

"You're not even the least bit excited? Nostalgic?" I asked, unconvinced.

He had heard these questions before, so I expected him to get annoyed. He answered coolly. "No. Not at all."

Another heavy pause followed. He was stretched out on his back, staring at the sky with his head close to mine. I decided to be bold.

"And your family? You're sure you don't want them there? We could still fit them in. The invitation would be a nice peace offering. It could bring some closure."

"I don't want them to be there," he said, his voice calm and decisive. "They're not my family anymore."

I offered him a sympathetic smile, but his eyes remained focused upward. I could feel him grow distant, as though he were being reeled into the sky.

A familiar roar broke the silence, and I remembered why we were there in the first place, why this had become one of our favourite spots over the years. I looked across the river at the twinkling lights of the airport as a jet took off toward us, its wheels drifting off the pavement with forceful grace. It sliced through the night sky, navigation lights blinking, before veering south to Los Angeles or Bogotá or beyond. We were both sitting up then, watching the plane arc high above the city as it disappeared into the darkness. I glanced at Elias through the corner of my eye. He was smiling.

PLAZA PEQUEÑA
Thirty-two hours after the crash

I know I am in Vancouver before I open my eyes. The scent is undeniable — damp and wild. The air is steeped in cedar and sweat and ocean, then carried by the breeze to purify the grit of the city. This is home.

My eyelids flutter open, and I find myself in a familiar place. Beams from the sun above filter through a haze of muted pink. Everything is still except for the branches that sway in the breeze. Surrounding me on all sides are tall brick walls painted white, each with six rows of shuttered windows stacked on top of one another. The courtyard is home to magnolia trees that bloom for only a few weeks of the year.

Something lands by my side with a dull thud. The pages of the book are worn with age, the cover faded to the point that the title is barely legible. It feels heavy in my hand as I decipher the letters: *Peter Pan.*

"Hey — that's my book!" a voice declares, piercing the stillness and echoing against the walls. I follow the sound to see a figure waving from the rooftop, directly above me. My eyes squint, but I can't quite see what he looks like. "Hang on," he says. "I'm coming down."

"What are you doing on the roof?" I shout back, but there's no answer.

I hold the book with both hands, breathing in the scent of its pages. All I can smell are flowers.

A few minutes pass before he emerges from the gate with such command that it startles me. There's a noble quality in the way he carries himself. His eyes are as dark as his hair, but they reflect the light like two satellites in a starless sky.

"Nice choice," I say, handing him the book.

"One day I am going to fly," the man says. "Just like Peter."

. . . . .

With my eyes closed, I can almost fool myself into believing I am in that courtyard so many kilometres and years away. The softness of the breeze on my skin. The living scent of spring.

A noise outside my door breaks the spell. What sounds like a pack of hyenas is roaming the halls. I prop myself up in bed to see the dim confines of my room at the Ōmeyōcān Hotel.

My tablet sits beside me. There's something comforting in the bluish light of its screen as I power it on. The words I typed earlier appear in jagged lines of text.

Dear friends,

By now, you've probably heard the news about Elias.

Please do not cancel your plans. Join me here at the same place and on the same day as the wedding, which will now be a celebration of Elias's extraordinary life.

All I ask is that you wear what you were planning to wear to the wedding. This is not a funeral, so let's save the black for another day.

Thank you for the messages of concern. I am doing fine. This island truly is paradise. I can't wait to see you all when you arrive.

Safe travels,
Coen

I read the message three times before hitting send.

"'Extraordinary life'?" I hear Elias say. "Nice one."

"You don't approve?" I put the tablet away and stretch my limbs until my body covers every corner of the bed.

"I like it. I probably would have done without telling everyone what not to wear, but it is your party."

"It's not my party. It's yours," I reply to the ceiling. "In fact, it's not a party at all. It's a celebration of life — your life. I don't want it to be all doom and gloom. Do you?"

"I guess not," he says. "You should have given it a theme. Remember the party that Vivi hosted years ago? Where everyone had to wear an outfit made of anything but clothes? Now that would be fun."

"You looked pretty sexy in your pizza-box shorts," I say with a smile. Elias had worn two cardboard pizza boxes wrapped around his midsection, and not much else. "It was definitely a bigger hit than my toilet-paper suit."

"I thought you looked very handsome, like an adorable mummy. Your costume ended up being more provocative than mine as it unravelled throughout the night."

I cringe. "I was wearing the least flattering underwear. Anyway, I don't think that would be a very appropriate theme for your celebration. I certainly don't want to see what my parents would show up in."

"I could lend your father my pizza-box outfit," Elias says. I howl with laughter at the visual until tears are in my eyes. I imagine tears being in his eyes too.

. . . . .

Isla de Espejos is a croissant-shaped sweep of sand and stone that curves around a deep lagoon. On the eastern edge sits the main village, a cluster of cobblestone lanes lined with eateries and shops. A few open-air cantinas are scattered between buildings, with lights strung above picnic tables and fluorescent Tecate beer signs hung on the walls. The streets are busy with friendly locals going about their business and tourists taking photos. The place possesses a laid-back, breezy, tropical charm that has a way of slowing time.

All lanes in the village converge at a picturesque square called Plaza Pequeña. Soaring high above one end are the twin bell towers of the cathedral. Statues of the Virgin and her entourage of saints guard the baroque facade — they watch over the people below, a barrier between human and god. Balconies wrap around the bell towers, suspended high above the square. The pinnacle of each is capped with an ornate cross atop an onion-shaped dome.

A wide circular lawn stretches over the centre of the square. Stone paths divide the grass into quadrants where tropical trees provide respite from the scorching sun. Water spouts from an ornate fountain where the paths meet.

I take the short walk to the village and find the streets bustling with people. Plaza Pequeña transforms into a buzzy outdoor market every evening, and the sun has just dipped behind the fringe of trees to the west. The stalls lining the outer edges of the square sell things like handwoven blankets, wooden dishes, and plenty of local sweets. Children dart through the crowds of families and tourists. Packs of teenaged boys and girls display themselves to each other on the grass, taunting and flirting. Young men fill the cantinas, gesturing wildly with their hands as they recount tales of their conquests.

An elderly woman approaches. Our eyes meet, and it takes a second for me to remember why I recognize her. She's the sad woman in the bright floral dress from the Terrace Bar yesterday. She wears a similar dress tonight, this time blue with hibiscus. I give her a polite smile. She shoots me a disturbed look before diverting course, shuffling away from me as quickly as her old legs can take her.

After imprisoning myself in my room for nearly thirty-two hours, it feels good to breathe fresh air. I hadn't thought to open the balcony doors. I kept the curtains tightly closed, peeking outside periodically to confirm that the level of daylight matched the time on the bedside clock. Time seemed to move either too quickly or too slowly. I had one meal while I was in there, ordered through room service. It was placed in front of my door, as instructed, and I retrieved it when I was sure the hall was empty. The shiny cloche on the tray hid a bowl of diced papaya and mango, which I forced myself to eat.

It took every crumb of energy to shower, shave, and dress myself. My skin appeared paler than usual, the bags beneath my eyes heavier, but the rest of me looked normal. Chestnut hair tidily parted along the side. The tiny cleft in my chin and dimple in my cheek cursing my face with an excess of youth.

After twenty minutes of steady breathing, I was ready to walk out the door. The hallway lamps were blinding. I could feel eyes on me as I hurried through the lobby, even though I didn't dare look at anyone's face. Now I wonder if their expressions were similar to that of the old woman I just passed in the square.

I managed to ask the concierge where I could find Maria, my wedding planner, and he directed me to Plaza Pequeña. After completing a full lap around the market, I spot her petite figure by the fountain in the middle of the circular lawn. With her white linen dress and hair flowing loosely around her face, I almost don't recognize her at first. She looks like a more relaxed version of the professional woman in the navy pantsuit who greeted me two days ago. A girl of about eight stands close by her side.

As I get closer, I see they're lighting candles on the ledge of the fountain. Similar candles appear in corners across Mexico, encased in tall cylinders of glass and wrapped in images of holy figures. The locals call them veladoras.

Her face creases with compassion as she notices me approaching. The sadness in her eyes moves me. This is Maria, the mother.

"Señor Coen, how are you feeling?" She places both hands on my cheeks in the way only mothers do.

"I'm fine," I say, but my voice comes out like a croak. The feeble smile I attempt is even less convincing.

"You are strong," she tells me, staring into the depths of my eyes. It sounds like she believes it, at least more than I do. "But you are not fine, not after what has happened. You must let yourself mourn."

"I've never been through something like this before."

"Of course, of course," she says reassuringly. She takes my clammy hand and leads me to the fountain. The little girl studies me with curiosity. "There is no right or wrong way to mourn. It is different for everyone. Let your heart decide."

I don't know what this means, but I nod.

"This is my daughter, Jacinta." The girl smiles before turning away shyly. She's wearing a lace sundress the colour of canaries.

Maria says something to her in Spanish with that scolding tone loved by mothers around the world. Jacinta offers a little curtsy and very quietly says, "Buenas noches."

Looking pleased, Maria turns to me. "We are lighting candles for Señor Elias and those poor people on that plane. It is a tragedy. Life can be unfair."

Now that's an understatement.

"We must honour the dead and listen to what they have to teach us," she goes on. "Life is fragile, like an egg. This, I know, is true."

My head continues to nod mindlessly. I wonder how long she plans to hold my hand.

The ledge of the fountain is covered in candles housed in glass jars of all sizes. Many feature the Virgin. She wears a powder-blue cloak in some and robes of white in others. There are candles depicting Christ nailed to the cross or surrounded by beams of light. Flaming hearts wrapped in thorns and pierced by swords are a common symbol — the sacred heart. Together they flicker ominously, casting a glow against the water. It's beautiful.

I notice for the first time that the centrepiece at the top of the fountain, above the highest of the three tiered basins, is a small statue of the Virgin. Her hands are crossed demurely in front of her chest. Her stone eyes look down at me with a vacant gaze.

"Isn't she lovely?" Maria asks, following my eyes. Stevie Wonder's voice immediately fills the tunnels of my mind.

"She is."

"Our Lady of Guadalupe," she continues. "Mexico's mother. Ever since she appeared to a peasant on a hillside hundreds of years ago, not too far from here, she has been our patron saint. Our very own Virgin."

I smile at Maria, and I can tell by her satisfied reaction that it's more believable this time. She finally releases my hand.

"Tell me about your love. What was he like?"

The question catches me off guard. I wince hearing Maria say "was" instead of "is."

"Elias was perfect," I respond slowly. "Handsome. Strong. He was everything to me. I suppose he still is and probably always will be. We were very happy together."

I imagine his face, every detail sharp and vivid. I wonder if he cut his hair, like he promised he would.

"When do you leave for home?" she asks, taking a seat on an empty section of the fountain's ledge. I sit next to her as Jacinta continues lighting candles.

"That's what I want to talk to you about. I'm not going home. Not yet, at least. We're not cancelling the event."

A look of confusion tightens her face.

"It won't be a wedding, of course," I go on. "It will be a celebration of life instead, for Elias."

"Do you mean a wake?"

"Sure, kind of," I say, uncertain. "It's a chance for everyone who loved Elias to come together and remember his life, rather than mourn his death. Funerals back home can be so grim. I don't want that for him, and neither would he."

She doesn't seem convinced. "This is a lovely idea, but you should be home, no? If Señor Elias's home is Canada, and your loved ones are in Canada, then his life should be celebrated there, in your home, where he belongs."

"No." The word shoots past my lips. My fists clench in defiance. "We were supposed to be married six days from today. It was meant to be the happiest day of our lives. We chose to do that on this island, in your hotel. If this is good enough for our wedding day, it's good enough for his funeral — I mean, *celebration of life.* So that's what we're going to do. Our guests arrive in four days. We need to be sure this event is as perfect as our wedding would have been. Do you understand, Maria?" The words are sharper than I intend. With a deep breath, my tone softens. "I need your help."

She looks at me. Some of the motherly tenderness is no longer there. "I understand," she says, patting my hand with hers. "As you wish. It will be a beautiful ceremony."

"Thank you. Really, thank you, Maria."

She turns to the ledge beside her and picks up a tall candle, its glass jar displaying a golden-haired angel in flowing white robes. His dovelike wings spread outward in a burst of white feathers while beams of yellow light radiate around him.

"Take this," she says, putting the candle in my hand. "Those we have lost live on beyond this world. They come back to us as long as they are remembered. You must honour your love."

He looks nothing like Elias, I think as I stare at the angel's peaceful face. "How do I honour him?"

"You create an ofrenda — an altar — in your home," she says. "For now, the Ōmeyōcān is your home, so place this candle in your room in front of a photograph of your love. Then you must find offerings. Gather your love's favourite foods, as well as incense and fruit. Put them on the altar. Do you see that woman over there with the flowers? Buy some marigolds from her. Place them around the candle. The scent will guide him back to you from the afterlife."

My mouth opens to decline, but I remain silent as I look at the flames reflecting on the surface of the water.

"Now this is important. When you return home to Canada, build another altar for him there with the same offerings: candles, photograph, incense, food, and marigolds. Every year, on Día de Muertos, he will return to you, but only if he is remembered."

She looks at me with such conviction that a sense of comfort wraps around me like a sweater. I consider telling her about my stance on religion but decide again to stay quiet. I just smile. "Thank you, Maria."

"He has not left you," she says. "They never leave us."

The candle feels heavy in my hand as I walk away. It seemed like Maria and I were the only people in the square while we talked by the fountain, but now the noise returns. The teenagers scream, wrestling each other on the grass. An audience has gathered around a group of impromptu dancers who twirl to the music of a mariachi band. Vendors try to outshout one another as they compete for the attention of customers.

I am making my way through the crowd, toward the hotel, when I come across the flower vendor Maria had pointed out. The woman appears to float in a pool of colourful petals. Baskets overflow with dahlias white as bone and sage as purple as bruised skin. Then I see the marigolds, each one a little burst of yellow and orange flames. The woman reaches toward her feet before holding up a long garland of the fiery petals. She hands it to me solemnly as though she knows exactly what I am looking for.

The courtyard of the Ōmeyōcān is a different place beneath the moonlight. The arched doorways that surround it, illuminated by lanterns, create a glowing necklace that flickers as people hurry through the halls. Lights have been strung up in the trees overhead. The magnolias give them a pale pink glimmer.

A wedding is underway. The bride is dazzling in white. The groom could be a prince from a faraway land. They hold each other closely as they dance beneath the trees, auburn hair cascading past her shoulders from a crown of white flowers. He looks into her eyes as though he's never seen anything so precious. She lays her head on his shoulder as if he could protect her from every danger in the world.

They're so lucky. The magnolias are in bloom.

From where I stand on the terrace, the scene below me could be a lavish ball from a fairy tale, one in which everyone lives happily ever after.

Wait and see. Life doesn't end happily.

I hear Elias's voice finish my thought. "It just ends."

As the band plays on, I tear myself away and step through the large doors that lead to the Terrace Bar. It's a relief to shut those doors behind me on the music and light outside, to step into this room that feels dim and accepting.

The space is furnished in dark cherry wood and sumptuous leather. A chandelier hangs from the centre of the ceiling. The tinted mirrors that cover the walls reflect the muted light, creating plenty of dark corners. It's a shadow-filled jewel box of a room, which I thought was a strange contrast to the airiness of the hotel when I first arrived three days ago. Now, I feel right at home.

Except for a few couples seated at tables in different corners, the room is empty. I sink into a cushioned stool at what has become my favourite spot at the end of the marble countertop that serves as the bar, as far away from everyone else as possible.

Gabriel, the bartender, wipes a glass clean with a towel. He is clad in black from head to toe: suede brogues, fitted pants with the cuffs rolled up just past the ankle, vest, collared shirt, goatee, thick hair pulled back in a knot. The only brightness on his body comes from the silver buckle on his belt that's in the shape of a human skull. The wall behind him is neatly stacked with glass bottles of different colours, glinting like gems. These are the jewels in the box.

"Coen, my friend," Gabriel says, sidling up to me with a glass in hand that might as well be embossed with my name. A knowing smile appears on his lips, his voice steady and smooth like the purr of a cello. "What will it be?"

"Surprise me. Something bitter and stiff."

"I know just the thing," he responds with what is either a micro-wink or an inadvertently sexy twitch of the eye. His sleeves are rolled up to the elbow, and I watch the muscles in his forearms flex and relax as he pours, shakes, muddles, and stirs. Before I know it, a glass tumbler sits in front of me holding an amber-hued liquid. Gabriel stands behind it, watching me expectantly with his arms crossed over his chest. I take a slow, measured sip and savour the rich potion of smoke, oak, and citrus.

"So?"

"You're a magician," I say, taking another long sip. "What do you call this?"

He pauses. "Tears of Men."

I let the words sink in before delivering my verdict. "I like it."

His smile widens, revealing more perfect teeth and higher cheekbones. In a place that has become so solemn so quickly, Gabriel has been a welcome distraction — not just for the steady stream of liquor he's been pouring into me over the last twenty-four hours, or the sexuality that steams from his pores, but because he has helped me feel normal again.

Of course, the circumstances preclude any and all semblance of normality, but the last thing I need is more pity. The entire hotel staff is currently treating me like I'm a Fabergé egg, but Gabriel talks to me as though he weren't a witness to my discovery that the man I loved had perished in the ocean.

I could use a distraction. I've spent most of the day dealing with the collective hysteria of family and friends. The messages of shock and sadness have escalated to concern and confusion. The celebration of life invitation has been met with a curious variety of reactions. Most people seem to have an opinion on acceptable methods of mourning. Though the responses have been courteous and carefully worded, I think my brother's words sum up the general feeling: "This is fucked up, but I guess it's your choice."

It astounds me that they don't appreciate how poetic the idea is — celebrating Elias's life in the same country where he was born on the same day that should have been our wedding.

The overall response is surprising and confusing, but, like Clark said, it's my choice.

I draw another mouthful from my glass, savouring the burn as it travels through my body. My eyes wander up to the television mounted on the wall behind Gabriel, the same screen that delivered the news two days earlier. The hotel has decided to set it exclusively to a British station. I would think people come to this island to escape the dreadfulness of real life put on perpetual display by the news.

"Don't you think the news is a bit bleak for such a beautiful place?"

"I do," Gabriel says, nodding his head. "And that is why I try not to watch it, even though management insists we leave this on." He gestures to the screen with a flick of the chin. "At least the sound can be muted. I like to live in a world I can smell and touch. I came to this island because here it is easier to forget about what is on the other side of the water."

"I wish it were that easy for me," I say, looking down at my glass.

"Well, you are here now, no?" He flashes me a smile, and I can't keep my face from going warm. "I know it is hard. Life, he is a bastard. We all do the best we can. Sometimes it works out. Other times ..." He trails off, not finding the words. "You are doing the best you can. It is all you can do. This bastard who is life will always get his way in the end."

I look up to see the sincerity on his face. The smile is gone. His eyes are sombre. It's the first time he's addressed the state I'm in.

"You're right," I say. "That's all I can do. That, and drink everything in sight." My half-hearted laughter echoes throughout the bar, amplifying how empty it sounds. I wink at him before I can stop myself, instantly regretting it.

"Well, I can help you with that." His smile returns, alleviating the embarrassment that simmers beneath my skin.

"Hey, has Maria talked to you about the event that's happening in five days?"

"There was a meeting this morning with the entire staff. She told us all about the changes. It will be a wake, yes?"

"Well, kind of. I like to think of it as a celebration of life, but sure, more or less a wake." My palms slam against the countertop with excitement. "You must tend the bar for us."

"I would be honoured," he says, an air of formality around him. "I am scheduled to be here that evening, and I believe Franco is supposed to be the bartender for your ... *celebration*. But I will talk to Maria. I am sure it would not be a problem if I switch with Franco."

"Perfect! And if there's a problem, tell Maria to talk to me. It would make me very happy if you were a part of it."

"Would it?" I hear Elias say. "Would it make you very happy for this puto to be there?"

"I am at your service," Gabriel says, bowing his head humbly.

"Who does he think he is?" Elias scoffs in that incredulous tone of his. "Pendejo."

I try to ignore him, but I've never found that easy to do.

"It's going to be perfect, Gabriel, like nothing you've ever seen before. The entire courtyard will be filled with lights and candles. Dinner is going to be spectacular. There will be cake for dessert. We're even bringing in a band from Mexico City. They're called Sangre del Pirata, and they're really hot right now in the Condesa clubs. It will be unforgettable. It will be worthy of Elias."

Out of breath, I pause to take a sip from my glass before realizing it's empty. Before I can say a word, another glass appears in front of me. I didn't notice Gabriel fixing a drink while I rambled on. He stands there, assessing me, before saying, "It sounds beautiful. I am sure Elias would be very proud."

"He would be," I say, convinced. "I forgot to mention the flowers. There will be flowers everywhere. Have I told you that I'm a botanist?"

Gabriel shakes his head.

"I have a thing for flowers. *Magnolia x soulangiana.* That's the species of magnolia tree outside in the courtyard." The liquor hugs me from the inside, making me warm. "What do you believe happens to us when we die?"

"I believe that we go to a different place," he says, not the least bit disturbed by the question. "Not heaven or hell. It is not necessarily better or worse than this place. Just different."

"So you don't believe in Jesus or Mary or any of that stuff?"

A gentle laugh slips past his lips. "No. None of that stuff. They are fairy tales forced on our people long ago. Religion is not for me. That does not mean I am not spiritual. My beliefs are just different."

"Maria told me to build an altar for Elias. She gave me a candle and said to surround it with flowers, incense, and his favourite food. The crazy thing is I did it! I made an altar. It's in my suite right now. There's even a bowl of cereal that I stole from breakfast this morning, just sitting there on my windowsill, soaking in milk. It's his favourite food. Anyone from home would think I've gone crazy if they saw it. I've never been religious, or even spiritual. It just … I don't know. It's comforting. I guess that's why people do it."

"It matters not what we believe," Gabriel says. The serious look has returned to the contours of his face. "Beliefs are useless. They mean nothing. Actions are what matter. How you make others feel is what matters. Truth is personal, not universal. You do not need to be Catholic to build an altar, just like you do not need to be Buddhist to meditate. If the ofrenda brings you peace, then let yourself be at peace."

He looks into my eyes so intensely I fear he can see everything underneath. I can't help but look away.

"It's my fault," I confess. "He's gone because of me."

"No, Coen. You know this is not true, yes?"

"But it is true. I picked the wedding date. I picked the date because of the trees. I wanted so badly for those fucking trees to be in bloom, and so I picked the date and if I hadn't, if it were another date, any other date, Elias would not have been on that flight, and he would still be here, and he would be alive, and we would —"

I cry. Right there, sitting at the counter, I cry. It comes out of nowhere and hits me hard, a series of tremors. My body convulses with each one, and my face is paralyzed, inanimate, a mountain. I'm embarrassed and want to cover myself with my hands, but they don't move. They grip the marble counter as though I will fall if I let go. Rivers run down my face, and it doesn't escape me how fitting it is that tears drip down my chin into the glass below. Tears of Men.

I can't see clearly, but I feel the warmth and smell the sweetness of Gabriel's breath against my skin. "Let yourself weep. Let it go."

After what could have been a minute or an hour, I sense the feeling return to my body. Composure comes over me quickly. I frantically wipe my face with my hands and I'm collected again, as though it never happened. It's the first time I've cried since the crash.

"I'm sorry," I say. I can't look at him.

"There is no reason to be sorry."

I am taking another sip of my cocktail when something catches my eye on the television. I look at Gabriel. "Could you turn the volume on?"

He sees the urgency in my eyes, and the sound is unmuted a second later.

"… three hundred and fourteen fatalities. The team of investigators, which includes authorities from Iceland, Canada, Germany, and France, is speculating that the crash might not have been accidental, but deliberate. News Cloud has obtained a radio transmission made to air traffic control in Keflavík, Iceland, less than one minute before the aircraft made impact."

Elias's face appears on the screen, the same photograph they used two days ago. He looks so handsome in his uniform. His dark eyes stare vacantly into mine. A red banner below him displays his name in stark white letters.

"Authorities have identified the voice in the transmission as belonging to First Officer Elias Santos, co-pilot of flight XI260. We are going to play this recording now. Although there is no explicit language, we would like to caution that some viewers may find the content disturbing."

Elias's face remains. There is a moment of silence. Static noise can be heard, then a man's voice, deep and calm.

"Pronto dios."

My body goes cold. The words are unfamiliar, but the voice has whispered to me in the morning and sung to me at night. It has shouted and screamed and laughed and cried with me.

"Elias Santos is Canadian; he resided in Vancouver for the past several years, but sources suggest he originated from Mexico. The words you just heard, pronto dios, are Spanish for 'soon god.'"

THE COURTYARD
Sixteen months before the crash

"Do I have to?" The expression on his face was part suspicious, part pleading.

"Yes," I said. "Come on. Be a good sport."

He stared at the striped necktie in his hand. With a reluctant exhale, he tied it around his head so that it covered his eyes. His hair was shorter back then, but it still bulged beneath the improvised blindfold.

"Just relax," I told him. It was a dark winter's day, and I had to let the engine run for a few minutes to defrost the windows. He sat stiffly in the passenger seat, clearly uncomfortable with not being able to see.

"How do you want me to relax? I can't see, and I don't know where you're taking me."

"Don't you trust me?"

"No comment."

The roads were black and shiny like an oil slick as we sped through the city. The rain had let up recently, and the street lights reflected in the still-wet pavement. It was that period in the year when it was easy to forget how sunlight felt against the skin. The entire city collectively dreamed of the warmth and adventure and sunset revelry that comes with the promise of spring. In the meantime we waited.

The grey winters had been difficult for Elias when he first arrived in Vancouver. It didn't help that he had moved from a tropical climate during the darkest time of year. Spring was beginning to emerge when we first met, life bursting from every bud with colour and the scent of wild things. I was excited to share the city with him as it bloomed, though I never minded the rain. I even missed it during the occasional dry spell. Elias was different. He let the rain get inside of him.

I tried making conversation as I drove through the busy streets, but Elias was too distracted. His hands gripped the sides of his seat, and his head jerked toward the sound of every screech of a tire or siren's wail. I would have found it funny had I not known how uncomfortable he was in cars to begin with.

"We're here," I announced as I parked on a quiet tree-lined street.

"I can take it off?"

"Not quite." I opened the passenger door and took Elias by the hand, carefully guiding him out of the car.

"Hijo de puta!" he cried as he hit his head on the door frame. "I don't like this."

I couldn't help but laugh. "We're almost there."

"And you think this is funny."

I did. Elias was usually so sure of himself; I took some pleasure in seeing how awkward he could be. All I had to do was take away his sight.

His posture stiffened as he heard the wrought-iron gates swing open. He took slow, deliberate steps to avoid tripping over the uneven bricks that made up the path we were walking along.

With one hand holding his and the other against the small of his back, I led him deep into the centre of our destination.

"We're here. You can take off the blindfold now."

My nerves hummed as he unfastened the necktie from around his head. He blinked rapidly a few times, waiting for his vision to adjust.

We were surrounded on all sides by tall brick walls painted white, but they looked silver in the moonlight. Rows upon rows of picture windows looked down on us like eyes. Some were dark while others emitted a warm glow from inside. Shining globes sat atop the lampposts. The trees weren't in bloom. Their branches formed a web that stretched around us, protection from the terrors of the night.

We were standing in the centre of the magnolia courtyard.

I waited eagerly to see the look on Elias's face, expecting a smile of recognition to appear. It was expressionless for the first few seconds, then his eyebrows crinkled and his lips pursed tightly together.

"Why are we here?" he asked, turning to me.

"Elias, this is where we first met." I was surprised that he didn't quite get the point of this.

"Yes. I can see that." He paused. "Why did you bring me here?"

"I spoke with the owner of the building, and she's willing to rent out the space for the day. We'll have to arrange everything ourselves, like catering and equipment and licences and whatnot, but isn't this place perfect? Elias, this is where I want us to get married."

He looked at me with the same blank expression, then squinted his eyes closed and rubbed them with his hands. After a moment he said, "This is not a good idea."

"Why not? It's perfect."

"It is not perfect, Coen."

"Sure, it's a little shabby, but I've already been thinking about how to spruce it up."

"Coen, listen to me."

"We can set up the chairs right down the middle, and this brick path here is where the aisle would be."

"Coen ..."

"The bar could go here, and there would be a table there for the guestbook. We could string up lights around the trees."

"Stop it. Listen to what I am saying."

"And the magnolias! We'll time it for when the magnolias are in —"

"Shut up!"

It felt like a slap, except he stood six feet away. We just looked at each other, so still one would have thought we were playing a game. I was confused. This wasn't how I had imagined this evening would go. It should have been a happy surprise. He should have removed his blindfold and looked at me as though I'd read his mind. He should have taken me in his arms and said how much he loved me. We should have held each other there for a while, underneath the trees.

Instead he stood there, looking more defeated than angry. "Coen, this is not a good idea."

"This is where we first met, right here in this courtyard. How is that not a good idea?"

"Let's not do this right now." He looked so tired then. "We're going to get married, just not here. We will find another place."

He made his way through the courtyard and down the brick path that was supposed to be our aisle. I felt troubled, but all I did was watch him walk away, imagining how he would look on our wedding day.

JARDÍN INGLÉS
Three days after the crash

I listen to the radio transmission of Elias's voice for what must be hours. I feel more baffled each time I hear it. His voice is so calm, like he's ordering a pizza for delivery. I record the four-second audio clip to my phone and play it on repeat until the words don't sound like words anymore. Until it is no longer a voice speaking but the wind.

Pronto dios.

His final words. Of the millions of words he could have chosen, he spoke those. He had no friends, no family. Only me. And even I don't know what this message means.

"What would you have wanted me to say?" he asks. It sounds like a challenge.

"*I'm sorry? I love you?* Anything else, Elias. Literally, any other words would have been better. Maybe something I could have understood without the bitch on TV having to tell me what my fiancé's final words mean."

"Hey now, that's not fair. It's not the lady's fault."

"You're right. It's yours."

A silent pause.

"You know I didn't crash the plane on purpose, right?" he says.

"I know."

"You're not going to ask me to explain?"

"You can't explain. You're dead."

Another pause.

"Then how do you know I didn't do it?"

"You just couldn't have done it," I respond, my voice sharp in the quiet room. "I will not believe you would have done that to me."

"And to those people on the plane."

"Yes, and to those people on the plane."

When I can't stand to listen to his voice anymore, I arrange a video chat with Vivi. The loneliness in my suite has become stifling. I need to see her face.

She had called several times after the clip was released. So had Decker, and then my parents. I didn't answer any of them. I let the phone ring and ring.

I also received messages from nearly everyone coming to the celebration of life. Each message was carefully crafted to show support, but the words couldn't hide their vague suspicion that my fiancé could very well have been a mass murderer. They said things like, "Maybe it would be best for you to come home, under the circumstances" and "You must be distraught; everyone would understand if you decided to cancel." I hated these words, so I started to hate the people who wrote them.

Vivi seems to agree with them.

"Cancel this thing and come home," she pleads through the screen. "Or stay there, and I'll come to you. Either way, you can't go on with this event. It's not right."

Normally my defences would be up, but I need the candour that only Vivi ever gives me. Sometimes she's my only tether to reality.

"You're right. This event might be a terrible idea. Going ahead with it would likely end in disaster."

She peers at me through the screen, and I can see she isn't fooled. "But?"

"But I can't cancel it now. That would be an admission of guilt. It would tell everyone what they're hearing on the news is true. I won't do that to him."

Her eyes are tired, but she hasn't been crying. She speaks slowly, choosing her words carefully. "Coen, how do you know he wouldn't have done this?"

"I can't believe you're asking me that," I say, shaking my head.

"It needs to be asked. You need to think and tell me whether or not Elias could have done this."

"You can't be serious." My fingertips are cold as they rub my temples in clockwise circles.

"Think, Coen!" she cries. "Could he have done this?"

"No! Of course not!" My voice is shrill, almost screaming. "Not to me. Not to himself. Not to those people. He's never hurt anyone. We were supposed to be married this week. He knew I was waiting here for him. We were happy. He wouldn't have done this to me."

We look at each other as though we're in one of the staring contests we used to play years ago. The first one to blink loses.

After a long and heavy silence, she blinks. "Okay. That's all I need to hear." Her face seems to release the tension that had tightened it. "I'm sorry I had to ask that, but I honestly don't know what's real anymore. You heard the recording. That was his voice. The airport in Iceland tried radioing the cockpit as the plane was going down. There was no answer. Why wouldn't he have answered?"

"I don't know," I say, helpless and lost. "Maybe there was a malfunction. Maybe he was dealing with something else that was happening in the cockpit. Maybe the other pilot was a Russian spy. I don't know. All I know is that Elias did not intend to crash the plane."

"No. He did not." She looks down and contemplates this as if to convince herself. Finally, her chin rises, her eyes meet mine, and I know she has made up her mind. We can move on now.

"Do you remember that photo I showed you a long time ago?" I ask. "The one of young Elias?"

She nods.

"There's an old hardcover book on the shelf in the living room. The cover is green, and the text is faded so badly you can barely read the title. It's beside that wooden bird Elias got in Amsterdam. The photo is tucked inside the pages. Bring it here with you, okay?"

"Wait." She disappears into my apartment, where she's been staying the past few days, and returns a minute later with the tattered photograph in her hands. She holds it up to the screen.

"That's the one. Don't forget to bring it here with you."

"You got it."

"And Vivi?"

"What?"

"I miss your stupid face."

I'm relieved to see her smile.

After we disconnect, I send the entire guest list an email only three sentences long:

If you believe that Elias could have done what the news is suggesting, please don't show up to the celebration. For everyone else, the show will go on. I'll see you here in paradise.

I thought I would feel bold and empowered after hitting send, but I don't. I just feel claustrophobic.

Needing to clear my head, I take a few deep breaths while splayed across the bed before I venture out of my suite and into the hall.

Walking through the hotel has become something to dread. I can feel the eyes burrowing into me, even though I no longer look up to see their faces. As I keep my gaze directed to the floor, I can see their feet stall while I pass as though they're incapable of walking and pitying me at the same time. I've discovered the best routes to take to encounter the fewest people, but I can't escape the hotel unless I go through either the front lobby or the courtyard toward the beach.

Circular in shape, the hotel's lobby is a gallery of light and air. The front entrance opens to the island outside with no barrier other than three large sets of ornate gates that only close late at night. There's always a doorman and a valet standing guard with flowers pinned to the lapels of their matching taupe suits. The ceiling is a cone of glass that distorts the sky above, projecting its shadows and rays throughout the room below in kaleidoscopic motion. With the white walls and marble floors amplifying the light, it always seems brighter inside than it does outside.

I keep my eyes on the floor and see a pair of delicate feet in high-heeled shoes the colour of flamingo feathers. I stop abruptly and look up, but it's too late. The woman collides with me and falls to the floor, spilling the contents of her handbag.

"I'm so sorry," I say, getting on my knees to collect her things: a pocket mirror, a notebook, various vials of makeup and lotion.

To my surprise, she laughs and it sounds like a songbird. "I am as clumsy as a baby giraffe," she says in an English accent that is both refined and jovial. She continues to laugh, still sitting on the floor with her dress fanned around herself in fronds of green silk. Thick waves of mahogany hair spill over lovely shoulders. There is warmth in her eyes.

She takes the hand I offer, and I hoist the woman to her feet. She almost trips over her heels on the way up; her baby giraffe comment was no exaggeration. Once she is steady, I return to my knees to retrieve the rest of her scattered belongings.

"Marble floors and high heels are not a friendly combination," she says with another songbird's laugh.

Exasperated, I hand the purse back to her. "Sorry again," I say before turning around and heading straight for the exit as quickly as I can.

The woman calls out after me, but I don't look back. As I emerge from the hotel, the humid air floods my lungs and the heat washes over my skin. I look directly at the blazing sun, feeling its flares pierce my eyes until orbs streak across my vision.

I cross the hotel grounds and pass a few similar-looking resorts, each one its own little fortress of decontextualized luxury. Eventually the resorts disappear, and it's a relief to enter an area where real people seem to live. The streets are lined with houses painted in bright, sunny colours, the walls and doors with opposing yet complementary hues.

My shirt sticks to my back as I make my way farther from the ocean breeze. The racing thoughts in my mind begin to slow down when I stumble upon a path leading into a dense forest of tropical flora. The green tangle of leaves looks inviting, luring me into its cool, quiet shade. I'm still lost in my thoughts when I find myself in front of a house of glass.

It stands unexpectedly in the middle of the forest. About eight elephants could fit inside, the unit of measurement that first comes to mind. The frame is an ornate maze of thin metal tendrils that hold together hundreds of panes of glass. They form a straight, square grid in some portions of the exterior, then burst into whimsical curves in others.

The little building must have been magnificent at one point in time, but it now looks as though it was abandoned long ago. The frame is infected with rust, though flashes of rich green paint remain. Many of the glass panes are either missing or reduced to jagged teeth. Nature is slowly assuming possession of the house, vines and branches wrapping around its body as though her intention is to swallow it whole.

Where did this come from?

I step through the open doorway, which no longer has actual doors. The floor is littered with fragments of what were probably once tiles. The shrubs and roots that now cover the ground must have burst through the floor like a chick emerging from its shell. Other than a few glass bottles nestled in the undergrowth, there are no recent signs of humanity. It is yet another beautiful thing that man once loved but has long since forgotten.

There's a clear patch of earth near the centre of the room where I lay my body down, resting my head on my hands to gaze up at the patchwork of metal and glass above me. The rays of sunlight able to pierce through the canopy of trees are muted. It seems quieter inside, even though the walls have more openings than glass left. It's a peaceful place.

"Señor Coen?" A familiar voice breaks the silence. I bolt upright to see Maria standing in the open doorway. Her long hair is pulled back in a tight bun. She's wearing heels and a blazer the colour of cayenne pepper. Maria, the professional, has returned.

"Maria?" I ask, surprised. "Where did you come from?"

"I am so sorry. I hope I am not disturbing you. My house is nearby. I was on my way to the hotel when I saw you go into the forest. I called your name, but you did not hear me."

. I must have been too absorbed in my own thoughts to notice the sounds of the real world. "No worries," I say. "It's good to have some company. Pull up a seat if you'd like." I smile and gesture to the ground beside me.

She returns the smile, relieved. To my surprise, she takes me up on the offer, lowering herself to the ground more gracefully than expected considering the constraints of her outfit.

"I wanted to see how you are doing," she says. "I hope you are not too stressed."

"I'm doing great!" I say with an unnatural amount of enthusiasm, far more than I intend. "I mean, I'm fine. I'm not stressed. At least, that's not how I would describe it."

"I am happy to hear this."

My legs begin to seize up ever so slightly. I extend my body on the ground, stretching my limbs as far as I can. Maria does the same. The moment is surreal, lying on the ground with my wedding planner in an abandoned house of glass.

"This place must have been so beautiful once upon a time," I say.

"It was," she responds in a wistful tone. "It was a greenhouse filled with the loveliest flowers. Like you say, once upon a time."

"A greenhouse? In Mexico?"

"It was not just an ordinary greenhouse. Let me tell you the story."

. . . . .

A long time ago, a man and his wife travelled to Isla de Espejos from their home in England. They were both young and beautiful. They came here to escape the pressures of their lives back home. The island cast its spell.

As construction began on the home of their dreams, they lived in a little wooden house beside the sea that was painted bright yellow like the sun. Every day, they would bathe in the ocean. Every night, they would shop at the village market, charming the locals with their kindness. The islanders called them el príncipe and la princesa — the prince and princess. These enchanting foreigners seemed so perfect, so happy.

One day, we heard the news: the princess was with child! Word spread across the island like a joyful breeze, and within hours everyone knew. A celebration was thrown in the centre of town, right in Plaza Pequeña. Lights and papel picado were strung up all across the square. There was a stage in front of the cathedral where bands played throughout the night. The prince and princess, along with their new friends, danced and sang and celebrated until the sun rose over the lagoon the next morning.

Nine months passed and the princess gave birth to a precious girl. We called her Princesita — the little princess. She was the island's daughter.

Their new house had been completed in time for the birth. It was painted white except for the gabled roof, which was yellow like their little house by the sea. Wrapped around the main floor was a veranda with wicker chairs and tables. A balcony ran along the second floor, where the princess would often be seen painting with her daughter nearby.

They would host guests for tea, inviting anyone they met. Rich or poor, it didn't matter. They would sit on the veranda and show their guests how to have a proper afternoon tea the English way: how much cream to pour, how to hold the cup. When Princesita was older, she would help serve the cream, sugar, and biscuits. To this day, you may notice the locals having tea every afternoon, just as they were taught.

The prince and princess didn't miss anything about England except the flowers. The princess would often tell the locals about how fragrant the flowers were in the countryside. She wished she could grow them here, but the climate was not right.

The prince had an idea. He gathered some of the islanders, and they spent months building a greenhouse in the woods. On his next trip to England, he brought back seeds, soil, and everything he needed for an English garden. The greenhouse was specially designed so the wildflowers would thrive.

One day, the princess was blindfolded and led by the hand by her beloved husband and daughter. They walked across the lawn, into the woods, to the greenhouse. Some say she burst into tears when she saw her gift; she was so happy. Her prince had brought the English countryside all the way to her new home in Mexico. This happened right here in this glass house. The islanders call it el Jardín Inglés — the English Garden.

The years went on, and they continued to live their blessed lives. Princesita lived up to her name, growing more beautiful as she became older. Her hair was the colour of the sun. During these years, the wildflowers in the English Garden bloomed as though they would never die.

Then one day, something changed. The prince and princess stopped coming to the village. They stopped having guests over for tea. Whenever anyone went knocking at their door, there would be no answer. Sometimes, the princess would be seen swimming in the sea. Other times, the prince would be spotted sitting outside on the veranda. They were never seen together, and nobody ever saw Princesita.

Most troubling of all is that the English Garden was left to die. First, the flowers started to wilt. Seeing the neglect, some of the locals took it upon themselves to tend to the garden every week. They did everything they could to keep it alive, but nothing worked. Like a disease, each flower decayed until the English Garden contained nothing but death.

One morning, very early, the two princesses sailed away from the island. Witnesses say they were both dressed entirely in white with wide hats and long silk gloves. Nobody spoke to them or saw their faces, but they could see Princesita's golden hair as she boarded the boat.

The prince left the island three days later, also by sea. He was dressed in black and looked a decade older than his age, the lines that once creased his face when he smiled now sunken and weary. None of them ever came back.

No one knows what happened in that house. We can only imagine what could have made such a perfect, joyful, loving family become so cold and closed off to the world. Some say Princesita became very ill, which was too much for the mother and father to bear. Others say the princess discovered that her prince had fallen in love with another woman. This happened many years ago when I was a young girl, so I do not expect we will ever know the truth.

To this day, the islanders tell this story to their children as a warning. Do not be fooled by happiness. It can wilt and die, especially when kept in a house of glass.

. . . . .

I see the decay around me and try to imagine the greenhouse filled with colour and life. The pain in my chest begins to throb.

"That might be the saddest story I've ever heard," I say. It's not an exaggeration.

"Sadness is part of life," Maria responds. "Without sadness, happiness would mean nothing."

"Just like how life would be pointless if it weren't for death."

Maria's story has filled the glass house with a gloom that's tangible. It has a taste and a scent. It surrounds us.

"I let happiness fool me once," Maria says. She turns her head toward me for permission to go on.

"What happened?" I find myself eager to hear more, as though I'm craving more misery, am addicted to it.

"I always dreamed of travelling to Spain," she says. "There, I would swim in the Mediterranean and get lost in the halls of the Alhambra, dine on paella and dance the flamenco in the streets. But then I fell in love with José. He was handsome and strong. I was young and silly. José promised to take me to Spain one day, and I believed him. He told me he loved me and, again, I believed him. You have heard this story before, I am sure. It happens to young, silly girls and boys every day.

"I gave myself to him. Anything and everything he wanted, I gave to him. One day I learned I was with child. José seemed so happy. We would be married, be a family. We would raise this child together. We would watch the sun rise and set in Spain. All of this he told me, and all of it I believed."

Maria appears younger in the light filtered through the panes of glass above. Something hopeful shines in her eyes, a wilful naïveté, despite knowing full well how this story ends.

"I was fooled," she says, her voice barely louder than a whisper. "All of those words meant nothing. José met another woman, and they left the island together. I do not even know where they went. I accepted the truth — my dreams were nothing more than dreams — and gave birth to my beloved Jacinta. I have no regrets, but José changed me. His promises, his lies. Now, I do not believe the words that people say."

"José deceived you. He didn't deserve your love. You and Jacinta are better off without him."

"Perhaps," she says. "My point is that one never really knows the truth inside another's heart. Sometimes their intentions are hidden away."

I turn my head toward her, and she's already looking at me. Our eyes meet, and I realize this isn't just another story. It's a parable with a lesson, and it's directed at me.

"What are you trying to tell me?" I ask. My legs ache. I can feel the gentle prick of a needle, then another.

"Even the people closest to you can hide behind a mask. You think you know them when in fact their true selves are strangers. It is not your fault. People are deceitful. You can never truly know anyone other than yourself."

The needles are sharper now, and the anger washes over me suddenly. "You know nothing about me," I say. "You know nothing about Elias."

"Señor Coen, be calm," she says. "I am trying to help you."

"Then please stop. I am sorry for what José did to you, but don't you dare think it has anything to do with me. I know Elias. He would never have abandoned me."

My throat tightens. I need to get out of here. My legs throb as I struggle to stand. My fists open and close to keep from going numb.

"I only want to help." Maria is still sitting on the floor, looking up at me with such pity.

"Then just do your job."

I stride out of the English Garden as quickly as I can, relieved to breathe in air that isn't poisoned by its gloom.

There are two kinds of silence between lovers. There is the sort you can sink into like a favourite old chair — comfortable and broken in, with the satisfaction of knowing that the familiarity has been earned. Then there is the sort as tense as a piano string, when both parties know that one wrong word is all it would take for it to snap.

I have always found silence unsettling. *Are they bored by me? Am I not interesting enough?* I often felt the need to fill these quiet interludes with noise, a mundane observation or question I didn't care to hear the answer to, simply to avoid the heightened sense of self-awareness that comes with the quiet.

Elias helped me gain some control over this fear. He had always been a curiously inconsistent man. As with other aspects of his personality, his conversational ability would go from one extreme to the other with no discernible trigger. He could talk emphatically for hours on any given subject, then retreat to his cave of silence from which he would not be coaxed out. It made dinner parties interesting as I never knew which Elias would be present — the conversationalist or the mute. It was the same in private and, after several failed attempts to maintain a steady hum of dialogue between us, I learned to settle into the regular quiet he needed.

That night we drove in silence, and it wasn't the comfortable kind. Tension heated the car as if it were consuming the chilliness of the winter air and replacing it with the warm simmer of resentment. Elias sat rigidly in the passenger seat, staring out the windshield rather intensely at the street lights that passed by. I tried to concentrate on driving but couldn't help ruminating on our last conversation. It played over and over in my mind.

Earlier that day, I had made the mistake of leaving a browser window open on the computer we shared. It was nothing scandalous: just a map of the Mexican state of Veracruz and a list of auto repair shops in the region. Elias didn't have to be a detective to realize I was searching for his family.

I expected him to be angry, but I had underestimated the volume of his anger. My usual methods of avoiding conflict didn't work as he confronted me, hands twitching and sweat forming along the base of his thick hair. He let me explain myself, and I had nothing useful to say. I couldn't articulate why I was searching for his family based on the small amount of information he had given me. I had no end goal in mind, no reasonable motive. I wouldn't have taken any sort of action if I was successful in locating them. The only explanation I could offer was curiosity, which was reductive and not quite accurate.

"It's none of your business!" he had shouted. "My family does not concern you. I have told you everything you need to know."

I let him berate me, which seemed to make him more upset. There was no use in fighting back or trying to explain myself further. I didn't want the argument to escalate, but I didn't apologize either. Why was it such a crime to show interest in my partner's past?

"You will never do this again, do you hear me? You will not ask about them. You will not look for information on them. As far as you're concerned, they do not exist. Do you understand?" he had said, his index finger pointed steadily at my face. I think I hated him then.

There we were, two hours later, driving through the city in silence toward a Christmas party, of all things. We should have cancelled, but that would have required some degree of interaction and agreement. Besides, we were both too stubborn to take such drastic action. We showered, dressed, and headed out the door as planned, on schedule, and with minimal acknowledgement of each other's existence.

I usually feel a tired brand of dread when arriving at a party, as though my body simultaneously recognizes how draining it will be and its potential for social embarrassment. This time I felt relieved as Decker opened the door with his signature cheer. We needed the noise of people and music to drown out the silence between us.

"Merry Christmas, boys!" Decker said, wearing a knitted sweater depicting a winter barnyard scene, complete with a red barn and three inexplicable reindeer. He pulled us in for one of his wholehearted hugs. I watched Elias smile broadly as he greeted Decker with such warmth and grace.

Man, he's good.

Decker attempted to take our coats while juggling the bottle of elderflower tonic and German stollen we had brought for him. He stayed away from alcohol — his mother has always had a troublesome relationship with the bottle — but I had witnessed him experiment with beer once in university. It turned out that drunk Decker was a less tidy, less sensible version of the very tidy and very sensible young man I had grown to love. I haven't seen him touch alcohol since.

His shoebox-sized apartment wasn't exactly a spacious venue for a large gathering, but that never stopped him from hosting them. They usually involved a gauntlet of people impossible to cross without being intercepted for conversations or introductions, and that night was no different. The general rule for one of Decker's parties was to avoid wearing white as someone would inevitably bump into you with a glass of red wine or other such dark-tinted liquid. The space felt even more cramped with strings of Christmas lights dangling from the ceiling, as well as the fact that every guest seemed to be wearing an elaborate dress or a woolly, festive sweater.

We hadn't even made it past the front hall when the first interception of the night happened. Decker's girlfriend, Samantha, pounced on us like a stealthy, chipper panther in a dress the colour of Merlot. *Strategic colour choice*, I thought as she pulled us both in for a three-way hug, smothering me in her long blond hair. She smelled like cinnamon.

We chatted with Samantha briefly until she was pulled away by another guest. I didn't have a chance to say a word before Elias walked away from me and into the kitchen. It was clear that he intended to ignore me for the rest of the night.

I went straight for the bar and poured myself a glass of wine, which I guzzled in less time than it took to find the alcohol content on the label: 13.5 percent. I refilled my glass with a sloshing purple torrent while scanning the room for Elias. He was talking to Mason, one of Decker's squash-league buddies and arguably the most attractive man in the room.

Strategic choice in conversation partner.

The wine left my mouth feeling dry and raw, though I had barely tasted it.

Two can play at that game.

I searched for a handsome man who could tell me jokes I would laugh at loudly, but I couldn't avoid being intercepted by old university friends, most of whom were female and not conducive to stoking the flames of jealousy.

After what felt like a never-ending drip of the same conversation — What's new? How have you been? How's work? — I was relieved to see Vivi step into the room. Amid the blur of ironic sweaters and jewel-toned holiday attire, Vivi stood out like a vampire in a crowd of silly elves. She wore a leather jacket over a slinky black dress, her delicate neck bound by a velvet choker. Even the shade of red on her lips was distinct in the room saturated with a similar colour.

"How much have you had to drink?" She interrogated me without even the pretense of a greeting.

"Merry Christmas to you too. Only a couple glasses, if you insist on being my mother."

"You already have that constipated look you get whenever you drink, so slow down. I saw your car outside."

"What look? And I'm fine, although it would be nice if I didn't always have to be the designated driver."

"Elias doesn't drive and you refuse to take cabs or transit, so that doesn't leave many other options, does it? Just slow it down with the wine. Your teeth are already purple."

Vivi was right, as always, even about the teeth. I tried to be discreet as I rubbed them with the sleeve of my shirt.

"Speaking of Elias, he doesn't seem like his usual antisocial self," she said after confirming my teeth were restored to an acceptable shade. "I just saw him with Mason. What the hell would they have to talk about?"

"He's pissed at me, and now he's trying to prove something. What exactly, I don't know. Maybe that he doesn't need me as much as I think he does. Or that he could find someone far more attractive than I am. It's pointless. I already know both of these things are true."

"What did you do?" Vivi asked, looking at me with her smoky eyes as though she'd already drawn the conclusion I was at fault.

After placing my wineglass clumsily on a shelf, my fingers struggled to undo the top button of my shirt's collar. The room felt suddenly warmer, the air stifling. The collar loosened at last, and the skin of my neck felt like heated rubber as I inhaled deeply.

"Let's get some air," I said, pulling Vivi away from the suffocating noise and warmth toward the balcony. This was our typical escape route for when our extroversion reserves began to dry up. Thanks to the winter chill, we had the balcony to ourselves. Vivi lit a cigarette. The end burned more brightly than the pale light that drifted from a single lamp above the door. The city lights twinkled around us in the dark.

Yaletown back then was among my least loved neighbourhoods in the city, a place of dilettantes and pretenders, but it was difficult to ignore its allure from our vantage point on the thirty-third floor. Its residential towers competed for the sky, creating canyons of glass and concrete. We were surrounded by uniform boxes of light suspended in the air, each one a tidy compartment of people and possessions that represented a life.

In one box across the street, a young woman held yoga poses on the carpeted floor while two small children in pyjamas spun around her. They climbed over and under furniture, mouths open with squeals I couldn't hear, but were unsuccessful in disturbing their mother's state of peace.

Another box in the building next door revealed a grey-haired woman wrapped in a blanket. She sat pensively by the window sipping wine from a glass, the uncorked bottle on the table next to her. There were no Christmas decorations, no coloured lights.

In the box four levels below her, two athletic young men kissed each other on a couch as the television cast a seductive glow on their contorting bodies. An innocent movie night had evolved into something else.

Their windows were screens displaying vignettes of everyday life, as though each box were its own reality show or zoo exhibit. The city was filled with people who were inside looking inside somewhere else. Everyone was both spectator and performer. The scene could go from mundane to lonesome to impassioned by looking left or right or up or down.

I wondered what a spectator would have thought about the scene that played out in my apartment earlier in the evening — and cringed.

"So tell me. What did you do?" Vivi asked, smoke billowing from her red lips. I never admitted to her that she was one of the few people who could still make this habit look cool in our overly informed age.

She was silent while I recounted what had happened, her eyes squinting and relaxing at various points as she waited to deliver her verdict. I thought I'd been successful in eliciting sympathy through my biased version of events when she said, "You shouldn't stick your nose where it doesn't belong." I was about to interject in defence when she continued. "But Elias definitely overreacted. You've been together for five years now, right? You know hardly anything about his family, or his past. He can't keep that from you and expect you not to care."

"Right? It's not like I would have tried contacting them. His parents are heartless goons. He's gotten on with his life and doesn't want anything to do with them. I am fully on his side with that."

"Then what possessed you to track them down to begin with?" she asked with a skeptical gleam in her eyes and the cigarette poised between her fingertips.

"I guess I just wanted to know more. Perhaps see what they look like. Find out what their names are. I don't know anything about what happened besides what Elias told me years ago, and he's refused to talk about it ever since. The only way to learn anything new would be to find it on my own."

"Well, give it a rest, Sherlock," she said, punching me playfully just below the collarbone. The pain was unexpected, and I flinched more dramatically than I should have.

"What's wrong?" she asked, shooting me a look of suspicion and concern.

"Nothing." I tried to shrug it off with a feeble laugh, knowing it would only insult Vivi's ability to see through every mask I wear. Without a word, she grabbed my shirt and undid a few buttons, pulling the sides apart so violently I thought the remaining buttons would pop off. I wished I were invisible underneath, that my bare skin would be hidden beneath the dim light.

"This is happening again?" Her eyes travelled from my chest to my face, and I knew the lonely lamp above us was enough to expose me. I wanted to change the subject while another part of me hoped she'd be outraged, but her voice remained unnervingly calm. "Did this happen tonight?"

"It's not a big deal. I'm fine." I shivered in the cold, gently pushing her hands away. My fingers felt unsteady as they buttoned my shirt back up. "I don't want to talk about it."

She searched my eyes, then turned away, marched back inside, and closed the balcony door loudly behind her. My first instinct was to follow after her, to stop her, but my legs wouldn't move. I stood outside in the cold and watched her through the window. I watched as she pushed her way through the crowd. I watched her take Elias firmly by the arm, pulling him away from the conversation he was having. I watched the look on his face go from confused to indignant, then I couldn't watch anymore. Time to change the channel.

I turned to the balcony's edge and looked into the glowing boxes across the street. The young family was now cuddled up on the couch, the children giggling along to the book their mother was reading to them. The grey-haired woman was no longer visible in her box, but the wineglass and bottle sat on the table, both empty. The box with the two athletic boys was now dark. The show was over.

I gazed out at the lives on display around me, safe in my darkness and my silence.

OTRA LUNA
Four days after the crash

"She had her whole life ahead of her. It was just beginning. Holly had such big dreams. She was going to start medical school in the fall. She always wanted to be a pediatrician, you know. Holly just wanted to help ..."

The woman on the television can't finish her sentence. She seemed composed during most of the interview, but all of a sudden her face distorts as she chokes on her words. It must be surreal to her. One moment, her life is ordinary, then she remembers that her only daughter, the future pediatrician, perished in the ocean while flying home from a study-abroad year in Berlin. I wonder if it's the realization that she's referring to Holly in the past tense that triggers the grief.

I found these stories comforting for a short while. I watched the news coverage and read the articles that paraded these poor, unlucky souls in front of a mournful, entertained audience.

I read about the twenty-seven-year-old German science prodigy who was on his way to lead a groundbreaking study. It was expected to revolutionize our understanding of human genetics.

I watched an interview with a thirty-six-year-old Canadian dentist who had taken an earlier flight than his wife because of an error with the booking. He didn't learn what happened to her until after his flight touched down safely at the airport. He was inconsolable.

I stared at the photos a Dutch family had posted twenty minutes before boarding the doomed plane, while they waited at the airport. They had sandy-blond hair and wore matching nylon windbreakers in bright colours. Their photos were goofy. They formed a human pyramid in one shot — the parents on the bottom, the two young sons on top. In another, they pretended to drink out of different bottles of liquor in the duty-free shop, the boys making comical drunk faces.

I indulged in the tragedy of these people and those they left behind. I mourned for them and with them. They made me feel less alone. In a strange way, I found comfort in meeting the people who had accompanied Elias on his final flight. Although it would have been far less tragic had he been alone, a sick, selfish part of me is glad he wasn't.

The initial feeling of solace has mutated into something numb. The more stories I hear, the less real it seems, the duller my senses become. The throbbing pain continues to grow within my chest, but the rest of me feels nothing, even as I watch Holly's poor mother grapple with her loss for the whole world to see. It probably doesn't help that I've replaced sleep with staring at the news over the last few nights.

"Turn off the TV," I hear Elias say. "You've had enough."

"Don't tell me what to do," I respond as I stretch my limbs across the bed.

"You need to sleep."

"I need much more than sleep."

"You know I love you. Right?" His voice is gentler now.

"*Loved.* Past tense."

"Stop it."

"If you loved me so much, then why aren't you here?"

"I am here. I am right here with you."

"You are so full of shit."

"It's true," he says. "Do you think a crashing plane could take me away from you? That death means I just disappear? Evaporate? Like it or not, dear, you are stuck with me. I am going through all of this with you."

I let the silence hang above us with the air held in my lungs before letting it out with a ragged sigh. "I would rather you be here, alive."

"So would I. But the universe doesn't work the way we want it to."

"The universe is a sewer."

Elias chuckles in agreement.

"You were supposed to arrive this morning," I say, my voice quiet. "I was excited to show you around the hotel. I know you were skeptical, but I think you would have loved it. We're scheduled to taste cakes today, you and me. How am I supposed to pick a cake on my own?"

"I'll be there with you. Do we really need a cake anyhow?"

"Yes," I respond flatly. "It's a celebration, and celebrations come with cake."

"Whatever you say, dear. We shall have cake then."

Elias appears on the television screen, the same photograph that has been shared around the world over the past few days. He looks fearless in his pilot's uniform.

"Investigators continue their search for clues to the cause behind this fatal crash," the familiar messenger announces. The pale blue colour of her blouse complements the red banner beneath Elias proclaiming his name. Her voice is bright and buoyant. "Much of the attention is being focused on Elias Santos, co-pilot of flight XI260. It does not appear as though Santos was affiliated with extremist groups, although details are still being uncovered. We can confirm that Santos passed all standard health examinations that pilots routinely undergo, though we do not yet know the details behind his history of mental health."

"Classy," I say. "When lacking evidence, just question his sanity."

"They're just doing their job," Elias says, frustratingly objective even in death.

"Can't you see what they're implying?"

"They're simply investigating all possible explanations."

"There is nothing wrong with your mental state," I say, clutching the bedsheet beneath me.

He doesn't respond.

. . . . .

When Decker de Gannes was a young boy, his mother once left him with his brother and sister in their beat-up van while she got wasted in a bar on whatever anyone would buy her. He was only seven at the time, and his siblings weren't much older. They waited in the parking lot for hours, huddling together for warmth as the night got darker and the air got colder.

Their mother finally walked out of the bar with some help from a new friend of hers. She would have collapsed to the ground if there hadn't been someone to hold. Decker watched as she followed her new friend to his car, climbed inside, and drove away. Not knowing what else to do, they slept in the van, shivering in the cold until their mother returned late the following afternoon.

Decker told me this story one night as we lay on the lawn outside my dorm, staring up at the stars. Our first psych midterm was the following morning, and we were taking a break from a particularly gruelling study session to get stoned. I thought he must have been joking at first, but one look at him confirmed he was serious.

At first glance, you'd be forgiven for writing Decker off as nothing more than your typical entitled, arrogant, narcissistic jock. I was guilty of that. He had reminded me of my brother, Clark, when I first met him.

Decker was charismatic and beautiful, with an athlete's physique and a thick mess of blond hair. There was always a smile on his face and an entourage of similarly attractive people hovering around him. He should have been the worst kind of person you would find on campus, and it was easy for me to avoid his orbit. Imagine my surprise, and suspicion, when he'd go out of his way to speak to me in public, when he showed a genuine interest in being my friend.

I tend to think the worst of people. Sometimes I'm guilty of typecasting them as two-dimensional caricatures, more like characters in my head than real humans. Decker surprised me. He was kind. He was gentle. He was perceptive and compassionate. He would never exclude, insult, or belittle anyone. Considering how much joy Vivi and I got from mocking everyone we came in contact with, Decker was annoyingly decent.

Vivi and I came from a stratum of privilege we resented. We were embarrassed by our bourgeois families. I suppose we still are, though it would be more embarrassing to admit that, at our age, we still care enough to be embarrassed.

I hated how my parents tried to groom me to be a younger version of my father, like Clark was — respectable, urbane, desperately conventional.

Vivi never could bear the weight of her family's expectations, explaining why she became an artist instead of a surgeon.

The proper thing to do would have been to show gratitude for our privilege. Instead, we ridiculed it.

Decker had no privilege to ridicule. He worked for everything in his life because his mother certainly wouldn't do it for him. Getting into university had been an obsession for him, graduating high school at the top of his class and earning every scholarship he could apply for. When everyone else was getting sauced at basement parties, he studied. When he wasn't studying, he bussed tables and installed drywall to keep his family fed.

Before Decker moved out to live on campus, his mother said she was ashamed of him for abandoning her. He made the two-hour journey by public transit every weekend to visit, spending most of his time cleaning the house or doing the laundry. I convinced him to let me tag along once, and it was difficult to reconcile how a person like Decker could be produced in an environment like the one I saw there. His mother followed us from room to room as he did the chores, mocking and menacing, a bone-dry desert thirsty for sympathy. A plastic cup never left her hand.

Decker couldn't hide his pride on graduation day. He was the first person in his family to earn a degree. But when he walked across the stage amid roars of applause, looking like the son every parent dreams of raising, I could see a moment of sadness flash behind his eyes. His mother hadn't shown up. His brother and sister, who grew up to be self-destructive and perpetually adrift, weren't there either. While everyone took photos with their families, Decker went to his dorm to fine-tune his resumé.

I bet people often wonder why he is friends with me and Vivi. We are petty and cynical, while he is caring and warm-hearted. I don't know what his explanation would be, but I do know why I'm friends with him: he makes me feel like I'm a better person than I am.

"I'm worried about you," Decker says. His face is different through the fuzzy resolution of the video-chat window on my tablet. There are creases around his eyes, and the ends of his mouth angle down like little hooks.

"You've got nothing to worry about," I reply, impressing myself with how normal my voice sounds. "I'm fine. Under the circumstances, I would say I'm doing better than fine. I'm good, even." I smile to prove my point, and he looks at me as though a lizard has crawled out of my mouth.

"That's the thing. You shouldn't be good. You shouldn't be fine. You should be a wreck. You should be with the people who care about you. Instead, you're alone on a deserted island."

An incredulous laugh escapes me, and the sound reminds me of Elias. "Why does everyone think this island is deserted? There are plenty of people here. There's even a gourmet churro shop. Tell me: Do deserted islands have churro shops?"

"You know I'd do anything to be there with you now, right?" There's so much earnestness in his voice it's almost pathetic. My eyes drill into his, willing them not to tear up. I don't need to see him crying for me.

"I know. I'm just happy that I'll see you tomorrow. You have a pregnant wife to look after. I'm lucky you'll be here at all. Sam needs you more than I do."

Do I really believe this? I'm not so sure. A part of me wants nothing more than for Decker and Vivi to drop everything to be with me, as though I were the only thing that mattered. Another slightly more insistent part of me wants them to forget I exist so they can go on with their lives, and I can go on with being alone on my deserted island.

"Sam feels awful that she can't be there at all," he says.

"I can't really hold that against her. If the doctor says not to fly, she shouldn't fly."

"Remember the last time we all took a flight together?" Decker asks, a nostalgic grin lighting up his handsome face.

"You mean when Sam threw up all over me on the way home from Jamaica?"

He laughs and it sounds like music. "I will never forget the look on your face. Pure disgust."

"I still don't understand why she decided to hurl on me instead of you, the boyfriend sitting on her other side. I'm sure a psychiatrist would have a field day analyzing Sam's subconscious motivation for turning left instead of right at that critical moment."

"It was revenge," he says. "You were really pissing her off that day."

"I think she knew that throwing up on you would have affected her odds of a ring in the future. Smart girl."

"Watching her cover you in vomit made me love her even more. That's what sealed the deal, to tell you the truth."

"Oh, shut your mouth," I say with a laugh.

"I'm just happy we didn't eat the same Jamaican patties she did. I warned her that the cart looked dodgy."

Decker and I sit in silence, smiling at the memory of Sam's embarrassed face, my white linen shirt covered in what resembled butternut squash soup, and the flight attendants' stifled giggles as they helped me out of my seat.

"I don't think I've ever seen Elias more embarrassed than he was on that flight," I say, remembering how unhelpful and self-conscious he had been. I regret ruining the moment by bringing him up, but I can't help it. "You would think he'd been the one covered in orange sludge."

Decker pauses to consider this. "I guess it can be easy to forget to laugh when you're too busy thinking."

. . . . .

Elias looks like a ghost. His night-sky eyes are flat and unseeing, their satellites dimmer than usual. The expression on his face is inhuman — not happy or sad or excited or calm but void of detectable emotion. I thought I loved this photograph. He looked invincible. Now that it's been blown up to this size, as though it were a portrait of Napoleon hanging in the Louvre, the larger-than-life-sized face of Elias looks alien. Lifeless.

"It's not right," I say. Maria's eyes dart in my direction, weary. "He doesn't look like himself."

"This is the picture you chose," she explains gently like I must have experienced a lapse in memory. "You chose the size and the frame too."

"Yes, I realize that." I try not to sound irritated, but the impatience bubbles under my skin, warm and satisfying. I let the negativity wash over me. It reminds me of how it feels to drift to sleep after fending it off until the end of a movie. The weakening of resistance. The sweet rush of submission.

"So what would you like us to do?" Maria asks.

"Change it. We need another photo. He needs to look alive. He needs to look like himself." The face stares back at me from behind the glass, caged within the handcrafted tin frame displayed on the easel in Maria's office. Its eyes aim past the sharp descent of its nose, a hawk's beak — no, a vulture's — as though gazing at its own vacant reflection.

"Si, señor. You can send me another photo. We will change it." Maria studies the face. I know she can't stand to look at me now, more out of pity than frustration.

Maria hasn't been the same since our encounter in the English Garden. The motherly warmth is gone, as is the playful sense of humour. There is only one Maria available to me now: the efficient professional. Her pity is the only thing that tempers the iciness between us. I see it in her eyes and in the way she pauses before every response. I would prefer the cold.

"What about the band?" I ask. "They're all set?"

"Yes, they will arrive the morning of the event," Maria says, still looking at the face. "On the first ferry of the day. We will be sure the sound check is complete in the afternoon. You have nothing to worry about."

"And the flowers? I want flowers on every table, on the bar, at the entrance, along the banisters, everywhere."

"Yes, there will be flowers, just like we discussed. We will have roses, lilies, marigolds, and, of course, the magnolias. It will be lovely."

"I hate flowers," I hear Elias say.

Be quiet. You don't hate flowers. Nobody hates flowers.

"Whatever you say, dear. It is your party."

"Señor?" Maria's manicured eyebrows are raised. I must have looked like I had drifted away.

"Sorry. What were you saying?"

"The cakes. Are you ready to sample them?"

Ah, yes. The cakes. How I had looked forward to tasting these cakes. Of course, the original plan involved my future husband being by my side as we sampled them. We would have giggled at the silliness of the process, nibbling at thin slivers while determined to choose the perfect one, like we were self-important judges in a televised baking competition. He would comment on the texture of one, while I would critique the flavour combination of another. We would disagree and defend our choices as though the outcome of this decision would leave an everlasting imprint on our lives. Finally, one of us would succumb to the other, and we would put forth our final decision, united. Perhaps I would playfully smear some frosting on Elias's cheek. He would smile and retaliate. We would leave the room happy, smeared in frosting, and having chosen a cake.

"Of course," I say with resignation. "The cakes."

Maria offers a terse smile, then leads me out of her office. I'm relieved to get away from the face behind the glass. We make our way through a hallway lined with doors before entering the lobby. Prisms of sunlight reflect throughout the room, forcing my eyes to squint. I hear greetings from staff members directed at me. My head nods, but I can't look at them.

The hotel is calm today. The guests are wasting away on the beach or harassing the locals in town. There is only a handful of intruders in khaki shorts and straw hats to avert my face from.

We climb a spiralling flight of stairs and enter the hotel's restaurant. I haven't eaten here — I haven't eaten much besides the occasional dish delivered by room service — but I know every detail about it from studying the hotel's website over the last fourteen months. Otra Luna is supposedly the island's top restaurant. Its owner, Ramona Merida, is part of the elite band of chefs from the capital and Oaxaca credited with revolutionizing Mexican cuisine over the past two decades.

Ramona prides herself on marrying ingredients from the land and the sea. As one critic put it, "Ramona Merida has transformed the humble concept of surf 'n' turf, creating a delicate harmony between earth and sea that allows the flavours to sing like a siren's call." Her signature dish is octopus grilled with lime, paired with pork tenderloin rubbed in chile adobo. It is served in a shallow clay bowl covered by a green purée of avocado and coriander, garnished with twists of zucchini blossoms. The slightly charred tentacles of the octopus wrap around the tenderloin like the kraken pulling an ill-fated ship into the murky sea.

The air in the restaurant is cool and soft. Light filters through the gauze-like curtains that cover the windows. Broad leaves spill from large ceramic pots, giving the space a wild, organic ambiance. The walls are decorated with brightly coloured masks depicting the Aztecs' fanciful interpretation of jaguars, their white eyes standing watch over the room below. Best of all, it's empty.

Maria motions for me to sit in one of the many bentwood chairs neatly arranged around linen-covered tables. She disappears through a door and returns minutes later with a middle-aged man wearing a typical chef's uniform of black pants and white double-breasted jacket. He pushes a cart with three plates, each one displaying a triangle of cake.

"Where's Chef Merida?" I ask.

Maria and the man swap glances. She gives me a tentative smile. "Chef Merida does not work here full-time. She lives in Mexico City."

"That's disappointing." Did I actually expect Chef Merida to guide me through this trivial tasting? I can't tell.

"She created the entire menu though, and visits once in a while to meet with the kitchen staff," Maria explains. "She even leads the dinner service on occasion."

"But she's not here now."

"No, unfortunately, she is not. Chef Merida has another restaurant in the capital where she plays a more hands-on role. This is our pastry chef, Javier," she goes on, gesturing to the man beside her. "Javier is known as the best on Isla de Espejos. Chef Merida chose him herself."

The man turns to me with a hopeful look, hands clasped modestly behind his back. "Mucho gusto, Javier," I say with a strained smile.

Maria takes a seat across the table from me as Javier wheels the cart beside us. He picks up one delicate dish at a time, carefully placing them on the table. Each cake is a bold, bright wedge of colour against the stark white of the porcelain and linen.

Javier introduces each slice with the panache of a circus ringmaster. The first option is encased in a shell of white frosting, its insides the colour of lemons.

Elias's voice whispers into my ear: "This isn't your wedding anymore."

You're right! I remember now. This isn't my wedding anymore. Because you're dead, and nobody wants to marry a corpse.

"You say that like it's my fault."

Is it not?

"Tell me, dear, how I might be to blame."

You were flying the plane, right? And it crashed.

"I did not crash that plane." He sounds defensive now, like he does when he's been cornered.

Perhaps not intentionally, but your job was to keep the plane in the air, was it not?

"Señor?" Maria and Javier look at me from across the table, eyes narrowed.

"Sorry. What did you say?"

Javier glances at Maria, then turns to me and says, "What do you think?"

"What do I think?"

"Of the cake," Maria clarifies, her words now tinged with the slightest trace of impatience.

"Oh! Yes, the cake. It's good. Wonderful, actually."

Javier smiles, relieved, and gestures to the second option. The sponge is deep crimson with a rich, dark coat — blood orange and chocolate ganache. I slice off the triangle's tip with my fork and wrap my mouth around it.

"It's morbid, no? Blood cake at a funeral?" Elias says with that tone of disapproval I know so well.

I choke. I inhaled too sharply, and the cake is now lodged in my throat. The violent sound of coughing echoes throughout the quiet room. Alarmed, Maria and Javier come toward me, but I ward them off with my left palm while beating on my chest with the other hand. I cough until I can breathe again.

"Are you okay?" Maria asks, now standing.

"I'm fine!" I say, breathing forcefully, my left palm still held in the air. "Maybe that was an omen. This cake has bad juju." I laugh, but they look at me like I'm the one that's cursed.

"I warned you about that cake," Elias says.

"What's next?" I look at Javier with intensified eagerness.

He hesitates before introducing the final option. Triangles of white sponge, bubbly and light, are sealed with thin layers of ivory cream. "Tres leches cake is very common in our country," Javier explains. "The cake is soaked in three different kinds of milk, hence the name. It is a simple treat, but we have created a more refined version for you."

I imagine what the full-sized cake would look like — an imposing pyramid of radiant white, inside and out. It's beautiful.

"You want to serve this cake at my funeral?" asks Elias with that incredulous tone of his.

Is there something wrong with this cake?

"Dear, that is a wedding cake."

Dear, they are all wedding cakes. These cakes are meant for weddings.

"Exactly. Not funerals."

This is not your fucking funeral!

"Ah, yes. That's right. I meant *celebration of life*."

Javier and Maria watch expectantly as I chew, but it's suddenly difficult to swallow. Their gaze drifts over my shoulder, and I hear the sharp clack of heels against tiles behind me. I turn around, my mouth still filled with cake, to see a familiar face.

The woman is striking. She enters with her dress billowing around her like a cloud of sheer silk several shades of green. Her face is partially covered by a wide-brimmed hat, but the waves of mahogany hair are distinct. It takes a moment to remember how I know this woman before it comes to me: she's the clumsy giraffe I knocked to the lobby floor the other day.

"Look at those cakes," the woman says sweetly, her English accent ringing through the room like the trill of piano keys.

"Señora, this is a private tasting," Maria answers.

"Oh, I didn't mean to interrupt," the woman says, blushing. "I must have gotten a little lost. I'll just be on my way then."

"Stay." The word leaves my mouth before I realize I'm saying it. I clear my throat, trying to hide my surprise. "You can help me choose."

"Really? It would be my pleasure," the woman says with a smile. She takes a seat beside me, smelling like a tropical flower. Maria flashes me a disapproving look but doesn't say a word.

"I'm having trouble deciding," I say. The truth is I need to be around someone who doesn't think I'm a pitiful mess. The woman's presence is refreshing at what may be the saddest cake tasting to ever take place.

"What's the occasion?" she asks, expecting my answer to be predictably ordinary, pleasant, not the least bit disturbing.

I consider the appropriate degree of honesty before saying, "It's just a celebration." She returns my smile, convinced.

Javier, looking relieved there is now someone new to alleviate the tension in the room, introduces the three cakes with renewed vigour. The woman listens intently, studying each slice with care before tasting. She closes her eyes after each bite to focus her attention on the flavours, weighing the merits of each option, intent on reaching an indisputable conclusion. I watch her, admiring how seriously she's treating this responsibility. The woman is the perfect cake-tasting companion.

"What do you think?" I ask after she's savoured the last bite with a flutter of eyelashes.

"We must know," says Elias with mock anticipation.

"I like all three. You really can't go wrong. But if you want my opinion, I would have to go with the tres leches cake. They're all delicious, but this one is special. It's pure and uncomplicated."

Maria and I exchange glances. "Pure and uncomplicated," I repeat, thinking over her words. "I couldn't agree more."

After finalizing the decision with Maria and Javier, the woman and I leave Otra Luna and wander toward the ocean. I learn that her name is Raina Babel. She's travelling alone.

"I was supposed to come here with my husband," she tells me. "Well, the man who was supposed to be my husband. This was meant to be our honeymoon. We had been planning it for months. It is still rather surreal that I'm here."

I think about whether or not to ask the obvious question, but she anticipates my hesitation.

"You're wondering why I'm on my honeymoon alone. It's okay. I don't mind telling you. It's simple, really. Honeymoons are for newlyweds, and we didn't get married."

"I'm sorry to hear that," I say, not sure of the appropriate response.

Raina laughs. "Don't be. Do you ever feel like something isn't quite right, even though everyone tells you it should be?"

I nod, but she can read the uncertainty on my face.

"I met Paul at a party hosted by a mutual friend of ours," she continues. "We graduated from the same uni and ran in similar social circles, but our paths didn't cross for years.

"I was a terrible, pathetic mess. My boyfriend at the time

had recently broken my heart. He was a cruel boy, disturbingly narcissistic. I look back now and count my lucky stars I didn't waste any more of my life on that tosser. But at the time, I was so embarrassingly sad.

"The only reason I decided to attend this party was because I knew my ex was going to be there. I was delusional. I thought he would take one look at me and fall madly back in love. I'm sure now this wouldn't have been possible. He was never in love with me in the first place. I swear he didn't even notice I was there. He was too busy putting his hands on every other girl in the room.

"I was so upset that I grabbed my things and ran out of the flat as quickly as I could. That was when I met Paul. I didn't see him at first. I was walking out the door and, before I knew it, I was on the floor. We had turned the corner at the exact same time and crashed right into one another! I am such a clumsy giraffe. And there we were, a heap of limbs on the hallway floor. He was such a gentleman. He kept apologizing as he helped me to my feet, then he picked up my things that were scattered everywhere."

"I can actually see that happening," I say with a soft smile. "You might not have recognized me, but we ran into each other in the lobby the other day. Literally. I had to hoist you off the floor."

"Oh dear, it was you! How embarrassing. I'm sorry again for being such a klutz. I am truly helpless."

"It's okay. I could do a better job myself of watching where I'm going. My head has been in the clouds lately. So what happened next, after you met Paul?"

"I was smitten from the very beginning. We went back inside the party together until we got bored and decided to find a late-night kebab. Then everything just unfolded from there.

"Paul was perfect. He was handsome. Well educated. Gainfully employed, which is always a nice bonus. My friends liked him.

My parents adored him. He treated me like the most important woman in the world. From that very first moment on the hallway floor, he showed me nothing but respect and kindness.

"When Paul proposed five years later, everyone was thrilled. They told me how lucky I was to be engaged to this flawless man. They were right. I was lucky. I was going to get everything every young woman dreams about. I could see how much Paul loved me. I could see how happy everyone was for me, for us. The problem was I didn't *feel* anything.

"I knew I should have been happy, but I didn't feel happiness. I floated through the engagement in a cloud of doubt, and soon doubt became the only thing I could feel. Eventually, doubt gave way to guilt for not feeling the way I should, for being inexplicably flawed. I went through the motions and played the part of the blushing bride-to-be, but the doubt and the guilt ate away at me slowly. I researched wedding venues, signed invitations, attended dress fittings, all the while wondering if the wedding would even take place, if I would actually go through with it. I suppose I assumed I would be too weak to stop it.

"The worst part is that nobody seemed to realize there was something wrong. My friends, my family, my fiancé — none of them noticed anything out of the ordinary. I'm sure I put on a very convincing show, but I would have hoped that someone, anyone, would have known me well enough to realize there was something the matter. Nobody did.

"I called off the engagement three weeks ago. The wedding was scheduled for last Saturday. I told Paul during dinner. It wasn't planned. I intended to go through with the wedding, to succumb to it, but we were eating peas and chicken, and I realized that I never liked peas and chicken — and that I didn't want Paul. It just came out of my mouth before I could stop it. I told him I didn't want to marry him.

"He laughed at first. He thought I was cracking a joke. Then he understood that I wasn't. He pleaded. Then he cried. Then he called me a selfish bitch. I like to think that deep down he knew we were never meant to be together, but I'm not sure.

"He's right though. I am a selfish bitch. I wasted six years of his life, and I can't justify how or why. I suppose it was just easier to go along for the ride than to take the wheel. It's easy to believe you're happy and in love when there's no reason to think otherwise. But when you're confronted with something as permanent as marriage, the truth finds a way to surface."

The sun begins its slow descent behind us, casting a fiery glow across the beach. Raina looks even more brilliant in this light, and I find it difficult to imagine a sad, cold version of this woman. There is so much life in her.

She turns to me as her hair dances in the breeze. "Do you think I'm a despicable person?"

"Of course not" is my response, delivered by reflex rather than honesty. Deserting one's fiancé three weeks before the wedding is not a decent thing to do. That's undeniable. But surely it's more respectable than going through with it and prolonging a relationship void of love. Who am I to judge, anyway?

"Paul deserved honesty, and that's what you gave him." My words are slow and thoughtful. "It would not have hurt any less if you had left him one year before the wedding or rejected his proposal outright. Sure, it would have saved you both a great deal of trouble, but the result is no different. Like you said, the truth is not always evident. Sometimes it needs to be forced out. The important thing is you recognized your truth, and you did something about it."

Raina looks at me in silence with an expression of relief, possibly gratitude, before letting out a musical laugh. "Listen to me, burdening you with my tales of woe. You didn't sign up for this."

"It's no bother. I'm happy you told me."

"Enough about silly me. I want to know your story," she says, linking her arm in mine.

I was afraid this would happen. "Oh, I'm not all that interesting," I say with a nervous laugh.

"Why don't you start by telling me why you were tasting cakes by yourself? What's this mysterious celebration you're planning?"

"It's my wedding," I blurt out before I've had the chance to formulate what to say. Raina's face lights up, and I hurriedly correct myself. "Shit. It's not my wedding. I mean, not anymore, at least." She now looks confused.

I take a deep breath before going on. "What I mean to say is it was supposed to be my wedding. I was supposed to get married in three days, here, at the Ōmeyōcān."

"What happened?"

My throat tightens, closing around the salty air I try to inhale. "He died. My fiancé died a few days ago, unexpectedly."

Raina stops walking. Our bare feet sink into the sand as the ocean's waves pool around us, then recede, in and out, in time with our breathing. For the first time today, it seems like Raina is at a loss for words. She looks at me, then down at our feet, then back at me. "I'm so sorry."

"Thank you," I say, not knowing how to respond.

"How did he ...?" she asks, unable to finish the question.

"A plane. It crashed."

A look of recognition flashes across her eyes.

"He was one of the pilots." I regret the words as soon as they leave my mouth.

The recognition becomes a look of revelation. "No ..."

Stupid. I am stupid.

"That plane near Iceland ..." she says.

I am such a fool.

Raina might have been the only person in the hotel unaware of how fascinatingly tragic I am, and now I've ruined that special distinction.

"That man was your fiancé?"

"He was."

I don't know what else to say. I want to hate this woman for calling Elias "that man." I want to hate her for forcing this out of me, but I don't. We are the same, Raina and I. We had everything, and now we have nothing. We chose this perfect island to usher in a new era in our perfect lives, but instead we are here, alone, with no possible way of ignoring how imperfect we are.

. . . . .

I return to my room, and it's a relief. It has become my refuge, so dark and warm and still, from the cruel, pitying world outside.

My walk with Raina left me feeling ill at ease. Something she said, about how she felt with Paul, struck a nerve. The throbbing in my chest has returned.

I can't stop seeing the look on her face when she realized who should have been sitting beside me in the restaurant today. The sadness would be expected, but there was apprehension as well. I don't think she doubted I was telling the truth, but there was something in her eyes that hinted at her sudden discomfort with me, as though my fiancé's death said something about who I am. It lasted for a moment if at all, but I can't get that look out of my mind.

I stand over the altar I built for Elias on the windowsill. The bowl of cereal has become a thick, reddish soup and the edges of the candles are black with ash, but the marigolds are still bold and bright. Thinking about how silly it is, I light the candles until they flicker together like a chorus of saints framed by the indigo sky. The candle of the angel that Maria gave me stands proudly in the middle, taller than the others.

"It's beautiful," Elias says.

"You're not going to lecture me on how vulgar and disrespectful this display is to your beliefs?"

"No. If it brings you peace, then it's not silly or vulgar or disrespectful. I just want you to be happy."

I stand in silence for a long time, watching the reflection of the flames on the window. The throbbing in my chest has worsened.

I walk over to the nightstand and pick up the book I brought from home. Tucked between the pages is a folded sheet of paper. I open it slowly, feeling how smooth and crisp it is against my fingers.

It's a note from Elias. He wrote it before leaving for Berlin, the morning after our last night together when we watched the planes from our spot on Iona Beach. I woke up that morning to find his side of the bed empty, the lingering smell of his skin on the sheets. There was a note on the kitchen counter in the same spot he always left them. He wrote them so frequently that I stopped saving them long ago, but this one I kept. This one was special. Now, it's the last.

My dear,

You're sleeping so soundly, I didn't want to wake you. I will always remember last night. It is more difficult than usual to leave you this time, but don't worry about me. Take care of yourself in Mexico. We shall have our happy ending.

See you in the sky.
E.

"Can we eat?" Clark asked. He sat slouched in his favourite armchair, arms dangled over the sides in a performative show of impatience.

"Let's just give him another few minutes," I answered, looking at my phone. No calls, no messages. "It's not like him to not show up."

"Sure, little brother. He's always been so dependable." The sarcasm was as thick as his chestnut hair. "Maybe he's afraid of Mom's cooking." He laughed in that ugly, arrogant way of his.

Clark and I were at our parents' house in Deep Cove, a suburban village on the outskirts of the city, for our weekly family dinner. The ritual has become irregular these days, planned for whenever we can find the time, but back then my mother made sure we met every Sunday.

Elias and I had been together for almost four years by that point, and he refused to take part in the Caraway family Sunday dinner. When I first invited him after he moved in with me, I didn't blame him for not wanting to join. These dinners could be gruelling: Dad describing which beloved civic institution he planned to demolish next, Mom fussing over every little thing, Clark just existing at all. Over time though, it began to bother me that Elias seemed to have no desire to spend time with my family and that my family didn't seem to mind.

This changed the week prior. Elias asked unexpectedly if he could join us for dinner. It caught me by surprise, but I was elated. I was also nervous about the idea of Elias, Clark, Mom, Dad, and me sitting down together for a civilized meal. The stakes were high. I knew this dinner would set the dynamic between Elias and my family, and there was much that could go wrong. I forbade my mother from patronizing him with her distorted idea of Mexican cuisine. We decided to play it safe with a simple, rustic menu of coq au vin and garlic mashed potatoes, with butter tarts for dessert.

The meal was keeping warm in the oven while we waited. Elias was supposed to have arrived an hour earlier. He wasn't picking up my phone calls or answering my messages.

"Honey, I'm sure he's fine," said Mom. "Traffic can be horrendous on the bridge this time of night."

"It's Sunday," Clark said, "and he doesn't drive."

"Hush," she snapped back. "He's taking a cab, isn't he? I'm sure he's just stuck in traffic, Sunday or not."

"Can you try him again?" Clark's face wore a trademark expression of his, a perfect fusion of boredom and impatience and contempt. "He's an hour late. If he doesn't have the decency to notify us, then I don't see why we need to extend the courtesy of waiting for him all night."

Choosing not to respond, I stepped into the hall to call Elias for the seventh time. I'd been able to stay relatively calm, but I could sense the shadow approaching. It tickled the hairs on the back of my neck, sent flashes through my fingertips. I focused on bringing air into my lungs as the phone rang. Elias's recorded voice sounded distant after the fourth ring. "Hello, you have reached Elias Santos ..."

The hum in my ears began, dull but steady. I had to get out of there.

"I have to go," I said to everyone in the kitchen as I passed them on the way to the front entrance.

"Coen, where are you going?" I heard my mother protest. Ignoring her, I slipped on my shoes and headed into the darkness.

I drove with the windows rolled down, letting the icy air numb my skin. My fists gripped the steering wheel as I made my way over the bridge, the ocean black like tar underneath, then through the lights of the city toward home.

I don't know what I expected to find when I walked through the door. I searched our apartment, shouting his name, but it didn't take long for me to see it was empty. There was no note on the kitchen counter. His shoes and jacket were missing from the coat closet. There was no sign of him.

It took all my energy to keep the pricking of the needles at bay. The ringing in my ears remained a steady hum. My hands shook as I called Vivi and Decker, neither of whom had any idea where Elias would be. Realizing there was nobody else in our lives Elias would feasibly be with, my hands shook even harder as I called the nearest hospital. Then the second nearest. Then the third. It took over an hour to get through and confirm that nobody matching his name or appearance had been admitted.

I walked laps around every tidy, compact room for hours, checking my phone obsessively while drinking wine. I held my breath every time the phone rang, but it was my parents, Vivi, Decker.

I anticipated the worst, as I always did. I waited for the police to call to tell me there had been a horrible accident. It was a familiar prophecy. Elias would be late coming home by fifteen minutes, and my mind would imagine him falling on train tracks or being run over by a truck. I couldn't help it.

The only thing worse was the idea of Elias simply vanishing. No horrific accident. No tragic death. Just gone.

Elias always showed up eventually. He would return home without fanfare, and I would silently reprimand myself for letting my imagination run away from me. I always knew that one day it wouldn't just be my imagination. One day he wouldn't return.

It was past midnight when I heard the front door open. The shadow disappeared as soon as the key clicked in the lock. I don't think I felt relieved, or thankful, or angry. I felt nothing.

Elias entered the room slowly, his face grim. I think it was guilt, but I can't say for sure. We stood there looking at one another.

"Where were you?" The sound of my voice startled me as it broke the silence.

"I needed to be alone."

I paused before repeating, "Where were you?"

"That's not important. I should have answered your calls. It was wrong of me to let you worry. I know that. I'm sorry."

"Where were you?"

I felt so tired then. My mind was cloudy and my legs ached, but I needed an answer from Elias.

"Coen, I told you. It doesn't matter. I'm sorry."

"Of all the days, you had to disappear today. Why? To humiliate me in front of my family? In front of Clark?"

"What are you talking about?"

"We waited for you for over an hour. Imagine how stupid I looked not being able to explain where you were or why you weren't showing up."

"Coen, I was never going to your parents' for dinner," he said carefully.

"You were supposed to be there when you were done."

"Listen to me. That was not the plan."

"Don't you dare," I said, my voice fraught. "You always do this. You know you're in the wrong, so you try to turn it around on me, to make it seem like I'm the wrong one. You have been missing for hours. I've been calling you. I've been calling hospitals. Don't try to make this about me."

It was becoming harder to breathe, and I couldn't help but choke on my words, but I was able to say what I needed to. I expected Elias to be defensive. He just stood there, silent.

"I got my licence today," he said finally. "I'm a pilot."

I didn't know how to respond. I looked at him. He looked at me.

"That's great. Isn't it?" I managed to say, barely louder than a whisper.

"It is."

"Then why aren't you happy?"

"I just needed to be alone."

I never discovered where he was that evening. I never found out why he didn't show up for dinner or answer my calls. We were both so exhausted that we went to bed, and neither of us brought it up the next morning. It was easier that way.

Instead, we decided to celebrate. When I first met Elias, becoming a commercial airline pilot was his only dream. We knew his training would eventually lead to his certification — he took it more seriously than anything, and he had become one of the top prospects — but there had always been suspicion lurking in the back of his mind that something would go wrong. But it didn't, so we celebrated.

After dinner at our favourite Persian eatery, we went to a haunted carnival being held on the other side of town. We laughed and screamed as we wandered through the fairgrounds, where actors dressed as killer clowns jumped at us through the fog. I don't think I've ever seen Elias laugh as much as he did that night. I guess he could finally let his mind rest, be free to laugh instead of think.

A few months later, Elias was hired as first officer for a major airline. His pride was palpable. The night before his first flight, I walked in on him staring at his uniform hanging on a hook behind our bedroom door. He looked at me and smiled.

I woke up the next morning, and he was gone. I wanted to see him before he left, to kiss him goodbye, but I had slept through the alarm. He must have decided not to wake me. Instead, there was a note on the kitchen counter.

My dear,

I am off to fly around the globe. But worry not! I will return. And when I do, we shall celebrate. Do not miss me too much. I love you.

See you from the sky.
E.

ESPEJO ROTO
Five days after the crash

At one point in time, the Aztecs were the most feared and powerful people in this land of dusty plains and soaring mountains. They commanded an entire empire from the centre of their universe: Tenochtitlan, their island capital in a vast lake cradled within the Valley of Mexico.

Rulers and councilmen congregated in the capital with ambitions of expanding the empire across Mesoamerica, while commoners farmed the land and raised families. They built cities and alliances and pyramids, making enemies along the way. But that didn't matter. They were untouchable.

Then along came Hernán Cortés and his conquistadors. When they dropped anchor near the coast, not far from Isla de Espejos, the Aztecs mistook these strange men — with fairer skin and weapons that shot thunder — as gods. The ruler of the Aztecs, Moctezuma II, sent gifts of gold to the Spaniards before receiving them in his capital as a gesture of peace.

What happened next? Just another tragic display of the impressive human capacity for destruction. Cortés's heart didn't grow three times larger, and there was no surprise happy ending. The Spaniards imprisoned Moctezuma II within the walls of his own city before murdering him. Thousands of Aztecs were killed in battle. The Spaniards razed Tenochtitlan to the ground and built their capital of New Spain directly on its grave. All that is left of the great Aztec capital are the ruins of its once-mighty pyramids. They rest, defeated, in the main square at the centre of Mexico City, a reminder of how greatness can fall when trust is misplaced.

A vague feeling of dread stirs within my belly as if my body senses an impending attack. The vessel drifting toward me is not a galleon filled with Spaniards but a double-decker ferry carrying people who know me from a distant home.

It's arrival day. Everyone has flown in from a faraway land and now sails into the lagoon of my island fortress. The sanctuary I've created is about to come under siege. This is my Tenochtitlan. My Neverland.

The faces of these people may be familiar, but they are foreign nonetheless. They don't know this island like I do. They cannot know how it feels to be me. They will step off the boat like they belong here and attempt to deceive me with their sympathetic words, but I know better. They will never belong, and they could never understand. We are different now.

I awoke this morning with a ringing in my ears and the sheets wrapped around my body like a protective cocoon. The room was dark and still. The only indication of morning were the slivers of light peeking along the edges of the blinds that covered every window.

Elias's altar rested by the window nearest the bed, looking less reverent today. The candles must have burned through the night. The wax had melted away, leaving hollow pillars of glass coated in black ash. The marigolds appeared duller, less alive. The display was more forlorn than holy.

"I apologize for my amateur attempt at an altar," I said, sitting up in bed.

There was no answer.

"Even an atheist like you doesn't deserve this convenience-store version of spirituality."

Silence.

I scanned the room, expecting Elias's voice to project out of nowhere, like an audible version of him springing from the closet to get a jump out of me. There was nothing but the burned-out candles and his last note to me lying on the nightstand.

I read the note again. Then again. For years, Elias signed off his notes in the same reliable way.

See you from the sky.

This last note was different. Not significantly so but different nonetheless.

See you in the sky.

I crumpled the paper in my hand and let it drop to the floor.

The unsettled feeling that clouded my thoughts only seemed to get worse, foggier, as the day wore on. Now, standing on the pier with the sun warming my skin, the breeze streaming through my hair, and the most important people in my life so close to being reunited with me after having travelled so far, I realize how defective I am. A normal person would be happy, or at least relieved, rather than whatever it is I'm feeling now.

As the boat is moored to the pier, I am pulled back to reality by a pair of deceptively strong arms that wrap around me. All of a sudden, I am surrounded by noise and movement. Another familiar body holds me from behind. They smell like coffee and vanilla and sweat.

"Babe, I am never letting you spend this much time away from me ever again, do you hear me?" Vivi says, holding my face in her perfect piano-playing hands.

"I'm never letting you go, ever," Decker shouts from behind me, his muscular arms clenched like a vise around my chest. "I'm the Rose to your Jack."

I surrender myself to them as they hold me and shout things at me, first smiling and bright-eyed, then smiling and teary-eyed. I can't think of anything to say. I just watch them in a stupor, soaking in their energy. For the first time in days, I feel like my old self. The unease that had gripped me just minutes before has melted away into something warm. I had forgotten how much I need these people in my life, how lost and alone I am without them. As they shake me and hold me, I feel hopeful. I am still human. I can survive this.

"Say something, damn it!" Vivi screams at me, simultaneously laughing and crying.

"Welcome to paradise!" The words tumble from my mouth like I've dropped a fistful of coins. They do the trick. Vivi smiles and wraps her arms around me again as Decker tightens his grip.

When they finally release me, I am swept away by an undertow of faces and hugs and good perfume and bad perfume. The pier feels so impossibly crowded with people and luggage that I'm sure it will collapse beneath the weight. I float through the scene as though on a marvelous drug. Familiar faces swarm around me, vying for my attention.

I make facial expressions and say words, wondering if they will be the ones people want to see and hear. Condolences are offered like little gifts of sadness, and I'm sure my careless responses are deemed inadequate. But that's fine with me. This is my island. I can relax the usual control I assert over myself. Plus, Vivi and Decker stay close by my side. They're my sentinels, my defenders.

My senses sharpen when I see my mother and father. They look less imposing in their matching resort-wear outfits of khaki shorts and polo shirts in complementary pastels, but my lungs inhale deeply in preparation nonetheless.

I've always been an outsider in my family. At some point in time, we must have accepted that we would never truly understand one another. I used to place the blame on them for not trying hard enough. Then I placed the blame on myself for being too difficult to love. Now I know we are all at fault.

My mother approaches with her arms open, engulfing me. "My poor son," she says, arms outstretched to cradle my face in her hands. Her eyes are unblemished by tears, not that I'd expect otherwise, but they appear to corroborate the compassion in her voice. "You don't deserve this."

It takes me by surprise when she buries her face against my shoulder and begins to sob, shaking rhythmically with each hiccup. My father stands behind her, unsure of what to do. He decides the most appropriate action would be to pat her on the back in the most mechanical of comforting gestures.

"It's okay, Mom," I say, feeling as helpless as my father. I rub her back while trying to avoid colliding with my father's patting hand. "I'm doing fine. Really, I am." I look at her and force a smile only she would believe. She smiles back and pulls away.

With a sharp inhale, I turn to my father. He offers a sympathetic look and extends his right arm. "It's good to see you, son."

"Likewise," I respond, taking his hand in mine. After a second's hesitation, he catches me off guard by pulling me in for an embrace. Now he's patting my back.

"It's a terrible thing," he says. "Remember that we love you and that we're here for you."

"Thanks, Dad," I say, not knowing where to put my hands. "I'm happy you're both here."

He takes a step back and studies me with an uncommon tenderness in his intense eyes. We three Caraways stand together in a triangle of what may be the sincerest moment we've shared in years when I glance past my father's shoulder. I had almost forgotten about someone.

My brother stands there, looking solemn and uncertain. He's dressed like an outcast from a yacht club, wearing seersucker shorts that are rolled up above his knees and a matching blazer, with the accoutrements you would expect to complete this look: plain white T-shirt, tortoiseshell sunglasses, braided belt, leather boat shoes. I've done a decent job of remaining calm up to this point, but my muscles tighten now.

Clark Caraway was born two years before me, the same year as Elias, and we've shared everything since the day I was born. From our genes to our education to the colour of our hair, the similarities in our origins should have resulted in other parallels. But I can't think of two people more different than me and my brother.

When I was eight years old, Clark and I built a fort together in the woods behind our house. It took several weeks. We collected old pallets and plywood that we convinced shop owners to give to us. We even scavenged a few pieces from back alleys. Once the materials were gathered and the plans were drawn, we began construction. Clark took charge of the hammering while I helped by holding things in place. We had fun. It was the only time we did something I imagined brothers should do together.

We were proud of our accomplishment. I couldn't wait to hang out with my brother in the fort that we had built together. I figured we would have sleepovers there, play games, or just sit inside and talk. It would be our special place.

I was wrong. Clark invited his boorish friends over the day we finished building, and they took over the fort. I wasn't allowed inside or anywhere near them. It was theirs now, not ours. It always had been. That's when I learned that Clark would never be anything more than someone who shared my family name.

Now we stand here on the pier, looking at one another with uncertainty, waiting to see who makes the first move. The breeze streams through his thick chestnut hair, which I know has been meticulously styled to appear windswept. With the older, taller, stronger, more charismatic Caraway brother standing in front of me, it feels like I'm staring at the actor who'd be cast to play me in the Hollywood version of my life.

After an uncomfortable silence a few seconds too long, Clark grins broadly and walks toward me with his arms outstretched. My body tenses up as he grabs me by the head. He gives it a playful shake before wrapping himself around me in a hug, smothering me with his cologne that smells like tobacco rolled in leather. "Little bro," he says. "It's good to see you."

He releases and assesses me, tucking his sunglasses into the pocket of his blazer. His stupid grin softens into something else, lips pursed and eyes squinted. "This is a nightmare. I can't imagine what you must be going through."

I don't know what to do or say, so I just nod my head in agreement.

You definitely don't have any idea.

"Listen, if there is anything I can do, anything at all, you tell me," he goes on. "I'm here for you, Coenhead."

I wince as he says this last word, a name that never really caught on despite Clark's best efforts. He thought it was clever when he first came up with it, and he hasn't given up over twenty years later.

"I'll keep that in mind," I say. Vivi and Decker hear the subtle hint of sarcasm; Clark does not.

"I don't want to interrupt this Caraway family moment," Vivi says, "but we should get going. The shuttles are waiting."

She knows when it's time to pull me out of a situation, especially when it involves my family. Everyone can see that she's right. Only two vans remain from the fleet sent by the hotel.

"All right then," Clark says, grabbing his suitcase and slinging a duffel bag over his shoulder. "Let's get this party started."

Everyone looks at him, and he realizes what he has said. Decker catches my eye with a knowing glance and shakes his head ever so slightly.

"I mean …" Clark stammers. "You know what I mean."

Vivi and Decker sit on either side of me in the rear of the van like a human shield. My parents sit in the middle row while Clark takes the front seat beside the driver. I try not to think about the patronizing small talk the driver is likely being subjected to.

We make our way past the palm trees and fruit stands that line the road, speeding toward the hotel I've confined myself in for the past few days. It's surreal. Everyone talks with such rhythmic timing that it feels scripted, like there's an unspoken understanding that silence cannot be allowed. My mother asks a question, then my father interjects before I can speak, then Decker jumps in with a quirky anecdote from their flight this morning. Everything flows with mechanical efficiency. The mood in the van is cautiously upbeat, cheerful almost. Everyone does their part to mitigate awkwardness, extinguishing any hint of darkness by keeping things buoyant and distracted. It's an impressive feat of collective repression.

As I would expect, Elias's name is not uttered once. His existence is not even alluded to. I suppose there will be time for Elias, but this post-reunion drive will not be it.

• • • • •

"This concerns me."

Vivi examines the altar that sits dejectedly on my windowsill. She studies each offering with bemusement on her face and her arms crossed over her chest. "Seriously, Coen. This is disturbing."

"What do you mean?" I say, betraying my defensiveness. "It's a harmless tribute."

"You don't believe in god. You don't believe in any of this. I just find it alarming that you spend a week alone on a Mexican island and now you're all of a sudden making offerings to angels and virgins."

"Maybe you'd start doing uncharacteristic things if you lost your fiancé a week before your wedding day."

Vivi pauses, sighs, and closes her eyes. "It just doesn't seem like you. That's all I'm trying to say."

"I think it's nice," Decker chimes in, eyeing the bowl of soggy gruel that was once Elias's favourite cereal. "It's no different than those makeshift memorials that pop up on highways where cars have crashed. It's a way to honour someone's life, to remember them."

"Thank you," I say, walking over to the bed. I lay myself down as my legs begin to ache. "See? Decker gets it."

"I guess," Vivi says, unconvinced. "Isn't this supposed to lure Elias's spirit back from the underworld?"

"Something like that," I say. "According to my wedding planner, at least. That wouldn't be so bad, would it? Guiding his spirit back here?"

"No," she agrees, taking a seat beside me on the bed. She runs her fingers through my hair. "It wouldn't be so bad."

The drive from the pier to the hotel was more tolerable than I had anticipated it would be. It felt good to be surrounded by familiar voices. Even so, I was relieved to part ways from the others as they retreated to their rooms. It has been a tiring day of emotional shifts, first dread, then elation, then restraint. Vivi and Decker let me recharge for an hour before ambushing me in my room, dressed for the evening's festivities: a welcome reception at the Terrace Bar with all forty-four guests, then dinner at Otra Luna.

"Should we head over?" Decker asks, glancing at his watch. "It's almost time."

"A few more minutes," I say, eyes closed. "I just need a few minutes."

"For sure, bud," he says. "Take all the time you need. You should be fashionably late anyway. Make an entrance."

"Exactly."

"I'm worried about you," Vivi says in her gentlest of tones, spreading herself beside me on the bed.

"You have no reason to worry," I assure her. "Considering the circumstances, I really am feeling fine. Is it the altar? Does it really bother you that much?"

"It's not just that. It's everything. The fact that we're here on this island. The fact that you haven't been home since the crash. The fact that your wedding is now a funeral but still feels more like a wedding."

They both look at me with caution and anticipation, the expression one wears when they have finally gathered the courage to say what has been on their mind.

I let her words hang in the air. I swear they're holding their breath. Finally, I look at them and say, "This isn't a wedding. It's not a funeral either. It's a celebration of life."

The two of them glance at each other so quickly it's barely perceptible. "Of course," Vivi says. "You're right. But what about the gift baskets? Maybe those weren't a good idea."

"What's wrong with the gift baskets?" I ask. "You don't like them?"

"They're lovely. That's not the point. Gift baskets are a great idea for a wedding but pretty fucking weird for a celebration of life, don't you think?" Vivi's tone is less gentle now.

A gift basket was placed in every guest's room to welcome them to the hotel, filled with things like miniature bottles of wine and scented candles. Tucked in front was a card with a personalized message and an itinerary of the upcoming festivities. I had worked with Maria weeks ago on customizing the baskets for the wedding. The only thing that was changed recently was the message on the cards before Maria's team placed them in each suite earlier today.

"I wasn't going to throw out all those baskets. That stuff cost a lot of money."

"I get it," Vivi says. "I just want to understand your state of mind right now. I want to know that you're handling all of this in a healthy way, but there are more alarm bells going off than I would like, babe. Like gift baskets. And altars. I mean, we're on our way to a cocktail party, for fuck's sake."

"Vivi," Decker interjects. "Enough." He sits beside me and puts his arm around my shoulders. "We are your closest friends, Coen. We're on your side. We're just worried about you."

"What should I be doing then?" I ask. "Tell me, please. I would love for someone to just tell me what to do. What is the right and proper and normal thing to do in this situation? I clearly haven't got a clue."

"I told you that first day!" Vivi cries. She springs off the bed and begins pacing the room. "Cancel everything. Come home. Be with the people who love you. Cry. Be an utter mess. Scream. Freak out. That's what you should have been doing. But you didn't listen to me. You locked yourself up on this island, alone. And now you're going to put yourself through this spectacle as though everything is normal. It's not normal, Coen. None of this is normal. I haven't seen you cry yet. I haven't seen you scream.

Every time I hear you say that you're fine, I cringe. I worry about you even more, because you shouldn't be *fine*."

She looks at me, empty now. A long, laboured breath deflates her lungs as it streams past her lips. I stand up from the bed and put my arms around her.

"I just need you both to trust me," I say. "None of this makes sense to you, but neither of you have gone through what I'm going through now. Everybody would handle this differently, and I'm doing it my way. I can't get through it alone though. I need you both to be there for me. Can you do that?"

There's a silent pause before Vivi nods. I look at Decker, and his hands grip my shoulders. "We're here for you," he says.

"Good," I say. "Now let's move. We're late."

. . . . .

The atmosphere in the Terrace Bar is even moodier than usual tonight. Every reflective surface, from cocktail tumblers to the mirror-panelled walls, glints like a gem as it catches the light.

Most of the guests have already arrived. They are dressed in rich-toned suit jackets and safe black dresses. I make my way through the room, shaking hands and kissing cheeks. I smile through the greetings and condolences. I don't care what they think. I am going to smile through this.

I pass the servers balancing trays of champagne, cringing at the smell of it in the air, and steer myself toward the bar. A broad smile appears on Gabriel's face as he sees me. As usual, he is dressed in black from head to toe. His goatee is slightly thicker tonight, and his sleeves are rolled up just past his elbows.

"Welcome, my friend."

"It's good to see you. I want you to meet a couple people, but I think they got lost in the crowd over there." I try to wave

Vivi and Decker over, but it looks like they've been cornered by two friends from university. I turn to Gabriel with a shrug. "I'll introduce you later."

"What are you having tonight?"

"Tears of Men," I say with a lopsided grin and a wink. There is no way I pulled that off.

"Coming right up," he says, winking back. Within thirty seconds, there is a glass in front of me with the familiar amber-coloured potion.

"¡Salud!" I tip my glass toward Gabriel before drawing a long, thirsty sip.

"It must feel nice, no?" he says. "Having your people around you again."

"It is nice. I missed them. It feels like I've been on this island for ages." I laugh, though I'm not sure why.

"It is not such a bad thing, is it?" Gabriel asks. "To be on this island forever?"

"No, it certainly is not. I can't think of a place I would rather be."

"But there is also nowhere quite like home, no?"

"No. I mean yes. You're right, I guess."

A pair of hands grabs me by the shoulders from behind. Vivi and Decker appear on either side of me, protectively close. Gabriel smiles and shakes their hands as I introduce them.

"Coen has told me much about the two of you," Gabriel says, mixing soda with tamarind juice for Decker and pouring Scotch on the rocks for Vivi.

"All good things, I'm sure," she says with a coy smile.

"Only the best and most lovely things." He passes the drinks across the bar, and we clink our glasses together.

"Are you also botanists?" Gabriel asks, leaning forward with his hands on the countertop.

Vivi and Decker glance at each other, their glasses frozen in front of their lips.

"I should say a few words," I say before either of them has a chance to respond. Vivi's eyebrows are crinkled as she lowers her glass.

"What do you mean?" Decker asks. "Like a speech?"

"Yeah. Just to break the ice, welcome everyone to the island."

"Are you sure you want to do that?" Vivi asks, but I'm already clinking my glass against the side of my ring to get the attention of everyone in the dim room.

Vivi and Decker exchange more glances in my peripheral vision as I continue clinking my glass. The people around the bar turn toward me, but those farther away are still chatting, oblivious to my pleas for attention. The music that had been playing in the background ends abruptly, presumably Gabriel's doing.

"Excuse me!" I shout. "Excuse me, everyone! Could I have your attention, please?"

A few more people notice my voice, but the heavy din of conversation persists from the back of the room. I look around helplessly. Taking a deep breath, I prepare to shout louder when a shrill whistle pierces the noise from behind me.

"Ladies and gentlemen, Señor Coen would like to say a few words," Gabriel says. His voice booms with authority, but he doesn't need to shout. He holds a microphone in front of his mouth, likely retrieved from behind the bar while I floundered in the noise. With a faint flex of the lips, he passes the microphone across the countertop to my unsteady hand.

The room becomes quiet in seconds. Everyone looks at me, waiting.

"Thank you, Gabriel," I say with a laugh I hope sounds casual and unfazed. I clear my throat, and the sound rumbles unflatteringly through the speakers. "Hello, everyone. If you haven't already met Gabriel here, you should. He whips up a mean drink. We've become very close over the past few days. He's been a welcome distraction, if you know what I mean." I laugh again. Nobody else seems to find it funny except for someone near the back of the crowd, who I imagine to be Clark.

"Anyway, we just want to welcome you all to paradise. We know you've come a long way to be here. Elias and I can't tell you how grateful we are. Elias certainly can't tell you because, well, you know, he's gone. But if he were still here …"

See you in the sky. Elias's voice is soft as a whisper. But it's not his voice. Not really.

"… he would have been really touched to see all of you. Very touched. And he would want you all to enjoy yourselves. We're in this exquisite hotel …"

See you in the sky. The voice is louder, reverberating through the tunnels of my ears. My mouth feels like a pit of ashes as the words tumble out.

"… on this dreamy island. Even though there will no longer be a wedding two days from now, it will still be a celebration. We are going to celebrate Elias's life in style. It's going to be perfect. It's going to be …"

SEE YOU IN THE SKY.

"… unforgettable! Please raise your glass with me. Let's toast — to paradise!"

There is an unexpected silence before a few scattered voices echo the toast. The only voice I can hear clearly is Clark's coming from somewhere to my left. Most people simply raise their glasses, surveying the room with self-conscious eyes.

Beads of sweat have formed along the top of my forehead. My face doesn't feel comfortable, like every expression is laboured and unnatural, but I force a smile.

"Please enjoy yourselves," I go on. "Have another drink. Come see Gabriel. He'll take good care of you. Dinner will be served in the restaurant in twenty minutes."

My lips remain stretched into a warped smile as my eyes sweep across the crowd. With a shake of the head, I spin around and set the microphone on the bar.

Did that go well?

Gabriel offers me an encouraging smile. "Another?"

"Please," I say, eagerly handing him my empty glass.

I hear my name from behind and detect the familiar scent of tropical flowers. Turning around, I see a radiant woman in a chiffon dress the colour of the sunset. Her hair is pulled up into a bouquet of curls.

"Raina," I say, kissing her on the cheek before wiping the sweat from my forehead. "I'm so happy you could make it." I mean it. I feel a rush of rejuvenation to see her here, to have someone by my side who understands what it means to be on this island.

"That was a touching speech," she says, placing a gentle hand on my forearm.

"Do you really think so?"

"It was lovely. And you're right. Gabriel here truly is a wizard."

Vivi interjects then, extending her hand toward the new arrival. "I'm Coen's friend, Vivi. Who might you be?"

Raina accepts her hand and introduces herself. "Coen and I just met the other day," she explains. "We tasted cakes together, and we found the perfect one. It's a long story. Actually, it's more sweet than long." She lets out a pretty laugh, and I see Vivi sharpen her gaze.

"Raina's vacationing on her own," I say. "I've invited her for dinner tonight."

"Which was very kind of you," Raina adds as her hand finds its way back to my forearm.

"On your own?" Vivi says. "I admire the independence."

"Well, that wasn't the original plan," Raina answers coolly. "My husband was supposed to be here with me. It's our honeymoon, after all. But he didn't end up becoming my husband, so I didn't bring him along. It's another long story, but less sweet this time. We have lots to talk about." She lets out another pretty laugh.

I can tell that Vivi doesn't quite know what to make of this new character. Despite being caught off guard by Raina's candour, she laughs politely. Decker waits until there's a break in the conversation before introducing himself, and Raina is more than happy to make his acquaintance. Her head tilts downward as she shakes Decker's hand, her gaze and touch lingering a second longer than necessary.

Somehow the topic of conversation turns to the sport of squash, which Decker and Raina discuss enthusiastically while Gabriel mixes the next round of drinks. Vivi catches my eye. "May I steal you away for a minute?" she asks, taking me by the hand.

We weave through the crowd. I avoid making eye contact with anyone, but it no longer seems necessary. They're not as eager to talk to me as they were earlier. Vivi pushes open the large doors, and we step onto the terrace overlooking the courtyard. The cool evening air wakes my senses, and I welcome the quiet as the doors close behind us.

"I had to get out of there," Vivi says, turning to me. "It was so stuffy and crowded. I sure as hell could use a cigarette."

"That's the last thing you need," I say in my lecturing tone. "But I'm proud of you for really committing this time."

"Thanks, babe. I'm proud too, even though it makes me want to slap people sometimes."

"You can slap me as long as you don't touch a cigarette."

She laughs. "Coen," she says, the word lingering on her lips, heavy with intent. "How are you doing? And don't say fine."

With a sigh, I take a moment to consider the question. "I'm tired," I say after some thought. "I'm confused. I feel helpless. I'm pretty sure I'll never be able to love again. Otherwise, I think I'm holding it together."

She looks at me, contemplating my answer. With a strained smile, she turns toward the view. The courtyard is peaceful tonight. There is no event being held below us. No celebration. No candles along the staircase. The stars above shine as brightly as the lights hanging from the trees below. The moon casts a glow on the ocean's waves in the distance.

"It's okay to feel helpless," she says. "It's okay to be heart-broken. I want you to know that we are going through this with you every step of the way. You're not alone. You know that, right?"

"I do. I meant what I said earlier. I wouldn't be able to sur-vive this without you."

"I want you to tell me the second you start to feel over-whelmed. Do you understand?"

"Yes."

"I mean it."

"I know. You don't need to worry about me anymore. I can handle this."

She peers into my eyes as though evaluating whether or not to believe me. After a few seconds, she turns back to the view. She's as convinced as she's going to be.

"It's beautiful, isn't it?" I ask.

"It is." Her response sounds distant. She scans the courtyard, leaning over the terrace's balustrade. "Did you know those trees would be here?"

"Of course. They're magnolias, just like the ones where Elias and I first met." I smile at the memory. She doesn't say another word, but she looks so pretty with the breeze in her hair.

. . . . .

Otra Luna is a different place tonight than the lonely room where I tasted cakes with Maria and Javier yesterday. The space is alive with movement and noise. Candles flicker on every tabletop while geometric light fixtures bathe the room in a creamy glow. Servers dressed in taupe slacks and crisp white shirts dart throughout the room with hurried precision, carrying glasses and revealing dishes and charming guests with the panache of performers in a theatre. The atmosphere is buzzy and inviting, augmented by the sounds of laughing, chatting, glasses clinking, chairs moving, and shoes clicking against the ornately tiled floors.

A section of the restaurant has been cordoned off for our party. The staff has arranged seven large round tables for us, rather than the more easily configured square tables the other guests are seated at. I thought this occasion called for a more convivial seating arrangement, although I'm starting to question that decision. The carved jaguar masks stare down at us from the walls, their mouths twisted into menacing snarls painted red, and I know this must be Mictlan — the underworld.

Raina sits to my left. Vivi and Decker sit to my right. My brother, father, and mother round out the rest of the table. Raina and Decker are doing a fantastic job of keeping the conversation buoyant, as I knew they would, but I can already sense the discomfort I will have to endure tonight.

"Honey, how many drinks have you had?" asks my mother, looking at the tumbler in my hand.

"Mother, must I remind you that I'm a thirty-one-year-old man? The degree of intoxication I choose to obtain is no longer your concern."

Raina laughs brightly while everyone else looks down at their food.

"Your mother's right, Coen. Just take it easy on the tequila," says my father with a nod of the head to signify that the matter is settled.

"It's not tequila. It's mescal."

"Did anyone else get the scallops?" Decker asks, looking around the table. "Wow! Stunning. They're like ocean-flavoured butter."

"I got the scallops!" Raina says, delighted. "They are divine."

"This restaurant is owned by Ramona Merida," I explain, "one of the top chefs in the country. They say she has revolutionized Mexican cuisine."

Clark smirks. "You make her sound like some kind of national hero," he says, leaning back in his chair. The top three buttons of his chambray shirt are undone, which annoyed me when I saw him earlier in the evening.

I know the smart response would be to ignore him. As usual, I can't help myself when it comes to my brother. "She's accomplished far more than you ever will."

"You obviously haven't tried my homemade fish-stick fajitas," he says, laughing loudly.

"Please stop talking, Clark." Vivi shoots him a glance like a poisoned dart.

I don't see Maria coming before she materializes beside me. "How are we enjoying dinner?" she asks, smiling graciously. Expressions of approval resound around the table. "You know, this restaurant is owned by one of the top chefs in Mexico."

"Yes, we've heard," Clark says snidely. He shoves a spoonful of escamoles into his mouth. I sit back in my chair, pleased, deciding against telling him that he's chewing on ant larvae. He probably thinks it's rice.

"The first course was very impressive," Decker responds to Maria, flashing his most charming grin.

"Enjoy the rest of your meal," she says with a slight bow of the head before moving on to the next table.

I already feel full when the main course arrives. This is the most I've eaten in days. Each dish is culinary art, a delicate structure of colours and textures mounted on discs moulded from earth. I look at the dish in front of me — the kraken pulling the ill-fated ship into the sea. I finally get to try the lime octopus and pork tenderloin that I've read so much about.

"I must say, the food here is exquisite," remarks my mother, breathing in the aromas from the walnut-crusted barracuda in front of her. "Did Elias ever cook for you like this?"

It is the first time his name has been mentioned since my family arrived on the island. A hush falls as everyone at the table waits to hear the response.

"He definitely never spoiled me with fish-stick fajitas," I say, glancing at Clark. I cut the tension with a laugh, and everyone joins out of relief as Clark shoots me a sarcastic smile.

"Do you remember the first time Elias was supposed to come over for Sunday dinner?" my mother goes on. "It was years ago now. I made your favourite dish."

"You made coq au vin. I remember."

"Whatever happened that night?" she asks. "You just ran off with no explanation. We were worried about you."

"I told you. He got the dates mixed up. He felt awful about it."

"I hope he did," she responds. "I spent the entire afternoon cooking for that boy. We had leftovers for days. You would think he would have been more considerate."

"It doesn't matter anymore, does it?" I say, hoping for someone to change the subject. My knife slices a tentacle, grating loudly against the bottom of the clay bowl.

"Don't talk to your mother like that," my father says half-heartedly.

"You called him like thirty times," Clark chimes in, looking skeptical. "He forgets he's supposed to have dinner with his boyfriend's family, for the first time ever, then he doesn't even pick up his phone? What was he doing?"

"We don't need to talk about this now," Vivi interjects. She scans the table with her eyes as though delivering a warning.

"Something came up," I say, feeling the need to defend myself and Elias. It comes out weak and unconvincing. "I can't remember. It was a long time ago. Let's just drop it."

"Maybe it was a sign," Clark says. His eyes avert downward as soon as the words leave his mouth.

There is a short moment of silence. My mind warns me against responding, but the words form before I can stop them. "A sign of what?"

Another hush settles over the table as Clark decides whether or not to go on. I think he might have even surprised himself with where his carelessness has taken him. Perhaps he regrets it.

"Nothing," he says dismissively.

"No. It's not nothing," I press on. "What did you mean by that? What sign?"

He inhales deeply before saying, "A sign that maybe he wasn't such an upstanding guy."

"I swear to god —" Vivi begins.

"No, I want to hear this," I say. "Go on, Clark."

"Listen," he says, holding up his palms in defence. "I know this is neither the time nor the place, and I want you to know I am very deeply sorry for what happened to you, but are we all going to pretend that Elias was this perfect saint?"

Everybody is looking down at their plates now.

He continues. "We are all just trying to hold it together and be sensitive, but it doesn't serve any of us to be so wilfully ignorant. Were you even happy with him, little brother? What about that time you had to spend the weekend at my place because he locked you out of your own apartment?"

"Excuse me?" my mother says with theatrical shock.

"Yeah, that happened," Clark says. He's on a roll now. "Vivi was in Hong Kong. Coen didn't want to bother Decker and Sam. He spent the entire weekend hiding out at my place until Elias let him back in — to his own apartment."

"Let's talk about something else," Decker says helplessly. He looks at Raina for support, but she remains silent.

My mouth is a tinderbox. It's difficult to swallow. "We had a fight. That's all. It wasn't a big deal." The words are limp, lifeless.

"This wasn't the only time something like this happened. Vivi, tell him. You know more than anyone." Clark fixes his gaze on her, coaxing her to speak.

"Elias was a good man," she says decisively.

"Was he though?" Clark asks. He looks around the table, and everyone reaches their own conclusion. "How could we tell? We didn't know anything about him. Tell us, Coen. What do you know about his family? About his past?"

"I don't need to explain anything to you," I manage to stammer.

"I just … I remember seeing the wedding invitation," he goes on. "The two of you are laughing. You look so happy. I want to believe it. I really do. But I know how good you are at pretending." He pauses, looking down at his lap as he fidgets with his napkin. "We are all here to pay our respects, but I think now more than ever, under the circumstances, we all need to allow ourselves to be honest with each other."

"Clark, why don't you just go? Get out of here. You are obviously not here to be part of this celebration, so just go." The words come out like a verbal slap.

He looks at me with a hint of hurt in his eyes. "No. I'm here for you."

"I would rather you leave."

"Enough, gentlemen," my father says loudly. A few people from the surrounding tables look in our direction. "This has gone far enough. Let's be civilized and enjoy our dinner as a family."

My cousin Taylor flashes me an inquisitive glance from his seat at the table behind my father, and I look away. I notice my mother staring down at her plate, her fork in one hand and knife in the other, unmoving.

"I'm not going to sit here while this narcissistic ape slanders Elias," I say.

"Don't talk about your brother like that," my mother says firmly. She is visibly upset now. "He just cares about you, Coen. He worries about you. Don't you see that?"

"He cares about no one but himself," I shoot back. "He just had to make this about him, as though he's doing me a favour by imparting his wisdom on me. He thinks I care about his opinion. He thinks we all do. I couldn't care less what he has to say. He knows nothing about Elias. He knows nothing about me. He doesn't have a right to an opinion."

Everyone around us must be looking now, but I blur them from my vision. It would have been impossible to keep my voice down. These words were waiting to be said, and they deserved to be said with command.

"We are all here because we care about you," my mother says. "But your brother has a point. You can see that, can't you?" She looks around the table for support.

"Does he?" I ask. "Tell me. What's his point?"

"You've seen what they're saying on the news," says my mother, gently but with determination. "You understand what they're saying he did, don't you? I wasn't going to bring this up, but what if it's true? Perhaps you're better off this way."

A commotion erupts as everyone around the table starts talking at once with varying levels of volume. It all sounds like noise to me. I can't look anyone in the face. Not my mother. Not my brother. I have no words to speak. My head feels heavy.

I think I feel the static of the shadow's touch on my fingertips when suddenly Vivi pulls me up by the arm. It takes a second for my vision to focus. When it does, I can see she's not happy. "We have to go, Coen," she says. Chair legs scrape across the tiled floor as Decker and Raina stand up. I look down at the table. The dishes have hardly been touched. I've only taken a few bites of my octopus. My father and mother are saying things to us, but they remain in their seats. Clark is sullen and silent. Every eye in the restaurant is directed at us. Vivi takes me by the hand and leads me toward the exit with Raina and Decker close behind. The jaguars watch as we make our escape.

The cool night air helps settle my senses when we emerge from the hotel. Vivi grips my hand so tightly it hurts. "Your family never ceases to amaze me," she says, looking astonished. "They truly are the portrait of modern dysfunction. I would have expected that from Clark, but your mother — how tactless." She releases me from her grip and throws her hands up in the air as if surrendering herself to the indecency of it all. She looks at me, and her anger has softened into something that resembles a compassionate cousin of helplessness, like how you would look at a wounded animal you know you won't be able to save. "I'm sorry you had to go through that, babe."

"The Caraways were certainly in fine form tonight," Decker says, giving me a reassuring shake with his arm around my shoulders. "They do care about you though. This entire situation is so absurd; they're trying to make sense of it just like the rest of us. They're ill-equipped for this, but that doesn't mean their intentions aren't good."

I take several steps back to look each of them in the eye. "What do you think?" I ask. "Did Elias do it? Did he crash that plane?"

We are standing on the side of the road now. It's dark, but I can see them glance at each other underneath the moonlight. It scares me that I don't know what their answers will be.

"No." Decker is the first to respond. "Elias wouldn't have done that."

"I've been thinking about this for days," Vivi says. "He didn't do it."

Raina turns to me, and her eyes are sympathetic. "I didn't know him, and I barely know you, but I don't think you would have agreed to marry a man who would do such a thing."

The four of us stand on the pavement like we're taking part in a pagan ritual, facing one another from our separate corners, awash in the pale light of the moon.

"Well, then it's settled," I say. "Now let's go somewhere and get wasted."

"I'm not sure that's the best solution right now," Decker says, perennially sensible.

"Seriously, I need to get my mind off all of this tragic bullshit for a few hours. We're on a tropical island. We're together. Let's just be normal for one night."

"That's actually not such a bad idea," Vivi says, looking at Decker. He shrugs and locks his arm around my neck.

We walk toward the village and enter the first bar we come across. The exterior of the wide rectangular building was once a vivid shade of orange, but now much of the paint has chipped away to reveal the dull grey underneath. The shining neon sign above the door tells us where we are. Espejo Roto.

We step through the doors and enter what looks like a carnival funhouse circa 1987. The walls are lined with mirrors, reflecting our reflections into eternity. Candy-coloured lights pulse overhead, not quite in sync with the beat of the Latin pop music blaring through the speakers. A few dozen locals gyrate on the dance floor, itself a vortex of reflection and light intensified by the mirror ball spinning from the ceiling. Velvet curtains the colour of blood are draped throughout the room, belted by thick tasselled ropes. Even more conspicuous are the decorative carousel horses suspended on poles in various places.

We seat ourselves at an empty table in a corner and order a round of drinks from a black-clad woman who looks like an undertaker.

"It's refreshing to be in a bar that has escaped the reclaimed-wood-and-filament-bulb aesthetic that represents inoffensive good taste these days," Vivi says, admiring the carousel horse suspended behind her.

"Coen loves a merry-go-round," Decker says with a mischievous smirk. "N'est-ce pas, monsieur?"

"There's a story here," Raina says, tapping her palms on the tabletop. "Tell me!"

"It's stupid," I say. "It's just something dumb that happened long, long ago."

"Coen's just embarrassed," Vivi says, poking my arm with a teasing red-tipped finger.

"So here's what happened," Decker begins. "As how all the best stories start, we were being a nuisance in the south of France.

Coen is right. This did happen a long, long time ago. The three of us were spending the summer backpacking through Europe, you see. We met these two Danish guys while strolling along the boardwalk, and we all proceeded to get fabulously and glamorously intoxicated, as one does whilst in the French Riviera. That is, everyone but me, since I'm an angel."

"Decker was so innocent and pure back then," Vivi pipes in. "I suppose he still is. Let's not forget to mention that Coen was hopelessly enamoured with one of the Danes, who had this Prince Charming thing going on: blond locks, baby-blue eyes, European chivalry, the whole package."

"He sounds dreamy!" Raina squeals.

"Oh, he was," Decker confirms.

"Stop it!" I plead.

"He was an undeniable dreamboat," Decker goes on. "He was also wearing the deepest V-neck imaginable, which gave us all a good eyeful of his bronzed, hairless chest. So there we were, having a ball drinking everything in sight when Coen had the best idea. He wanted to break into the carousel in the park. It was closed, so there was a net wrapped around the entire thing. It was very uncharacteristic of Coen to make such a reckless suggestion, but I think being in the presence of Prince Charming might have emboldened him, if you know what I mean."

"I do," Raina says with a wink.

"Being the only sober one of the lot, I tried to talk them out of what was surely a hare-brained idea, but of course I got vetoed," Decker continues. "The five of us raced each other to the carousel and climbed the net. The break-in was a success. We rode the horses. We took photos. Prince Charming was so enchanted by how daring our friend Coen was. Then things went horribly wrong. Two flashlight beams appeared out of nowhere, and we could hear someone shouting in French. La police! Of course, we panicked. We scaled the net as quickly as we could, then started sprinting across the park away from the flashlights, only to realize there were only four of us. Coen was missing in action!"

I almost forgot about Decker's masterful skill as a storyteller. His hands dart around himself for emphasis, and I can imagine the scene like it were yesterday. Raina is on the edge of her seat in anticipation for the story's pièce de résistance, which I know is coming.

"Being the loyal friends that we were, we couldn't leave him behind. Once we got back to the carousel, this is what we saw: poor Coen hanging from the net, upside down, wearing nothing but a shirt and his underwear. His foot had gotten tangled in the net as he made his escape. His pants were so tight that they split right down the seam. We had to help the policemen untangle him while he was half-naked. The cops found it so funny that they let us off with a warning."

My face goes flush with embarrassment, but I laugh along. The rest of them are howling. "Those were my favourite pants," I say.

"If it weren't for Coen's tight undies, it could have been a long and interesting night in a French jail cell," Vivi says. "He saved the day. At least, his undies did."

"Was Prince Charming even more enchanted to find that you were as clumsy and flawed as the rest of us mortals?" Raina asks.

"I doubt he was ever enchanted by me. It probably didn't help that I was so visibly terrified by the cops."

"You did look like you were going to start crying at any moment," Vivi confirms.

"Who needs Prince Charming and his deep V-neck, anyway?" Raina asks.

"We have all the charm we can handle right here," Decker says, hooking his muscular arm around my neck.

"I'll drink to that," I say, clinking my glass with theirs.

"Let's dance," Decker says excitedly. "I need to move."

"I think I'm okay right here," I say. "You go and move that body of yours."

He takes Vivi by the hand and the two of them saunter over to the dance floor, shaking their hips along the way. Raina and I watch them move like clownish ballroom dancers. The expressions on their faces are deadly serious as he twirls her, then she dips him, then he lifts her off her feet and spins around.

"Your friends are a riot," Raina says. "I can tell how much they care about you."

"They are pretty awesome," I agree. "Sometimes I take them for granted, and I hate myself for doing that. In times like this when I really need them, they've never let me down. I'm lucky."

"Good people are not easy to come by. Hang on to them."

Vivi and Decker are now doing some sort of interpretive waltz while everyone around them grinds together in a uniform mass of shaking and sliding.

Raina turns to face me. "Let's dance."

"I'll pass," I say. "You go."

"Coen Caraway, you are here in this twisted carousel bar with your two closest friends and a strange Englishwoman you've just met. You are going to shake that skinny butt of yours, and you are going to like it." She stands and extends her hand. I don't have a choice in the matter.

I look at her, then at the dance floor, then back at her. With a sigh of surrender, I take her hand. She smiles triumphantly.

Vivi and Decker pounce on us as we join them beneath the spinning mirror ball, wrapping their arms around us, screaming. Then we dance. We jump up and down. We spin one another around. We dip. We shake. Everyone else looks at us with mocking amusement, but we don't care.

I forget about the throbbing in my chest, which has been steadily intensifying over the past few days. I forget about the smoke that has been clouding my mind. Everything fades away, replaced by the flashing lights and pounding bass. The only things that exist now are Decker's sweaty tangle of golden hair, Vivi's slender arms as they wave in the air, Raina's sunset dress as it glides around her body, and our neon-tinted reflections surrounding us. We move and dance and laugh all night. I catch a glimpse of us in the mirror, and we look immaculate. Happy, even.

MOUNT PLEASANT
Six years before the crash

"It's definitely orange Creamsicle."

"No way. It's close but not quite. The clouds need to be wispier to be Creamsicle. That's more like tangerine vanilla sundae."

Vivi and I often debated the colours of the sky. We used to spend hours lying on the lawn behind my parents' house, watching the sky turn from bubblegum blue to cotton candy to orange Creamsicle, then climax in a blaze of melted amber before dying out into a sea of India ink. No sky is quite like Vancouver's when the sun sets on a clear day.

"Tangerine vanilla sundae isn't a thing," she said, turning her head toward me.

Vivi and I were lying on a blanket on my apartment's outdoor terrace. The midsummer sky was a deep orange haze punctuated by pillowy clouds like scoops of vanilla ice cream.

"Tangerine vanilla sundae is certainly a thing," I said. "Look. That's it, right up there."

She considered this for a moment before saying, "Replace vanilla with marshmallow and I'll give it to you."

"Deal."

It was an important and exhausting day. Elias was moving out of his old studio suite and into my loft apartment in the heart of Mount Pleasant, a neighbourhood brimming with my favourite art-filled cafés and divey dance halls.

Gathering the courage to ask him had taken some time. It was a big step, the first time I would live with someone other than a roommate or a brother. I knew it was probably too soon — we had been together for only a couple years — but I reached a point when I could no longer be alone.

I pictured the two of us making breakfast together in the morning. He would set the table and prepare the coffee while I would fry the eggs. I imagined us covering the walls with photographs of ourselves laughing, travelling, and strolling hand in hand. He would insist on decorating the space with planes and aviation maps, which I would agree to so long as he didn't complain about my books and plants. We would compromise. We would collaborate. We would build a home together.

I wasn't used to dreaming like this. I was never one to let myself aspire to such contentment, so mundane yet seemingly unattainable. I suppose it had never occurred to me that I could have it. I wanted it this time.

He had hesitated when I finally asked him to move in with me. We had picked up coffees from his favourite café and were wandering through the neighbourhood, admiring the murals painted on the buildings. It was meticulously planned to appear casual and spontaneous. I popped the question while we sat on a park bench underneath the shade of cherry blossom trees. The resident dogs frolicked in the field in front of us. He paused and looked down at the coffee in his hands, but he said yes.

Decker and Elias spent the afternoon transporting his belongings while Vivi and I helped haul them up to my apartment. It wasn't a difficult job. Most of his old furniture had already been sold or donated. Everything he owned was packed neatly into a dozen cardboard boxes that now littered the floor. His entire life in boxes.

Now, Decker and Elias were picking up Thai food for dinner as Vivi and I gazed at the sky.

"It's still hard for me to believe how domesticated Coen Caraway has become," Vivi said.

"Domesticated? Never."

"This is the first step," she said. "The boyfriend moves in. Fine. Then the boyfriend becomes the husband. Then you adopt two children from Cambodia, or maybe one is Bolivian for the sake of diversity. You push them around in designer strollers. You vacation in Maui because it's easier than Madrid. Before you know it, you're wearing matching argyle sweaters and hosting family dinner night on Sundays."

"How dare you say such things."

Vivi laughed. "We mock it, but it would be a good life. It wouldn't be such a bad thing if everything I said came true."

"We spend so much energy rejecting everything that would associate us with our families, only to become a slightly altered version of them."

"Now that is dark."

"I know," I agreed with a laugh. "It's scary because it's true. I've always modelled myself to be the opposite of my father, of Clark. It's a waste of time really. We may be so fundamentally different in how we think and behave, but at the end of the day we all want the same basic things. To be loved. To feel safe. To attain something resembling happiness."

"It's okay to want those things, babe. It's nothing to be ashamed of."

"I always thought we were too enlightened for that, you and I, but now I'm not so sure. Truthfully, I think I do want the designer strollers. The argyle sweaters. The predictability. The comfort. I would take all of it if I could."

Vivi turned to me with a serious look in her eyes. "There is no reason why you couldn't have all of that."

I made a sound like a doubtful laugh. "Like you said, this is the first step. So far, so good. But do you really see me getting married? Or raising a family?"

"Why wouldn't I? Don't you?"

"It just seems idealistic," I said. "For Decker, sure. He'll get the white picket fence. And you'll get whatever you decide you want. It's different for me. I don't think I'm supposed to have a happy ending."

"Coen, look at me. Leave the past in the past. It doesn't own you. You deserve the life you want as much as anyone else. You deserve Elias. You deserve every good thing that comes your way. Don't rationalize yourself away from being happy."

Vivi spoke with conviction, but I was doubtful still.

"Do you think I'm making a mistake getting Elias to move in?" I asked, shifting my body on the floor to adjust my stiffening legs.

"Why would it be a mistake?"

"I just wonder if it's too soon. There are so many things I don't know about him. I want to believe that living together will bring us closer, that maybe he'll start opening up more. I have this feeling in my gut telling me it's not going to work out that way."

"I don't know if this will end up being a good decision," she replied thoughtfully. "But the decision has been made. We just spent the entire day hauling his entire life into your apartment. All you can do now is try your best to make things work and see what happens. It's better to regret the outcome of a decision than to regret not making the decision at all."

"You're right. There's no going back now."

"You might want to try being less insufferable though," Vivi said with a sly smile.

I responded by flicking her right breast. She gasped with exaggerated shock at the indecency, then stabbed her talon-like fingers into my armpits. I convulsed on the terrace floor, laughing uncontrollably as my nerves exploded beneath her touch. She knew my weaknesses.

"Surrender!" I screamed. "Surrender!"

She collapsed beside me, panting between giggles. "Don't throw a snowball if you're not prepared for an avalanche," she said.

We lay on the floor and savoured the quiet, the only sounds being our breathing and the occasional sizzle of a bus as it travelled along its electric wires. The sky had darkened into a calming shade of indigo — what Vivi liked to call raw denim — and I wondered what was taking so long for the boys to return with dinner.

"I want to show you something," I said, remembering what I had found earlier that day. I rolled onto my stomach and pushed myself up off the floor, careful not to strain my back, before running inside. I returned a minute later with something in my hand.

"Take a look at this."

Vivi sat up, curious. "Oh my god. Where did you find this?"

"It fell out of one of Elias's books."

"Is that him?"

"It must be. Look at him. He looks exactly the same, just miniature."

Elias appeared to be around eight years old. He wore tattered brown shorts and a wrinkled green shirt. No shoes. His hair was thick and wild. He looked at the camera with a curious expression, his arms hanging at his sides. A house made of concrete blocks with a corrugated metal roof stood behind him. Farther in the distance were two rectangular, industrial-looking buildings painted pale red. This faded photograph is the only evidence I've ever seen of Elias as a child.

THE PASSAGEWAY
Six days after the crash

I've always hated flying. Unlike Elias, I belong on the land.

Boarding an airplane requires the surrender of all control. It consumes my thoughts for the entire flight. I can feel it wake my nervous system, the cortisol rushing through my blood like tennis balls being released down a waterslide.

Logically, I know that being on a flight is one of the safest places I could be. It is a hypercontrolled environment in which every variable is governed by protocol and safeguards. When the needles begin to prick and my breath becomes shallow, logic doesn't bring much comfort.

Some flights are better than others, but I've learned a few methods to remain calm. I observe the other passengers making pleasant small talk and flipping through the duty-free catalogue. They always appear to be untroubled and trusting.

I watch the flight attendants go about their jobs. They tell passengers to buckle their seat belts. They hand out blankets and discard cups. From takeoff to turbulence to landing, they're unfazed. For them, this is routine and their manner is always placid. Sometimes they even look bored.

Above all else, I think about Elias, so strong and confident in his uniform. I imagine the pilot of my flight embodying the same qualities, even looking like him. This would always bring me a sense of security. I would trust someone like Elias.

He never knew how much I hated to fly. I never told him. I think I hid it well.

. . . . .

I wonder whose bed I'm in. This is now my seventh morning waking up in this same bed, in this room, on this island, and it still takes me several seconds to realize where I am, why my body isn't wrapped in the familiar texture of my sheets, why I can't feel the warmth radiating from another body beside me. It is my mind's cruel trick, to deny these foreign circumstances as my new reality so that I wake up each morning free of pain — just for a moment — before the same crushing realization.

The air is staler today. The smoke in my head is heavier. An image flashes through my mind. I am standing in a room of mirrors, looking at myself looking back at me, lights floating around my face in a kaleidoscope of colour. My skin is green, then blue, then purple. My face is distorted, eyes wild and teeth bared.

I don't remember how we got back to the hotel last night. I don't recall the time or crawling into bed. I only remember the movement and the reflections. I felt so free. It was euphoric. Now the memory disturbs me, as though I'm coming down from a spectacular high.

"Did you see me last night?" I ask aloud, a rattle in my voice. "I haven't moved like that in a long time."

Silence.

"Clark was delightful at dinner, wasn't he? He never does disappoint."

Nothing. I lie in silence for a minute before going on.

"I could really use you right now."

No answer.

"Where the hell are you? Where did you go? You said you wouldn't let me go through this alone."

I pull the sheets over my head. I close my eyes and breathe in, then out.

I remember seeing the wedding invitation.

I inhale, dragging the air into my lungs.

The two of you are laughing. You look so happy.

Out goes my breath as the sheet balloons around me.

I want to believe it.

Inhaling again, recycling the same tainted air.

I really do.

My breath escapes past my lips, a reluctant wind.

But I know.

In.

How good you are.

Out.

At pretending.

"Shut up!" The words burst from my lips like the wail of a creature that's been cornered, though the sound is muted with the pillows pressed against my ears. Clark's voice has replaced Elias's, and it refuses to be quiet.

• • • • •

I don't want to see people today. The very thought of it is exhausting. Then again, the only thing that seems worse right now is being alone and the prospect of what would come from that. I might have stayed in bed all day to find out, but the suffocating solitude of the room coupled with Clark's taunting voice drives me outside to face the world.

It is the day before Elias's celebration of life, and the sun hovers above like a hot coal. The sunglasses on my face help me avoid eye contact with people. I can be discreet in evading my guests, none of whom I want to encounter. I don't even entertain the idea of attending the luncheon that's part of the day's itinerary. I'm not able to be brave today.

Relief washes over me as I walk through the front entrance of the hotel into the warmth of the world outside. My aunt Sheila and her current boyfriend approach from the right. I veer sharply to the left. "Coen! Coen, honey!" she calls out, but I keep walking.

I am on my way to meet Vivi. She opted to explore the village over attending the luncheon. "I feel like death and smell like Scotch. There is no way I'm going to nibble on finger sandwiches today with the Caraway clan" was the message I received from her earlier.

As I walk across Plaza Pequeña, I see Vivi in a black cotton dress sitting on the ledge of the fountain. Her sunglasses are even darker than mine.

More candles surround the fountain than when I last visited. A few new additions catch my attention: images of a familiar face, cut out of newspapers and printed on cheap photocopy paper.

"I know," Vivi says. "It's morbid. The altar in your room is vanilla compared to this."

"I think it's beautiful."

"Do these people even know Elias? They cut out pictures of him from the newspaper."

"I think they know he is one of theirs."

The square is eerily quiet as we meander along the path that cuts across the circular lawn. We step inside a narrow passageway of cobblestones between two once-grand buildings, its walls draped in flowering vines. A hummingbird darts in front of us before hovering to the rooftops, whose edges are lined with clay pots overflowing with petals every shade of sunset.

Partway down the passage, we stumble upon an unexpected doorway leading into the courtyard of a quaint café. An elderly woman with a kind face greets us as we step inside. It is a peaceful setting, the only sounds being the wind chimes that hang in the trees, the hushed conversations of the other guests, and the television set perched on a table against a nearby wall.

The walls are covered in frames displaying old photographs of people and places. Judging by the vibrancy of the colours and the fashions that are worn, the ages of the photographs span decades. Some are black and white with frayed edges, while others are vintage Polaroids.

I pause on one sepia-toned photograph in particular. It looks like a celebration of some sort in the village square. The twin bell towers of the cathedral in the background are unmistakable. There are lights and paper streamers strung above the crowd, which is filled with smiling people.

A couple in the centre stand out from the rest. The woman's flowing hair is suspended mid-air, a cloud of gold. The man is rather debonair, wearing a fitted blazer over a striped Oxford shirt. In this moment, perfectly captured and memorialized on film, the two look into each other's eyes with what could only be love, faces laughing with genuine joy, hands holding hands, forever happy.

We take a seat beneath the shade of a leafy tree, at a table of glazed tiles that form a mosaic of peculiar patterns. I order a café con leche while Vivi orders a glass of Chenin Blanc. Judging by how the other customers speak and dress, they all appear to be locals. I notice an ornate teapot on each table, along with various vessels for sugar and cream. Everyone seems to be sipping from delicate porcelain cups.

"Earth to Coen. Are you there?"

"Sorry," I say. "I'm easily distracted today."

"I can't say that I blame you." She looks into her glass but doesn't take a sip. "How are you feeling about the event tomorrow?"

"Good," I say. "It's going to be unforgettable. I think we all need this. It will be healing."

Vivi is skeptical. "You can still call it off, you know. If it doesn't feel right or you start to feel overwhelmed, nobody would blame you for cancelling."

"For the hundredth time, I'm fine. Trust me. I can do this. I want this." I scan the room and catch the eyes of people around us. They quickly look away.

"Don't worry about them," Vivi says, noticing the glances.

"I want us all to honour his life," I continue. "I want to talk about the memories. Tomorrow won't be the day I imagined it to be, and that's just the way it is. That doesn't mean I'm going to let the day pass while curled up in the fetal position. This is my way of dealing with what has happened."

She looks at me, studies me, while taking a sip from her glass. Her red lips purse together. "I get it. You were right. There is no right way of dealing with a tragedy like this. There is no manual."

My mind contemplates whether or not to say what I'm about to say, but the words come out before I can make a decision.

"Besides, I should have been prepared. A part of me always knew this would happen."

Vivi's eyes narrow. She waits for me to go on.

"Everything was perfect: Elias, the hotel, this island. I was a fool for thinking I would have this fairy-tale wedding and live happily ever after. I fell for it. I believed I was going to get away with it. But all along, there was a voice that tried to warn me. It told me not to be fooled. I ignored it."

She reaches across the table and grabs my hands. "Babe, what happened was a tragic accident. I know it's tempting to believe that the universe is plotting against you. Terrible things happen, not because we deserve them, but because life is a series of events we can't always control. You had the strength to build something good, something happy. You can do it again."

"Was I happy though?" My voice quivers. "What Clark said at dinner — was I just pretending?"

Seconds pass as she formulates the right response, an answer that's honest yet cautious.

"Only you would know," she says finally.

"Do you remember when Elias first moved into my apartment? We were taking a break, lying on the balcony, looking at the sky. I told you then I wasn't supposed to have a happy ending. I was right."

Vivi's lips part to respond with what I'm sure would be a rebuttal, but something stops her. Her eyes focus on something past my right shoulder. Turning around in my seat, I see what has caught her attention.

It is me. More specifically, it is an image of me, on the television. It is the photograph of Elias and me laughing on the rooftop with the city sparkling behind us. It is our wedding invitation.

I stand up from my seat and dart to the television, turning up the volume.

"… was scheduled to be married tomorrow at a luxury resort on Isla de Espejos, an island in the Gulf of Mexico. Sources tell us the fiancé is Coen Caraway, the son of a prominent Canadian real estate developer, who is currently staying on the island and refusing to return home to Vancouver. Tomorrow's wedding has not been cancelled. Due to the tragic turn of events, Mr. Caraway will instead be hosting a celebration of Elias Santos's life, a private memorial held at the Ōmeyōcān Hotel with family and friends."

I stare at the screen in disbelief as the broadcast cuts from the unholy messenger's face to an image of the hotel. My hotel.

"News Cloud has obtained footage of Mr. Caraway from yesterday, making a bizarre toast in front of a room filled with guests."

The video appears to have been shot with a mobile phone. The footage is shaky and clarity is poor due to the low lighting in the Terrace Bar, but my face is visible. My speech is erratic. The glass in my hand is empty.

"It is unclear whether authorities have attempted to contact Mr. Caraway for questioning. The investigation into the horrific crash of flight XI260 is still underway. The harsh conditions of the Arctic Ocean have made it extremely challenging for crews searching for the remains of passengers. The body of First Officer Elias Santos has yet to be recovered."

The broadcast cuts away to another story, moving on as though it were nothing.

"Coen?" Vivi's hand is on my shoulder. I turn around to look at her, but neither of us knows what to say. All eyes in the café are on me. Their faces suggest sympathy or suspicion, or a little of both. One by one, they look away and continue sipping their tea. Moving on, as though it were nothing.

We pay our bill and make our retreat. The vine-covered passageway feels narrower now, its stone walls closing in on me the farther we go. Finally, we step onto a street, the sun blazing above us.

"Who would have done that?" Vivi asks. "Who would have taken that video?" Her voice is fevered and her hands are shaking, but she tries to remain calm.

"I don't know. I don't remember seeing anyone filming me. Do you think it was Clark?"

"He wouldn't have done that."

My head spins. I struggle to remember the scene last night in the Terrace Bar. I can see the dim glow of the chandelier hanging from the ceiling. I can see the reflections of light from the mirrored walls. I can see everyone looking at me, but I can't see their faces. In their place, there is nothing. No features. No expressions. Just a room of faceless people.

"We need to tell Maria," Vivi says. "That was an international news station. The world knows about this island now. They know about what's happening tomorrow. We need security."

I suddenly realize that I don't know where we are. We've been hurrying along unfamiliar streets. I can't tell which direction is the hotel.

"Seriously?" I say. "People aren't going to come here to sabotage the event. We're in the middle of nowhere."

"Don't you understand? The entire world thinks Elias is a killer. They blame him for the crash. They think over three hundred people are floating to the bottom of the ocean because of him. Regardless of what really happened, they think we are here celebrating the life of a mass murderer."

"They don't know what really happened. Nobody does. They have no reason to blame him or us. The media is sensationalizing all of this just like they do with everything."

"People will believe whatever they —"

She doesn't finish the thought. We've wandered down an unknown street, and it appears we are now at the edge of town.

A wide wall made of concrete blocks stands in front of us, spray-painted in bright strokes of yellow, purple, and green.

I passed plenty of graffiti on the drive from the airport in Veracruz to the ferry terminal a week ago. It lined the highways, covering the walls of buildings and overpasses. I admired it for how uniformly authoritative it appeared, as though each painted slogan were a rallying cry. I haven't come across anything like it since I arrived on the island, until now. The large capital letters are bold and angular, painted with purpose. With care.

PRONTO DIOS

"Airbus. A320?"

"Close," Elias said with a grin. "That's an A330. They're similar models, but the cabin on an A330 is wider. You're getting good at this." He looked at me, impressed, and tipped the neck of a beer bottle toward his mouth.

"If I'm going to date the planet's next great pilot, I might as well try to keep up." I clinked the neck of my bottle with his as the Airbus A330 flew overhead into the horizon, west of where we sat. The sun was beginning to dip, setting the sky on fire.

"Where do you think it's headed?" I asked, propping my arms on the log behind me while I dug my feet in the cooling sand. "I'm going to say Kathmandu. Or maybe Kazakhstan."

Elias laughed gently. "Judging by the airline, most likely Hong Kong."

"Hong Kong," I repeated quietly, as though I had never heard of the place before.

"But from there, who knows? Kathmandu, Kazakhstan — it could go anywhere. That's the beauty of the sky. There are no limits."

"Well, the stratosphere is pretty limiting."

Elias gave me a playful punch on the chest. "Smartass."

The sky turned quickly above our spot on Iona Beach. The melted amber began to soften and recede toward the horizon, revealing the India ink underneath. We could already see the moon hovering above the airport in the distance.

"What's your plan tonight?" I asked. "You staying the night with me?"

"I have no plan. I let the wind take me where it takes me. But if you're offering a warm bed and some company tonight, I wouldn't refuse."

"I suppose that could be arranged." I leaned against him, pressing his body against mine. Warmth radiated from his skin. He lifted his arm and wrapped it around my shoulders. "Besides, my place feels so empty. It's lonely there, so much space and nothing to fill it with."

"It's only been a month since you moved back in," he said, his voice quiet. "It must seem strange."

"I thought I would love being by myself again, but I was wrong. It's a good thing I have you." I smiled. Something flickered in the darkness of his eyes before he smiled back. "Plus," I went on, "aren't you happy to spend less time in that dark, dingy apartment of yours?"

"Dingy? What is this?"

I laughed. "It means dusty, gloomy, and downright awful."

"It's not that bad!" he said with exaggerated outrage.

Another airplane could be seen launching in the distance. It floated over the runway into the sky before veering away from us, south.

"I bet that one's going to Mexico." I peered at him through the corners of my eyes to catch his reaction.

"Perhaps." That's all he said.

Above us, the sky grew darker and the moon brighter. With a sip of beer, I decided to go for it.

"You never talk about your family," I said, attempting to sound nonchalant.

There was a pause. I could feel my nerves tingling. I couldn't bring myself to look at him, so I stared straight ahead at the ocean. Finally, he responded. "You're right. I don't."

I waited for him to say more. He remained silent.

"Why?" I asked, the intent now more evident in my voice. "You can tell me. You know that, right? You don't have to. I'm not going to force you to, but we've been together for almost a year now, and I feel like I barely know you. I don't even know what part of Mexico you're from. I don't know what your parents are like. I don't know if you even have parents."

I still couldn't look at him, but I could hear him breathing in a slow, measured rhythm. Even his breath wouldn't betray what he thought, felt.

"It's just that you know everything about me," I went on. "We've been through so much together already. We've become quite close, haven't we? I just hope you're not ashamed to talk to me about your past."

"I'm not ashamed." His words were sudden and firm. "I'm sorry. I want to tell you, but it's not something I like to talk about."

"That's okay. I understand. Just know that you can talk to me."

"I know that." Elias grabbed my hand. I turned to him, and the satellites in his eyes shone brightly, transmitting signals to who knows where. We sat there for a moment, looking at one another, not knowing what else to do or say. I could tell he was thinking. The muscles in his face made the subtlest of movements. His eyebrows. His lips.

"I'm going to tell you this only once," he said so quietly that I wouldn't have heard him had his face not been so close to mine. "I will tell you what you want to know. I will answer your questions. After tonight, I don't want to speak of it anymore. Do you understand?"

"I understand."

· · · · ·

I always knew I was different. I wasn't like the other children in my town. They were happy to be poor. They were satisfied with the crumbling streets, with the monotony. I dreamed of more.

My home was Veracruz, a region along the eastern edge of Mexico. It could be a place of magic. The coast was an endless seam of ochre and blue. Mountains stood watch over the land like giants cloaked in mist. The sky would turn the colour of burning sand whenever the sun began to descend.

My town, however, was poor and ugly. The streets were dusty. The houses were decaying. It was — dingy, yes?

My bedroom window faced a hideous cluster of buildings in the distance. They were painted a sad shade of red. I think this terrible place produced nuclear energy. I grew up looking at it every day from my bed, a reminder of how trapped we were between the beautiful and the ugly.

My parents were simple people. My father repaired cars in a garage beside our house. My mother greeted customers with sodas and sweets. They never expected much from life, so they were content with what they had: a business, a family, a home. They gave me everything they could. I always felt safe and loved. For that, I will always be grateful.

As a child, I spent much of my time with my father. He taught me everything he knew about cars. I would help him with the repairs, admiring his ability to take something dead and bring it back to life.

My mother spent most of her time with god. When she wasn't at church, she would be praying, or reading her Bible, or confessing. What a woman like her had to confess, I will never know.

We didn't have much money, but she always made sure I had a nice suit to wear to church. It'd often be a size too large, but I would still outgrow it within the year. When the suit no longer fit, she'd take me to the store and buy me another.

This was my life. Attending school in the day. Watching my father repair cars in the evening. Going to church on the weekend. The same cycle every day, month after month, year after year.

Of course, it wasn't quite as miserable as I make it sound. There were many warm people in our lives, and celebrations happened often. Mexico has a way of bringing laughter and colour to even the saddest corners. It was not all bad, but I wanted more. Back then, I dreamed of living in the city.

I imagined moving to DF — Distrito Federal, what you English speakers call Mexico City. I read about the athletes and celebrities who lived such glamorous lives there. I pictured myself shopping at the markets and sipping coffee in the cafés of Coyoacán. There, in the capital, I could be who I was meant to be.

I never believed that it would happen though. My mother and father had never stepped foot in DF. They would tell me about the gangs and the crime. Even the violence I romanticized. Anything would have been better than the monotony of my life in that forgettable town.

I was sixteen when I first fell in love. At least, I thought it was love at the time. My father hired a boy. Business was good, and he needed help I couldn't give him. I had lost interest in fixing cars when I realized my father was grooming me to become a mechanic. To take over the shop. To become him.

The boy was nineteen. His name was Miguel. He had hair that was black like a raven and shoulder blades I swore could sprout wings. He looked the same every day: white T-shirt stained black with grease, long hair pulled back in a knot. Another monotonous part of life, but this time it was captivating.

He was very kind to me. I would help him in the evenings, handing him tools and keeping him company. He would often join us for dinner. During the weekends, I'd linger near the shop when I knew Miguel would be taking his breaks. We'd spend them together, drinking sodas and playing cards.

He taught me about the stars. I was surprised by how much this grease-covered mechanic knew about astronomy. After the sun set, he would show me the constellations and explain their mythologies. One night he pointed out a very bright star he claimed was the planet Venus. He told me it was named after the ancient goddess of love and that, like love, it would consume a man in flames.

Everything changed the day after I turned seventeen. We sat in a car he'd been repairing in the shop, eating rice pudding left over from my birthday celebration the night before. It was evening, and we had decided to take a break while my parents were in the house.

I told him about my dream of moving to the city. He urged me to go. Not only was he the one person who believed I could do it, he encouraged me to. He didn't see there being a reason to fear the violence or the uncertainty.

"Escape this place," he said. "Do whatever it takes. Go as far as your feet will take you."

I asked him to come with me, but he had to stay in that awful place to care for his mother, who was very ill. "I dream about leaving here every day," he said. "Sometimes I wish I had wings so that I could fly far away."

Then I took him by the hand. I don't know what compelled me to do it. Something must have given me courage. Before I knew what was happening, his lips were on mine. Gently at first, then less so. He smelled like motor oil and sweat. He tasted like sugar. We pulled off each other's shirts, and my hands roamed over the firmness of his chest and the softness of his skin.

One second I was being consumed by the flames of this boy, the next he was pulled violently away from me. At first, I thought he had fallen out of the car door beside him. Then I realized he was being dragged onto the ground. There was screaming and shouting. Miguel scrambled to his feet, and I watched my father hit him across the face, knocking him back to the floor.

I was paralyzed for a second before I jumped out of the car and ran to Miguel's side. "Don't touch him!" I screamed at my father, who was shouting things I'll never repeat. Blood dripped from Miguel's lips. He looked at me with the saddest eyes, then got to his feet and ran away, out of the garage and out of my life.

That night changed me. My mother cried and prayed, her rosary clutched close to her heart. My father spewed his disgust, accusing Miguel of corrupting me, violating me.

When they became calmer, I told them that I loved Miguel. I knew what they would think, but I didn't know how they'd react. Even so, I wasn't frightened. I was angry. Miguel didn't violate me. They did.

I thought my father would be the one to reject me, but it was my mother who delivered the final blow. This woman I loved said something to me that broke my heart.

The next morning, they gave me some money they had saved and told me to leave. I couldn't return home until I repented for my sins. They would not support a son who was in open rebellion with god.

. . . . .

"Elias," I said, squeezing his hand. "I'm so angry for you."

The sun had slipped behind the edge of the earth, but the glow from the city's electric lights obscured the stars that looked down on us. The ocean crept closer to our feet.

"Faith is blind," he said, "and it can also be blinding. I don't hate them for what they did. They knew no better. Like I said, they were simple people. Besides, who knows what would have happened had they not thrown me out? I'd probably be rotting in that crumbling place."

"Sometimes a terrible thing can be the only catalyst for change."

"I think you're right."

"Even so, how could parents do that to their only son?"

"Remember this whenever you find yourself resenting your family," he said. "There are worse things than a dismissive father and a self-involved mother. They love you. They've proven that, haven't they?"

A chill rippled across my skin as my body stiffened. I pretended not to hear his question.

"What happened next?"

. . . . .

I took the money my parents offered and stuffed everything I owned into a backpack. I left without a word in the morning.

The streets of town seemed even greyer than usual that day. Uglier. I couldn't wait to leave, to know I would never see them again, but my first priority was to find Miguel. I was going to convince him to come with me. When I arrived at his home, I learned he didn't want to see me. He wanted nothing to do with me. I screamed his name from the street, but he wouldn't even come to the door. I never saw him again.

I spent that night on the floor of the bus station. I had enough money for a ticket to DF and probably three weeks of food if I was careful. I boarded the first bus in the morning. It was crowded and the drive was long, but I didn't mind. I had never felt so free.

My first few weeks in DF were a blur. The city was a living, breathing animal. Its veins and arteries connected every limb in the form of sun-seared pavement. Its blood was the constant rush of vehicles and humans, sustaining the vibrancy of the city while choking it with exhaust fumes and garbage. There was no heart. The entire concrete body pulsed as one entity.

It was both intoxicating and overwhelming. I felt like an outsider, even more than I did in my dusty hometown. I waited for the locals to identify me as alien, as someone who didn't belong, but nobody seemed to notice. Nobody cared. I was both nobody and everybody.

I scoured the city for days, looking for work and somewhere to live. I visited every shop, restaurant, and apartment building I could find, travelling from one corner of the city to another. Nothing. It took one week before I found hope.

Today, Condesa is one of the most fashionable districts in the capital. Its streets are lined with chic restaurants. Its residents have youth and money. Back then, it was different. Like much of the city itself, it was a more dangerous, less prosperous place than it is today.

I was walking along a quiet street when I stumbled upon a narrow bar beside a park. It was in the corner of a four-storey building made of brick, and there were tables and chairs scattered along the sidewalk. Inside the bar, the brick walls were painted black. The concrete floor was painted black. Even the counters were painted black. Dozens of dim, bare light bulbs hung from the ceiling at irregular angles throughout the black room, like stars in the night sky.

The man tending the bar was old, but he was built like a buffalo. He had thick white hair and skin tanned like leather. I'll admit I was intimidated, but I found the courage to ask him if I could speak to the manager. He examined me slowly and seriously. Then he smiled, transforming his entire face, and said in heavily accented Spanish, "You're looking at the manager. You're also looking at the bartender, the accountant, the dishwasher, and the owner."

The man was Canadian, but he'd been living in Mexico for many years. In Canada, he was John. In Mexico, he was Juan.

For the first time in a very long time, it felt like my luck was starting to turn. The head bartender had decided to move out of the city just a week prior. He used to live in an apartment directly above the bar, which Juan rented out. Not only was the job available, but the apartment as well.

It seemed too good to be true, but of course it wasn't going to be quite that easy. My mother and father didn't drink. I had never mixed a cocktail in my life.

"Listen," Juan said, "I'm going to give you one chance. It's a quiet night. Man the bar until we close so I can see what you're made of."

I was nervous, but I did my best. Juan sat at a table for most of the night, sipping mescal and watching me with amusement on his face.

Finally, it was closing time. I didn't feel very confident. I had broken two glasses and one guy told him I must be the worst bartender in town. When the room was empty, Juan told me to take a seat at his table. He looked me up and down, from my head to my feet. Then he asked me one question: "Why did you come to this city?"

I answered honestly. "To be free."

It must have been the right answer. He took a chance on me. Even though I had never tended a bar in my life, he gave me the job. Even though I had barely a coin to my name, he leased the apartment to me. I earned neither of these things. This was an act of kindness, and it changed my life.

The apartment was small and humble. Besides the bathroom, there was only one square room with a stove and refrigerator in a corner. There was one rectangular window that looked out onto the street and patio tables below. There was one bare light bulb in the centre of the ceiling, although the street lamps outside flooded the room with yellow throughout the night.

It was a simple place — just one of everything I needed to live comfortably — but to me it was paradise. Living in the city, in a home of my own, once seemed like an unattainable dream. Yet here I was, independent and ambitious, with a room that belonged to nobody else but me.

Juan and I spent much of our time together. We would meet downstairs in the bar every afternoon to prepare for opening, then work together until closing. I would tend the bar while he would chat with the customers. Another bartender would join us on the weekend. Gloria was a cynical, sarcastic woman in her thirties who seemed like she was born to get people drunk.

I was surprised by how much I enjoyed spending time with Juan. He lived in the apartment across the hall from mine, and I would often hear classical music coming from within. Some days he would knock on my door and invite me to join him for lunch or a trip to the market. We soon became friends.

I learned he was once a pilot. He had always dreamed of flying as a child, and he applied for aviation training as soon as he was old enough. Within a few years, he was travelling around the world, piloting airplanes that carried hundreds of passengers. He told me incredible stories of his adventures during layovers in faraway places. A romantic rendezvous or two with women in Paris. Drinking snake's blood with gangsters in Bangkok. Waking up on the beach in Rio, reeking of cachaça and covered in horsehair.

I listened to these stories, captivated. I'd never thought about what it would be like to fly. I'd never dreamed that I would ever travel by airplane or see the world outside of Mexico.

Late one night while we enjoyed a quiet drink after closing, I asked him what it felt like to fly.

"Like I'm free," he said.

Juan would often ask about my family and where I came from. I would always find a way to dodge his questions or change the subject. That night was different. I told him about my poor town with the crumbling streets. I told him about my dull father and my devout mother. I told him about Miguel.

By the end of my story, I was sure he would send me away, like my mother and father did. Instead, he put his hand on my shoulder and said, "Do not let your past determine your future."

"And what about you?" I asked, feeling bold. "On the day we met, you asked me why I came to this city. What's your answer?"

His face hardened, and I was scared I'd crossed a line. He glanced to the side, thinking, before turning to me with an expression I'd never seen before. I could only describe it as how my mother used to look when she confessed, a mixture of shame and surrender.

"Sometimes distance is the only cure," he said. "This city gives me what I need — a place where nobody will remember me when I'm gone."

Humans are impossible to satisfy. Once we achieve one dream, we set our sights on another. We always want more. This time in my life was the happiest I had ever been. I had a home that I rented with the money I earned at a job I had become good at. These things had seemed impossible just a few months earlier. Now that I had them, I wanted more.

I had been living in DF for one year when I began to dream about the world. Despite the immense sprawl of the city, it suddenly felt very small. I realized how much more there was beyond Mexico. I started to fantasize about the places Juan had described to me. The canals of Amsterdam. The skyscrapers of Hong Kong. I wanted this life he had lived twenty years ago.

Every Monday evening, the only night of the week the bar was closed, I would go to the same grassy field near the airport. I would lie on the grass and gaze at the sky. It was often the colour of burning sand at this time of night, just like it was above my ugly town.

I would watch the planes glide over the city, ascending and descending in streams that never seemed to stop. I imagined the places they were flying to and arriving from. Places with exotic names. Places with mysterious people.

At first, I reprimanded myself for thinking I would ever be able to see these places. It was a foolish notion, a childish day-dream. As the days and weeks and months wore on, the idea seemed less impossible.

I had been living in DF for two years when something happened that would change my life again. It was just another ordinary night: the bar had closed, and Juan and I were cleaning up.

I was laughing at something Juan had said when all of a sudden two men walked through the front door. They were clothed in black from head to toe. The hoods they wore covered their faces. They each had a gun, one pointing at Juan, the other pointing at me.

"Give us the money!" they shouted. We were too stunned to move at first, but then they screamed again, "Give us the money!" I dropped what was in my hands and stumbled to the cash register. One of the men instructed Juan to go to the back room. He knew about the safe.

The man kept his gun pointed at me, shouting. He was impatient. I couldn't think clearly. Finally, my fumbling hands were able to get the register open. The man told me to get to the ground, and I put my hands over my head. He came behind the bar and started grabbing the money.

I was crouched on the floor — it was sticky with spilled liquor — when the deafening sound of a gunshot rang throughout the black room. I froze. I thought it was me, that I had been shot. There was shouting. Then I heard the two men run out the front door.

I climbed to my feet, slowly. My ears were ringing. My hands were shaking. But I was alive. There were no bullet wounds.

I looked around the bar. It was so quiet, so peaceful. Besides the mop and dish rags that had been dropped on the floor, nothing seemed out of place. Everything looked as it should.

I called out to Juan. There was no answer. I called out his name a few more times, more quietly now as I made my way to the back room. There, I could see why he didn't respond.

Juan lay on the floor. The pool of blood underneath him expanded slowly, so red I couldn't believe it was real. I just stood there as the blood crept toward me. Soon it would cover the entire floor.

The door to the safe stood open. It was empty.

When the police arrived, they found Juan's gun on the floor beneath a desk. They concluded that he had reached for it while the intruder was distracted with emptying the safe. The gun flew from Juan's hand when he was shot.

The sun began to rise when the police left, bringing with them plastic bags of evidence and Juan's large, limp body. Once they were gone, I closed the barred gate and locked the door.

I spent that morning mopping up the blood. It was already beginning to darken and harden on the floor. I thought this would have been taken care of somehow at a crime scene, but nobody came to wash away these remnants of death.

The next few weeks were a haze. I would wake up every morning like it were just another day, as though everything were normal. Then I would remember what had happened. My apartment was so quiet, so lonely. There were no longer voices coming from inside the bar. No shadows or light. No clinking of glasses or laughter from the patio tables. Just silence and darkness.

Then one day I received a phone call. The man told me he was a lawyer. He needed to meet with me. It concerned Juan.

I met with the man the following day. To my surprise, I learned he wanted to discuss Juan's will. Juan had no family. He had revised the will just three months before his death, as though he had sensed the end was near. Everything he owned was to be passed on to me. It included the deed to the bar, the two apartments, and more money than I could ever dream of possessing.

I was shocked. I was embarrassed even. I didn't deserve any of this. I had not earned it. I didn't know how to own anything, let alone a business or property. My first instinct was to reject it all, to insist that it was a mistake. Then the lawyer passed me a note that Juan had written by hand: *My friend, be free.*

· · · · ·

"Elias." I didn't know what else to say.

The beach around us was deserted by then. I looked at him, my eyes struggling to make out his face in the darkness.

"Like you said, sometimes a terrible thing can be the only catalyst for change."

"What happened after you received the inheritance?"

"I sold everything," he said, his voice quiet and flat. "The bar. The apartments. I couldn't surround myself with those reminders. One night, I went to the grassy field for the last time. I contemplated what to do next as the airplanes flew overhead. Juan's final words to me repeated in my mind: 'My friend, be free.' Then I made a decision.

"I packed a few belongings. I went to the airport — it was my first time stepping foot inside of one — and purchased a one-way ticket to a place I'd never heard of until I met Juan. A city with an exotic name that Juan had called home once upon a time. Vancouver."

Silence settled between us, tempered by the sounds of waves rolling over the shore. The moon outlined his face in its pale light but revealed nothing else.

"Juan would be proud of you," I said. "You left that place and your past behind, just like you always dreamed of doing. And one day you'll be a pilot, like him. You are free, just like he wanted you to be."

"Am I?" he asked. "Free? I'm not so sure. There is only one thing that I feel. I've felt it every day since that last night in my poor town. I thought it would fade over time, but it lingers like a phantom."

"What is it?"

He turned his head to look at me then. The angle caught the glow of the moon, and I could see his face. The grave lines of his lips. The tiredness in his eyes.

"Guilt," he said.

THE CELEBRATION
Seven days after the crash

"Something to drink, sir?"

My eyes snap open and take a second to focus. "Pardon me?"

"Would you like something to drink?"

The woman looks pleasant and inoffensive. Her hazelnut hair is pulled back so tightly it stretches the skin on her forehead. The powder blue of her uniform is calming. She smiles at me with her mouth but not her eyes.

"I'll just have some water, please."

I watch as she pours from a tall bottle into a small plastic cup. She passes the cup to me, smiles again, and pushes her cart farther down the aisle behind me.

The cabin lights along the overhead compartments are dim, casting a soft blue glow on the people seated below. The few windows that aren't covered reveal the darkness outside and the sliver of flames along the horizon. The sun is either just rising or setting. Perhaps it is frozen alongside us.

The man seated beside me leans against my shoulder, smelling like champagne and cologne. I gently prop him up in his seat as his head rolls forward. He sleeps deeply, chest expanding and contracting with each heavy breath.

"I think he likes you," says the man across the aisle to my right. He is dressed in slim pants and a loose cotton shirt that's draped elegantly across his collarbones. From his boots to his hair pulled into a knot, he is clad in black like a cat in the night.

"Gabriel?" I ask, surprised. "What are you doing here?"

He flashes me a mysterious smile and leans back in his seat, leg outstretched across the aisle. "I could ask you the same thing, no?" He lifts a tumbler to his lips and sips slowly, consciously. I know what it is by its amber colour: Tears of Men.

"I'm going …" I realize I don't have the answer.

"Ah ha!" says Gabriel with a triumphant laugh. "As I thought. It is okay though. I do not know where I am going either." He tilts his glass toward me. "To only the best and most lovely things," he says before taking another long sip.

I shift uncomfortably in my seat when a voice projects over the speakers. The voice is familiar. Although the volume is crisp and clear, it somehow sounds faded, as if time has weakened its timbre.

"Ladies and gentlemen, this is your captain speaking. I'm happy to announce that we should have clear skies all the way to our final destination. So lie back and enjoy your flight. We are going to do this in style. It will be unforgettable."

I look out the windows again, and the sliver of light is fainter now. It must be night.

Two women in powder blue brush past my seat as they strut down the aisle toward the front. I look around and see people in powder blue stationed throughout the cabin. They no longer seem pleasant. Their expressions are grim.

"Hey, Coenhead." The man seated beside me is wide awake now. His cologne is familiar and overpowering. He glares at me with a mischievous look in his emerald eyes.

"Remember when we were kids?" Clark asks. "We built that fort together in the woods behind the house. Do you remember?"

"I remember."

"That was great, wasn't it? Just you and me. We must have spent all summer building that thing. Let's do it again. What do you say? Let's build a fort together."

"Clark, I don't know …" I don't finish the thought as my voice trails off. Something isn't right. I look past Clark and see my mother sitting on his other side. She's reading an old book with weathered pages. Next to her is my father, whose eyes are fixed on something in front of him.

I unbuckle my seat belt and stand up. Vivi and Decker are sitting a few rows behind me. Farther back is Raina. I see my aunt Sheila and her current boyfriend whose name I can never remember. There's my cousin Taylor and his girlfriend. Beside them sit Nina and Naomi, old friends from university.

"Señor Coen, you should take a seat," says a woman one row in front of me. She cranes her head to look into my eyes. It's Maria. She's wearing the same professional suit she wore on the day we met. "Relax. You are in good hands."

I sit down and look at Clark. "What's going on?"

"This is everything you ever wanted, isn't it?" His smile is unsettling.

The needles begin to stab deep beneath my skin. I sit back and concentrate on my breathing when I see the two women in powder blue at the far end of the aisle. They reach into an overhead compartment and pull something out. I watch as they lift the objects to their faces until their faces are gone. They have new faces now. Wild white eyes. Pointed snouts. Jagged yellow teeth. Twisted mouths painted red. I look behind me and see there are more women in powder blue, standing still with jaguar faces.

"Clark, something is wrong," I say. He's rigid in his seat as he stares straight ahead, his face calm and lifeless. "Clark, listen to me!" He doesn't respond.

I turn across the aisle to Gabriel. Before a word leaves my lips, I see that he's also staring straight ahead with the same calm expression on his face. There are slashes of red and black paint under his eyes and across his forehead. He looks like a warrior in a trance.

I twist around in my seat to see everyone around me. Their bodies are stiff and motionless as they stare ahead with lifeless eyes, faces slashed with red and black. Vivi turns her head to look directly at me, but it's not Vivi behind those eyes.

A tone chimes over the speakers before the voice returns. "Ladies and gentlemen, this is your captain speaking. We are about to begin our descent. Please buckle your seat belts and ensure that your seats are restored to their full upright positions. It has been a pleasure flying with you. I will never forget it. See you in the sky."

All of a sudden the plane lurches violently to the side, whipping us around in our seats as though we are on a rollercoaster. I hear myself scream but everyone else simply stares ahead, silent and unseeing.

Hundreds of yellow oxygen masks drop down from overhead. I grab the nearest one, frantically securing it to my face. Nobody else reaches for one. The masks swing wildly from side to side, a chorus of pendulums keeping time to the rocking beat of the plane, its conductor hidden away in the cockpit.

There is so much noise now as we dive faster, sharper. It sounds like a wind tunnel, the deafening rush of indistinguishable noise drowning out everything else except for a steady beep that pulses like a metronome.

I grip the armrests of my seat and close my eyes, bracing myself for impact. Any time now. The last thing I hear is Clark's voice. I feel the warmth of his breath so close to my ear, smell the stale champagne.

"This is everything you ever wanted, isn't it?"

• • • • •

The stillness in my room collides with the mayhem in my mind as I jolt back to consciousness, passing from one dimension to another, neither of which feels like reality. The impact is crushing, and I lie helplessly as I decompress. My body is slick with sweat, soaking the sheets that are tangled around me. The only sounds in the room are my pounding heart and fitful breathing. I am Lazarus returning from the land of the dead, a corpse trapped by life.

My mind spares me its trickery this morning. I know exactly where I am. I know what today is. The second my eyes open, I know. I am in suite 319 in the Ōmeyōcān Hotel. Today is my wedding day.

I lie here for what seems like hours, staring up at the feature-less ceiling above my bed, arms and legs spread outward like a star. Every now and then I hear footsteps in the hallway shuffle past my door, but mostly there is deep and penetrating stillness.

"Do you feel free?" I say to the silence.

I know that Elias won't answer. He has left me now.

"All you ever wanted was to be free. Now you finally are."

The quiet returns momentarily until it is pierced by three sharp raps on the door. Knock. Knock. Knock. The first one is loud and declarative, the second a little unsure, the third timid and apolo-getic. I don't move, hoping this person will go away. The knocks break the silence eight seconds later in the same diminuendo.

My body feels tremendously heavy as I place my feet on the carpeted floor, pull my bathrobe around myself, and make my way to the door.

Peering through the peephole, I'm surprised and a little suspicious to see my mother. She's dressed like she's on her way to play tennis, her eyes partly hidden beneath a white visor. There are no courts on the island.

My first instinct is to turn around and crawl back in bed, but curiosity gets the best of me.

"Good morning," I say, opening the door just wide enough for my face to be visible.

"Good morning, honey." She looks comically serious, every muscle in her face tensed up like a clenched fist.

"How did you find my room?"

"Decker told me where you were. May I come in?"

"I don't think that's a good idea."

"For heaven's sake, let me in. I have something important to say to you. Today is not the day to act like a stubborn child."

I reluctantly leave the door ajar and retreat back into the room, resisting the urge to slam the door on her. She follows in after me.

"I'd like to apologize for the other night," she says. "What I said at dinner was uncalled for. It was insensitive." She takes a seat beside me on the bed. I get up and sit in the armchair instead.

"You simply said what you believe," I respond. "What you believe is that my fiancé is a murderer. It is what it is. You're free to think what you wish, but I am not going to subject myself to hearing it. I'm not going to attempt to convince you otherwise."

"I never said that Elias did anything wrong," she responds. "You are twisting what happened in your mind. You do this."

The room feels suddenly small. Her presence consumes the air.

"I am twisting nothing. You made it very clear that you believe what you're hearing on the news. It doesn't matter what I say."

"Coen, my words didn't come out the way I wanted them to. What I was trying to say is that your father and I care about you very much. Your brother does too. We all came here for you. Elias is gone. It's a tragedy. But we are all still here. Don't forget that."

We look at one another from across the room before our eyes dart to the floor in unison.

"I know you never liked him," I say.

"That is not true."

"It is true. You never wanted me to marry him. You never trusted him."

"Your father and I did not know him. You wouldn't let us. How can I trust a man I barely know? Could I say without a doubt that Elias wouldn't have deliberately crashed that plane, like the authorities seem to believe he did? It would be impossible for me to say for certain. My priority is to protect my son. You were not on that plane. That is what matters to me."

"I'm happy that you got what you wanted."

"You may not believe this, but I will always be grateful for Elias," she says. It comes out like a confession as she clasps her hands in her lap.

I look at her suspiciously. This feels like a trap, but I take the bait.

"Why?"

She looks back at me, and I can't help but believe her.

"Because he saved you."

. . . . .

The magnolia blossoms are beginning to fall. The trees were in full bloom just a few days ago. They looked invincible, as though they would remain that way forever. Today, the petals have begun to break away. The pink cloud is paler, softer. The slightest breeze triggers a snowfall of withered flakes. I wince as people step on the petals that cover the ground.

Despite this reminder of death, the courtyard is alive. Young men in the hotel's taupe uniforms are setting the stage for tonight's event with methodical efficiency. They arrange chairs with precision. They shake out tablecloths like matadors.

"Señor!" Maria strides toward me, waving a clipboard in her hand. "Would you like to meet the band? They are just beginning to set up for a sound check."

She gestures for me to follow her, and we weave our way through the courtyard, past the fountain, toward the moon.

Underneath the terrace lies a mosaic of yellow and blue tiles. Unlike the pathways that wind throughout the courtyard, these tiles are irregularly shaped and sized. Some are jagged while others are bevelled. Together, they form a circle hugged on either side by the curve of the staircases that lead to the terrace above. I thought it represented the sun when I first arrived at the hotel. Gabriel was the one who told me I was wrong. It is the moon.

The stage has been erected in the centre of the yellow and blue tiles. Behind it, a veil of green vines cascades from the terrace above.

The band members of Sangre del Pirata busily set up their equipment onstage, adjusting knobs and uncoiling cords. I recognize them from my research. The two guitarists are brothers, identically athletic and baby-faced. The keyboardist is waifish with carefully manicured facial hair. The drummer is the vocalist's boyfriend, a severe-looking fellow who appears to take himself rather seriously. The stocky saxophonist has a friendlier face than the others. The vocalist, Carmen, is as sultry and seductive as her voice.

Maria gets their attention with a torrent of Spanish. They listen disinterestedly before looking at me with feigned enthusiasm. Jumping off the stage, one by one they greet me with outstretched hands. Their wide smiles seem rehearsed, except for the drummer who doesn't smile at all. He shakes my hand and assesses me with his eyes.

Once the introductions are over, one of the guitarists removes the felt hat from his head and says, "We are very sorry for your loss."

"It is a terrible tragedy," says his brother. As if on cue, all six of them bow their heads. Their hands dart from their foreheads to their chests, then from one shoulder to the other — the sign of the cross.

"Thank you," I say. "Tonight won't be about tragedy though. It will be a celebration."

Carmen begins to speak, then hesitates. Her eyelids flutter as she contemplates the words to use before going on. "How would you like us to change our music to suit this celebration?"

"You don't have to change anything," I answer. "You can stick to the set list that you had planned."

The six of them exchange furtive glances. "Some of the songs we were planning to perform may no longer be right for this event." Carmen speaks slowly, choosing her words with care. "They were chosen to get the guests dancing and to keep the energy high. Now that the event has changed, we think that the music may need to change as well."

"Why would anything need to change?" My tone betrays my impatience. "I still want people to dance. I still want the energy to be high. This is not a funeral."

"Of course, señor," Maria chimes in. "The music will be fit for the celebration this is." She looks at each of the band members to be sure they understand. They nod their heads.

"Of course," Carmen repeats. "We will not change a thing."

"I can't wait to see you in action," I say. "Everyone is going to love you. This will be a fabulous night."

They smile and echo one another's tentative expressions of agreement, but they don't seem convinced.

. . . . .

I only ever saw Elias cry once. I don't often tear up myself. I'm not tender like Decker. I'm not impassioned like Vivi. My life has taught me methods of self-preservation. Even so, Elias was often present when the tears did come. He knew what to do in these instances, how to comfort me. Over eight years, I only got one chance to reciprocate.

It happened a year ago. We rented a large house on Bowen Island for the weekend. It had soaring ceilings, wooden beams, and an enormous deck that looked out toward a grassy lawn. Past the lawn was a pebbly beach that embraced a swimming cove, its water clearer and greener than the ocean beyond. It was the weekend of our engagement party.

That afternoon, I peeked through the picture window from the second-floor landing and saw that guests were beginning to arrive. Vivi, Decker, and Samantha were on greeting duty downstairs while Elias and I prepared for our entrance. Everything was going according to plan except for one thing: Elias was nowhere to be found. I hadn't seen him for at least an hour.

I focused on getting dressed and decided to have faith that Elias would show up as expected. I was doing a fairly decent job of remaining calm until Samantha came upstairs to tell me all the guests had arrived. She must have been able to tell something was wrong, but she just smiled and retreated down the stairs.

It took several minutes to find Elias. I searched the entire floor, opening every closet door and getting down on my knees to peer underneath every bed. The thought of Elias hiding under a bed should have struck me as ridiculous, but it didn't.

Finally, I opened the door to a bathroom attached to one of the guest rooms and there he was, sitting on the floor, his back against the wall, his knees tucked in against his chest, his face in his hands.

At first I didn't know what I was looking at. It was Elias, but in a position I had never seen him in before. He turned toward me at the sound of the door and then quickly hid his face away, but it was enough time for me to see the pink hue in his eyes and the tears glistening on his cheek.

"What's wrong?" I asked.

"Just give me a minute, please. I'll meet you outside soon." His voice shook.

I walked over to his side and slid down to the ground with my back against the wall. We sat there for a while without saying a word. He wiped his eyes and stared at the floor in front of him, realizing there was no point in hiding his face from me.

I don't remember what was going through my mind, but I felt at peace. Perhaps it was reassuring to see that the man I loved was also susceptible to the inner ebbs and flows of being human. This time, I could be the strong one.

Eventually, I broke the silence. "We don't have to go through with this. It's okay if this isn't what you want," I said, calmly stating what I thought to be obvious.

He looked at me, surprised. "That has nothing to do with it," he said. "I'm not trying to call off the engagement. I want this."

It was my turn to be surprised. "Then why were you sitting on the bathroom floor, crying by yourself?"

He looked away, embarrassed, struggling to find an answer. I knew how he must have felt then. "Why?" is such an easy thing to ask. These questions always sounded like accusations to me. I hated how simplistic they were, as though expressing the shifting winds inside me as words were as simple as stating the colour of my eyes. I rarely understood these winds myself. Now I was the one compelling a man to justify his storm to someone who was sheltered from it.

"It's too much," Elias said. "This event. This life. Our future. You. I know I should feel happy and grateful. I want to feel this way. But all I feel is ..."

I waited for him to finish his thought, but he sat there in silence.

"How do you feel?" I asked gently.

I don't think he knew how to answer this question. He turned to me, the satellites in his eyes shining sharply, and I knew this would be the only answer he could offer.

"I don't deserve any of this."

"We only ever get what we deserve," I responded. He looked at me then, contemplating what I said, before leaning in to kiss me.

Now, standing here on our wedding day, as I look out over the courtyard of the Ōmeyōcān Hotel, I breathe in the scent of his aftershave and feel the dampness of his cheek against mine. He is here with me. We both got what we deserved.

"Are you ready?" Vivi looks brave in an attempt to instill the same quality in me.

The courtyard below is a scene from a fairy tale — my fairy tale. Candles flicker from linen-covered tables. Ornate vases overflow with tropical flowers of every shape and colour. Lights are strung above like supernovas. Heavy petals fall from the trees, their closed fists becoming open palms, but the pink cloud continues to hover overhead.

All of the guests have arrived. They sit at their assigned tables or linger near the bars, sipping wine and looking rather unsure of what to do with themselves. Carmen croons directly below us, her voice caressing the air like a warm breeze.

I take a deep breath and nod decisively. "I'm ready."

We step away from the edge of the terrace and slowly descend the curved staircase, Vivi to my left and Decker to my right. This would have been my grand entrance. I would have made my way down the west staircase while Elias descended from the east. Carmen would have been singing a jazz rendition of Ben E. King's "Stand by Me." We would have met at the bottom underneath the trees and the terrace and the twinkling lights. Our happiness in that moment would have been undeniable.

I look to the east when I reach the bottom, almost expecting to see Elias in his white suit looking back at me. Of course, he isn't there.

Vivi and Decker stay close to my side as I float through the scene. People greet me with conventional sympathy, their faces long and burdened. I counter with verve, smiling widely and embracing them with affection. I will not let them turn this night into a funeral.

My aunt Sheila approaches and kisses me on the cheek. "My poor, poor boy. I'm so sorry."

"I'm glad you could make it," I say, holding her hands in mine. "Isn't this island spectacular?"

She hesitates. "Yes, it certainly is. How are you doing, sweetheart? I can't imagine what you must be going through."

"I'm just happy to be here with all of you. How about you? How are things with …?"

"Charles," she says helpfully.

"Yes, Charles! How are things with the two of you?"

"We're fine. He was here a minute ago but had to pop up to the room because he forgot his eye drops, silly old man. His eyes get very dry despite the humid weather."

I laugh loudly before realizing she hadn't made a joke. Sheila offers a shaky smile.

"It sure is hot in hell," I say. "I mean, paradise." I laugh again, even more loudly this time.

After pardoning myself, I make my way to one of the bars set up beneath a tree. There stands Gabriel, shaking a cocktail with vigour as he chats with Nina and Naomi. The two women appear spellbound. As expected and against my instructions, he is dressed entirely in black, tonight in a thin silk tie and fitted tuxedo jacket with all but one button undone. His long hair is slicked back in its usual knot. The lanterns from the hallway behind him cast a brilliant glow, framing Gabriel with pillars and light. He is a dark angel.

Nina and Naomi walk away, speaking to each other in hushed tones with glasses in hand. I'm relieved they don't notice me standing there.

Gabriel spots me as I saunter toward him. He places his hands on the bar and grins mischievously.

"Coen, my friend. I was wondering when I would see you tonight. You have been keeping me in suspense."

"I like to retain an air of mystery," I say.

"You may be the most mysterious man I have ever met."

I try to conjure a witty response, but I come up empty-handed. Instead I laugh, almost certain it's obvious the sound is meant to fill the silence.

"Thank you again for being here tonight," I finally manage to say. "It means a lot to me. I hope it wasn't any trouble."

"It was no trouble at all," he says, leaning toward me with his elbows on the surface of the bar. "I am honoured to be here. Whatever you need, just tell me."

"I don't know what I would do without you."

"You would be very thirsty, my friend." He reaches below the counter for a couple bottles and begins mixing his potion. "My heart breaks for you tonight," he goes on as he stirs and pours. "This must be difficult for you. Remain strong."

"Don't let your heart break for me," I respond. "I'm not worth it."

"Worthy or not, it breaks." He places the glass in front of me with a brisk twitch of the eye. The lights behind Gabriel begin to flicker rapidly, transforming him into an ominous silhouette. For a split second, I see slashes of paint across his face, red as blood and black as night. It happens so quickly that I'm not sure if it happened at all.

I take a long sip of the potion, and it makes me bold. "Have you ever had your heart broken?" I ask.

"Every day," he says gravely.

"No, I mean really broken. Truly broken, just smashed into pieces."

"You are asking if I have ever suffered the carelessness of a lover. Yes, of course. We all have, no? For me though, that is not heartbreak. That is the sting of rejection. The shame of vulnerability. The cold slap of reality after a warming delusion."

"Those things sound heartbreaking to me."

"They seem so at the time but then the pain goes away," he says with a shrug. "It fades. The heart recovers and the mind forgets. True heartbreak never leaves you."

"Then what is the cause if not a careless lover?"

"You." His eyes peer into mine, and I can't look away. "People can bring you pain, but nothing will hurt more than the pain you inflict on yourself."

The lights flicker again, then stop. I think I see something lurking behind Gabriel. Something dark.

A commotion erupts behind me. I break away from Gabriel's hold to see a man being escorted out of the courtyard. He is dressed like the other guests, but I don't recognize him. The man's arms are gripped firmly by two large staff members who aren't outfitted in taupe like the others. Their dark uniforms distinguish them as security.

"Get your hands off me!" the man shouts with a Scandinavian accent, his face flush with anger. Soon he is gone.

I turn to face Gabriel. "Another one," he says, shaking his head.

I catch a shimmer of colour from the corner of my eye. Raina is glamorously dressed in a form-fitting gown made of metallic purple sequins that glitter in the light. She walks up to me without a word and kisses me tenderly on the cheek. Holding me by the hands, she takes a step back and studies my face.

"You are disturbingly handsome for a widower," she says.

"No, I'm not," I say. "That is, I'm not a widower. I was never married."

"Well, that's a relief."

Vivi appears by my side, seemingly from out of thin air, and links her arm around mine. "What are you two talking about?" she asks with her lips stretched tightly across her cheeks in her fakest of smiles.

"We were just debating the intricacies of being widowed," Raina says, punctuating the sentence with a melodic laugh. I join along, perhaps too enthusiastically.

"That sounds uplifting," Vivi responds, tightening her grip on my arm.

"She was just joking around," I explain.

"Can you believe that man who got tossed out a minute ago?" Raina says in an obvious attempt to change the subject. "Now how the hell did he get past security in the first place? Apparently he wasn't the first one either."

"I heard that some of the guests were being harassed in the village," Gabriel says as he wipes the surface of the bar with a white towel. "Those people are shameful."

Vivi's sleek black hair spins around her head like a whirling dervish as her eyes dart from Raina to Gabriel. She throws up her hands with an incredulous laugh, and it reminds me of Elias. "I don't think Coen needs to hear this right now."

"He's a grown man," Raina says. "I think he can handle it."

"Wait, why are you here again?" Vivi asks without a hint of humour.

"Okay," I say loudly, holding my hands up in front of me. "Everyone relax. We're all friends here, right?"

Raina looks at the ground while Gabriel slings his towel over his shoulder. Vivi glares at Raina's downturned head before saying, "Coen, let's take a walk before dinner is served. I don't think everyone has had a chance to see you yet." She asserts her link around my arm as she pulls me away.

"I'll see you both soon," I say to Raina and Gabriel.

I'm led toward the centre of the courtyard where a stone fountain bubbles beneath a canopy of branches and lights. Carmen's silky voice serenades the air from her pedestal, the vines from the terrace draped around her like a waterfall.

"That was really charming of you," I say, my voice hushed. "Raina is here to be supportive. You didn't have to shut her down like that."

"I don't trust her," Vivi says.

"You don't trust anyone."

"She doesn't know you. She hasn't earned the right to talk to you like that."

"Like what? I need you to be cool, okay? You're not my bodyguard."

"I just worry about you."

"Then stop!" It comes out more loudly than I intend, startling a few guests around us. A constricting sense of irritation begins to simmer beneath my skin.

"Coen, calm down."

"Don't tell me to calm down. Since you arrived you've been

treating me like I'm made of porcelain. It's suffocating, Vivi. I am not as fragile as you think I am."

She stands and stares, arms folded in front of her, red lips pressed tightly together. It looks as though she's deciding whether to give up, to throw in the towel. With a deep breath, she says, "You're right. I've been smothering. I'm just protective of you."

"You don't need to be. Just like Raina said, I'm a grown man."

We stand there in the centre of the courtyard, looking at each other, not knowing what to say, when I begin to laugh suddenly. I can't help it. Vivi watches as my body convulses.

"Are you okay?" She looks around hesitantly before taking a step toward me.

"I'm fine," I say, taking a step back. "I've never been better. I think I'll take a walk. I'll find you later, okay?"

She doesn't respond, defeated, as I hurry off.

I wander beneath the magnolia trees, smiling and greeting and kissing cheeks as though this is what I was born to do. This is my life now, combatting sympathy with grace. I congratulate my cousin Taylor on his latest promotion. I compliment Nina and Naomi on their choices in evening wear. I run into Charles and make a point to demonstrate how I remember his name. Some people seem confused by my selflessness. They want to talk about me. But I don't want to talk about me. I've had enough with talking about me.

It is a perfect evening. For the first time tonight, I notice the warmth of the air and the softness of the breeze that blows petals off the trees. One by one, they float to the ground, a reminder of the unstoppable lapse of time. The din of conversation combined with the vibrations of the music and the glow of the lights lends a dreamy quality to the scene around me.

This is exactly how I imagined this night.

This is everything you ever wanted, isn't it?

It feels like sand in my eyes. They squint harder with my palms rubbing in opposing circles. Everything glistens when I collide with someone so forcefully that I'm nearly knocked to the floor. He catches me as I fall, steadying me with strong hands.

"You okay, little bro?" Clark asks.

"I'm fine." I adjust my jacket, shaking off his hands.

"You should watch where you're going," he says with a tentative laugh.

"Thanks for the advice."

"Hey, I'm glad I ran into you — literally." Another awkward laugh. "I want to apologize for the other night. I was out of line. You know me. I can be a little clumsy with my words, but I mean well. I know that's not a legitimate excuse. I just want you to know that I feel like an asshole."

"Thanks for letting me know," I say, wondering if he can pick up the note of impatience in my voice.

"Are we cool?"

I look at him with disbelief. "No, Clark. We're not cool. It's not that easy. You don't get to say whatever you want, no matter how insulting or asinine, and then go on with life as though it were nothing. What you said was really dangerous. It was also very enlightening. Now I know how you really feel."

He stands there with his hands in the pockets of his pants. Then he takes them out and crosses his arms over his chest. He scratches the back of his head before his hands return to his pockets. I extract the tiniest drop of joy from watching his discomfort — this handsome, arrogant man in his bespoke suit the colour of the midnight sky. I've resented him for so long that I assumed he resented me too, but he seems sincere in his remorse.

"You're right, of course," he says. "It was stupid of me to think it would be that easy. Look, I went too far. I said things I didn't mean, but I also said things that are true. You might not believe this, but I care about you. I want you to be safe. I want you to be happy. I suppose my methods may need some work, but I want us to be able to talk to one another, to be honest with each other."

"Right. Be honest then. I know you weren't finished at dinner the other night. Tell me everything else you want to say."

He sharpens his gaze, sensing the challenge. "I'm not here to pick a fight, Coen."

"You want us to be honest with each other. I'm inviting you to be honest."

He studies me intently before saying, "I don't think you're doing as well as you want us to believe." He stops there, removing his hands from his pockets to hold them over his chest in a defensive stance. The lights strung above his head go dark, then illuminate again. They flicker erratically, but he doesn't seem to notice.

"Go on," I say.

He hesitates. "I don't think you're confronting the circumstances in a healthy way." He speaks with determination. "Nobody can blame you. None of us know what this must feel like for you now. We want to help, but you keep pushing back. I saw you shouting at Vivi earlier. She's your closest friend, and you're even shutting her out."

"I wasn't shouting."

"Yes, you were."

"I am doing just fine, Clark. Believe it or not, I don't need your help. I don't need anyone's help. There is nothing wrong with how I am dealing with this."

"Look at yourself!" he cries, exasperation beginning to show in his voice. "You're wearing a white tuxedo. Look at the giant photograph on that easel over there by the stage. It's not just Elias. It's Elias and *you*. It looks like the same photo from your wedding invitation. Is this a celebration of Elias's life? Or is it a celebration of the life you and Elias were supposed to have?"

"Shut up. You don't know what you're talking about, so just stop." I look around us and realize that people are sneaking glances at me. My eyes meet Carmen's onstage before she quickly looks away.

A heavyset security guard in a dark suit approaches, looking at us both with no-nonsense eyes. "Is there a problem, señor? Is this man giving you trouble?"

"Look, I'm his brother," Clark says with an incredulous laugh.

I consider requesting that Clark be escorted out of the event, but something stops me. "No, there's no problem. I'm fine. Thank you."

The guard takes another careful look at us before nodding and returning to his perch beside a pillar.

I don't even look at Clark when I say, "Just leave me alone. Please."

"You'll have to stop punishing me one day," he says as he walks away.

My legs begin to ache. Nobody seems to be looking at me now as I take a seat on a marble bench underneath a magnolia tree. Maria is talking to one of the suited guards, moving her hands emphatically. She still has her clipboard, but now she's dressed in a shimmering silver gown with a silk shawl draped around her shoulders. Her hair is pulled up into a bundle of curls. I have yet to meet this Maria — the lady.

My parents are already seated at their assigned table with an assortment of aunts and uncles, sipping wine and looking perturbed. I am sure my mother isn't pleased about their placement a safe distance from mine, which was a late amendment to the seating arrangement. After our last meal together, it's for the best. I've been mostly successful with avoiding them so far tonight.

Vivi appears to be polite but bored as she listens to my cousin Annabelle, likely recounting her latest sexual escapade. Vivi smiles and nods appropriately, but I can tell that her mind is somewhere else.

Nina and Naomi are back at the far bar, giggling along to whatever Gabriel is saying. I think his eyes catch mine for a second, but I can't tell for sure.

Raina and Decker stand near the stage. Decker must be telling one of his ridiculous stories while Raina laughs along between admiring glances. I can't blame the poor woman. He is Adonis in a dinner jacket.

The band looks and sounds exactly as I hoped they would, devastatingly youthful with an artistic air of tragedy. They are dressed as though they've stepped out of an opium den in turn-of-the-century Paris.

As the song crescendos to its end, Decker steps onto the stage with a wireless microphone in his hand. He was the natural choice to be our wedding's master of ceremonies. It may be a different event now, but he is still the best man for the job.

"Let's hear it for Sangre del Pirata!" he says amid the polite rumble of applause. "Good evening, everyone. I am Decker de Gannes, though most of you already know me. Coen asked that I be your host for the evening. I'm told that dinner will be served shortly, so please start making your way to your table. You will find a place card with your name at your assigned seat. ¡Buen provecho!"

I find myself disappointed that Decker opted against a more animated introduction. I would not have expected him to use the same material he had planned for the wedding reception, but it could have used a little more life.

I take my seat at the table nearest the stage along with Vivi, Decker, and Raina. We're joined by my cousin Taylor and his girlfriend, the last-minute trades for my parents and brother.

The seven courses of dinner progress in a blur. The conversation flows smoothly, but there's an undercurrent. Raina laughs impulsively at everything that is said. Decker has become a talk show host with his endless supply of thoughtful questions and entertaining anecdotes. Vivi has become the audience, withdrawn and reluctant.

I eat without paying any attention to the dishes. I taste nothing.

As our plates are cleared away and wineglasses refilled, I see Javier, the hotel's pastry chef, emerge from the service hallway that leads to the kitchen. He pushes a cart covered in rich purple linen. Atop the cart are three square tiers of cake that form a pyramid of sumptuous white frosting and flakes of gold. My breath catches in my throat.

Javier looks at me with a sympathetic smile. He places the cart beside the easel that displays the framed photograph of me and Elias. We're standing on that rooftop that seems so far away and long ago, holding one another, tears in our eyes with laughter, the city sparkling behind us like so many dying stars.

It's time. The conversation at our table becomes quiet as I stand. I walk over to the stage and pick up the wireless microphone. Beside me, the easel flaunts the framed image like evidence.

I motion for the band to stop playing, and they improvise a premature end to their song. A boom of feedback reverberates through the speakers, capturing everyone's attention.

"Good evening," I say. There is silence except for the sound of the ocean in the distance. All eyes are on me. "I thought I would say a few words before dessert is served. Speaking of dessert, look at this exquisite cake that the amazing staff of the Ōmeyōcān Hotel have created. In fact, Elias helped me choose the cake. It's a funny story. Raina over here was also instrumental. Stand up for everyone, Raina!"

She remains in her seat but waves her hand with a shy smile.

"I know I've said this before, but I want to thank you all again for taking part in this celebration. It is not the event it was originally intended to be, but it's a celebration nonetheless." An abrupt laugh escapes me. Everyone is sitting straight in their seat, attention fixed on me.

"Let me tell you about the day I met Elias. It happened eight long years ago, but it still feels like yesterday. It was the happiest day of my life."

A glance passes between Vivi and Decker. It's furtive, but I catch it.

"It was a spring afternoon at home in Vancouver. I was reading in my favourite courtyard. I loved that spot because it was filled with the most magnificent magnolia trees. They created a cloud of pink when the flowers were in bloom, which only happened for a few weeks of the year. They were in bloom that day. It was heaven, much like where we are tonight at the Ōmeyōcān."

My mother's face is bowed toward the floor. Her head shakes ever so slightly.

"All of a sudden, a book landed on the ground beside me. It was an old copy of *Peter Pan*. I looked up and there on the rooftop, peering down into the courtyard at me, was the most captivating man I had ever seen. He had dropped his book, you see. He came down to meet me, and he looked like a prince as he emerged from the gate. His hair was the darkest shade of black. So were his eyes. They'd reflect the light like satellites shining in the night sky. For those of you who don't believe in love at first sight, take it from me — it's real."

I hear a dull hum as my eyes land on Clark. It looks like he wants to say something, but my mother places her hand on his shoulder as a quiet restraint.

"Elias took a seat beside me on the ground. He held his book in his hand, and he said to me, 'One day I am going to fly. Just like Peter.'"

Vivi closes her eyes with a resigned sigh. I look around the room. Everyone appears so spectacularly sad.

"Elias was right. One day he would fly. All he ever dreamed about was the sky. The sky took him away from me. Maybe that's where he belonged all along."

See you in the sky.

The lights that criss-cross above the courtyard go dim for a second before brightening again.

I take a deep breath. "Elias changed my life. I never imagined myself having the things Elias gave me. A loving partner. Hope for a happy future in which anything would be possible. He saved me, didn't he, Mom?"

She forces a tight smile, despite the tears forming in her eyes.

Perhaps you're better off this way.

The lights above us flicker again as I feel one gentle stab of a needle deep beneath my skin. And then another.

"We built a life together. We made a home. We covered our walls with photos from our adventures. I let him fill the place with aviation maps and airplanes because he tolerated my plants and books, which were everywhere."

Another abrupt laugh escapes me, but nobody seems to join in. I look at Decker, hoping to see his wholesome grin, only to see his face set like stone. My gaze falls on Vivi, and there is something I don't often see in her eyes. Fear.

This is happening again?

I take another ragged inhale as the lanterns flicker from the columned halls that surround the courtyard. I should have seen it coming. It was lurking behind the light this entire time. As the needles become sharper, I can't deny its presence now.

The shadow embraces me, kissing the back of my neck. My skin goes cold while my blood burns hot.

"Elias and I were happy."

Maria stands beside a nearby pillar. The motherliness I was offered at one time has returned, her face soft with compassion.

Do not be fooled by happiness. It can wilt and die, especially when kept in a house of glass.

The shadow whispers in my ear, and the hum becomes louder.

"That day in the courtyard eight years ago was like a dream — a vivid, unbelievable dream. I anticipated waking up at any moment to find that none of it was real, but I never did. The dream just continued until I began to think there may be nothing to wake up from."

Gabriel watches me intently. His hands grip the bar he stands behind. His eyes are dark and piercing.

Nothing will hurt more than the pain you inflict on yourself.

"I suppose I've woken up now. It was just a dream after all."

The shadow holds me by the eyes and draws my vision toward Clark. He looks away.

You look so happy. I want to believe it. I really do. But I know how good you are at pretending.

The hum is louder now. The needles are sharper.

"Elias ..."

I look at his handsome face. His eyes are alive behind the glass of the frame. The city shimmers behind us like a curtain of stars.

"What happened to you?"

My laughing face in that moment is frozen, eyelids crinkled and teeth on display. We hold each other, undeniably in love. It was real. Wasn't it?

"You didn't want any of this, did you? You fucking coward." The words slip past my lips like they've been waiting for the time to be right. They would be inaudible without the microphone, such a quiet accusation. "Answer me!"

The shadow has taken control now. It grips my entire body — every limb, every organ. It is in my blood, flooding my veins with fear. It feels like fire as it simmers and smoulders. Every part of me screams.

I desperately attempt the focusing exercises I was taught long ago, but they won't help now. My vision focuses and blurs uncontrollably. When it's clear, I see the distress on their faces. They can see I've been consumed.

"You did this," I say, as though uncovering a terrible truth as my eyes scan the room. "All of you. You let this happen."

Tears stream down Vivi's face like thin strokes of black paint.

"None of you loved him. None of you gave a shit about him. You all let him die."

People stand from their seats now. There is noise I can't quite hear over the shadow's whispers.

"None of you wanted us to be happy. None of you believed in us. You just stood by and watched. Just like you did with me years ago, you stood and watched and did nothing."

Through the smokiness of my vision, I see a figure come toward me.

It's a shadow.

A jaguar.

A warrior.

An invader.

A demon.

A saint.

My arm swings at the figure. A dull sensation explodes in my fist as bone connects with bone. I fall on the figure, fists lashing out in front of me.

The smoke begins to clear as I'm pulled away by force. In an instant, the shadow is gone. I am sprawled on the ground with hands gripping my arms and legs. There are people standing all around me. I feel something coarse underneath me and realize that the ground is covered in shattered pebbles of glass. The easel and its frame are lying broken by my side. There is blood on my hands.

Movement and noise surround the figure I knocked to the ground. I wrench myself from the grip of the hands that hold me and climb to my feet. Stepping closer, I see that it wasn't a shadow after all. Neither demon nor saint.

There lies my brother. Blood is matted into his hair and caked on his face.

I can't look anymore.

Before I realize what is happening, I'm running. I run through the crowd. I run past the overturned chairs and beneath the dying magnolias. I run through the far gate and across the beach. The moon watches above me, a witness. I keep running until I feel the waves wash over me. I am cleansed in the coldness of the ocean. It relieves me of every weight I've ever had to bear.

"Let me be free," I say. "Let me be free."

Part Two

A New Year
and an Old Friend

THE CHAMBER
Eight years before the crash

I can't remember life before the shadow. It is closer to me than family. There have been times when it would come nearly every day. These were the bad years. Nowadays it often hides away, sometimes for months at a time. Then as soon as I dare believe it has left me for good, it returns for a visit. I used to find it amusing to read about Peter Pan chasing his mischievous shadow. My shadow chases me.

I was never afraid of the shadow as a young boy, even though I would sometimes find myself screaming in the middle of the night. I learned to be fearful as the years went by. With age came the understanding there was reason for fear.

Humans adapt. I learned how to manage. I met with specialists. I practised coping techniques. I swallowed whatever pills were prescribed before I flushed them down the toilet and refused to take more — they were not good for me. I figured out how to smile through the pain, how to get out of bed every day, how to be normal. I was doing well. There were days when I forgot the shadow existed at all.

Everything changed at the age of twenty-two. It was the beginning of a new year when I was reminded of something worse than the shadow. This was before Elias entered my life, though we'd been living in the same city for years at that point. He was so close yet still a stranger.

"Looking sharp," Clark said to me when I arrived at the party. I felt sharp. It had been a good year. After an era of feeling alienated in my sheltered suburb, university had given me a sense of belonging I'd never felt before. I was accepted despite my flaws. In fact, I was made more interesting because of them.

I had started to let myself take chances. I even spent the previous summer travelling through Europe with Vivi and Decker. We got into trouble and danced until sunrise and laughed like we would be young forever. It was an intoxicating feeling, what I could only describe as happiness. The more familiar this feeling became, the easier it was to forget about everything else.

As I stepped into the ballroom that evening, surrounded by beauty and success, I felt like I belonged there. Not because of my bespoke tuxedo. Not because of the elegant woman by my side, who also happened to be my closest friend. Not because my father was Calvin Caraway or because my mother sat on the board of the foundation throwing the event. I belonged because I was there to celebrate the start of a new year, like everyone else, and for the first time in a long time I was excited about what lay ahead.

Even Clark's nod of approval was welcome validation, though I was more interested in the man standing beside him.

"Happy new year," Adam said to me, the corners of his lips curling up into an easy smile. My nerves began to tickle as he grabbed my hand in his.

Adam had captivated me since the moment he entered Clark's apartment four months earlier, the muscles on his chest creating peaks and valleys underneath his fitted polo shirt. He gravitated to me during that barbecue Clark was hosting, and that summer had given me courage I'd never possessed before then. We spent the evening laughing as we discreetly observed and mocked Clark's vacuous friends. His spell had been cast.

I thought it unfortunate at the time that he was the loving husband of a woman named Theresa and the proud father of twin girls. On that first night, Adam had opened his wallet to reveal a photograph of his family. They were a daydream of wholesome good looks and commodified happiness. Normally, I would have scoffed at such a conventional life — more a Coca-Cola advertisement than a way to live — but I found myself admiring its simplicity. I wanted a sliver of what Adam had, perhaps a sliver of Adam himself. I sensed him wanting a part of what I had as well.

To complicate things further, Adam was Clark's boss at the real estate firm where he worked. It was inconvenient to find myself enamoured with a man who had a wife, two daughters, and an employee sharing the same DNA as me. Not that it mattered. I would never have acted upon my impulses, regardless of the circumstances. I certainly would never have predicted what would happen that New Year's Eve.

The night was a glittering, shimmering blur. I had never felt more assured of myself than I did that night. Perhaps it was the sparkle of the champagne, or the passing looks of approval from strangers, or the collective anticipation of forgetting what had passed and ushering in what was to come, but optimism warmed me from inside as Vivi and I glided through the room like we were untouchable.

Midnight came and we toasted beneath a shower of gold balloons as the band played "Auld Lang Syne." I kissed Vivi on the lips and my mother on the cheek. My father shook my hand,

and I pulled him in for a hug. Clark and I wrapped our arms around each other. "Happy new year, little brother," he said.

At one point in the night, long after midnight when the crowd had begun to thin, I found myself at the upstairs bar with Adam. He wasn't as tidy as he had been earlier. His bow tie hung loosely around his neck, and the top few buttons of his shirt were undone. It was also clear he was no longer in need of another drink. Even so, he looked like a movie star.

"What do you think of the champagne?" he asked, handing me a glass flute.

"It's the piss of the gods." I put the flute to my lips and emptied it in one gulp.

"You never cease to impress me, little Caraway," he said, putting his arm around my shoulders. I don't remember how long we stayed there on the edge of the balcony, talking and laughing over the revelry below.

Looking back, I wonder how things went so wrong. Did I laugh too loudly at his jokes? Did my eyes linger on his a second too long? I know now that I shouldn't have left the party with him, but I doubt I could have done anything to avoid what was to come. Even if I could have foreseen the outcome, I was powerless. It was inevitable. I was under his spell.

I followed him and the scent of the cologne I had grown to crave. We climbed into a cab to get out of the rain. Clark and Vivi and everyone else we were leaving behind didn't even cross my mind.

We arrived outside Adam's home, which was on the sixth floor of a stately brick apartment building. We didn't say much as we stepped through the front doors and into the elevator. The boldness from the champagne began to wear off. I could feel the tingle of nerves as we stood there silently while the elevator climbed slowly upward floor by floor.

He led me down a carpeted hall to a large wooden door that stood above a black welcome mat. "You'll have to forgive the mess," he said, unlocking the door and stepping inside. "The girls can be little hurricanes."

Adam fixed me a drink while I looked at the photographs hanging on the walls. His wife and daughters were spending the night with Adam's parents-in-law outside the city, but their beaming smiles surrounded me in this home that was theirs, not mine. The only thing that seemed sad in this room was the lonely Christmas tree standing in one corner, unlit and decorated in colour-coordinated ornaments.

"I'm not sure if anyone else is coming," he said as he handed me a glass. "I guess this happens with after-parties. Everyone gets all excited and then loses steam. We might be the last men standing."

If I had believed there would actually be an after-party, I probably would have left then. Instead, we clinked our glasses together and took a seat on the leather couch.

I don't recall the sequence of events that led to his mouth being on my mouth. There was no smooth segue, no warning. Before I knew what was happening, I was pressed firmly between the hardness of his body and the softness of the leather. The smell of his cologne and the champagne on his breath was intoxicating.

He threw his tuxedo jacket to the floor and tore off his shirt before doing the same to mine.

It was when he began to undo my pants that I realized this had gone too far. My ears began to hum. I could feel the prick of one needle, then two.

"I'm sorry," I said, smiling shyly. "We shouldn't be doing this."

Adam grinned at me. "What do you mean?"

"I'm really tired. I think I'm just going to head home."

"You're not going anywhere, little Caraway."

The ringing in my ears became louder.

"Adam, you have a wife. You have two kids."

His hand hit me against the face so unexpectedly that my body had no response, no reflex. I lay there frozen, the pain in my face spectacularly bright.

"You don't get to talk about my family." His tone simmered with disgust.

The shadow wrapped around me during everything that followed, warm and familiar like an old blanket. I found solace in its terror. As the needles spread throughout my body, I sank into the fear. My throat began to tighten — not by the hold of the shadow but by the hands of the man behind me as they closed around my neck. For once, the pain inside was overpowered by the pain outside.

I lay there, paralyzed, on the first morning of the new year as Adam reminded me that there is no escape from the darkness. No matter how much hope there may seem to be, life is deceitful. Happiness had fooled me.

His breath was warm against my ear. "This is everything you ever wanted, isn't it?"

. . . . .

I returned home later that morning and washed myself in the shower for hours, scrubbing until my skin was raw, until I could no longer smell him on my body. I sat on the tiled floor and let the water rain over my head, realizing it was futile. He was inside of me now.

The days that followed were dark. I could not sleep. I seldom left my apartment. There was a deep, throbbing pain in my chest. The shadow visited often.

I kept myself busy by cleaning. I scrubbed the floors. I sanitized every surface. I washed the laundry, then washed it again. I put my tuxedo in a garment bag and dropped it off for dry cleaning. I never picked it up.

There were multiple messages on my phone from Vivi and Clark trying to locate me after I had vanished from the party. I responded by telling them I was fine.

I scrolled through friends' posts online declaring their new year's resolutions and flaunting their celebratory photos. I tortured myself with this outpouring of aspiration from such hopeful people, musing how I had been one of them such a short time ago.

On day four, Vivi showed up at my door unannounced.

"You look like shit," she said as I opened the door. She was right. I did. Although my apartment was spotlessly clean and I was showering at least twice a day, the lack of sleep and nutrition was beginning to show on my ghostly face.

"Something terrible happened," I said.

Vivi visited almost every day. I was equally relieved and disappointed to learn she had no advice to give me. She always had an opinion. As much as I didn't want her telling me what I should be doing, it scared me that she had no idea.

The one thing she insisted on was that I talk to Clark. "He needs to know about this. He could help you."

By February, the pain in my chest had become unbearable. I dug out a hammer from the bottom of my linen closet. I don't know what was running through my mind except that I needed to do something. I stood in front of the bathroom mirror, my pale skin glowing beneath the glare of the light bulbs. Both hands clutched the handle of the hammer and swung it toward my bare chest.

It wasn't a hard swing, but it sent a wave of feeling that momentarily eclipsed the pain inside. I swung again, a little harder this time. Then again. My nerves flared in response to each blow, sending tendrils of relief throughout my body. Soon, my chest was crimson, the soreness smothering everything else.

Vivi screamed at me when she noticed the bruises a few days later, which had ripened into a rich purple colour like French wine. I didn't have the energy to calm her down. Instead, I sat on the couch and watched her break down into tears.

"If you aren't going to find help, I'm going to do it for you," she said. It was a threat. "I will tell your parents. I will tell Clark. I will find Adam myself, and you don't want to know what will happen then."

"Please don't do any of that," I said.

"Then talk to someone. Talk to Dr. Dana. Talk to your family. I don't know how to make you better, so you need to find someone who does."

"I can't go through all of that again," I said. "I thought it was over. I thought I could move on, that it was behind me. I can't go back now."

"You've come a long way," she said gently, kneeling in front of me with her hands clasped over mine. "You were able to put all of that in the past. You can do it again. You had help then, and you need help now. No one can do this alone."

I invited Clark over the next day. I had not seen his face or heard his voice since the party. Even though I made a valiant effort to appear normal, he could tell there was something wrong as soon as I opened the door.

"How has work been?" I asked, forcing a trembling smile.

"Work? I'm not here to talk about work. Look, Coen, what's going on? You've been avoiding our phone calls. No one has seen you in weeks. You need to tell me what's wrong."

He stood there in my kitchen, staring at me as he waited for an answer. I didn't know how to respond.

"Take a seat," I said, gesturing to the dining table. "Let me get you a beer."

"I don't want a beer. I want you to talk to me."

I sat across the table, placing a bottle in front of him and a glass of water in front of myself. Clark sat motionless and waited.

"Something bad happened," I said finally.

He continued to stare.

"It involves Adam. On New Year's Eve."

"What happened? Vivi thought she saw you take off together. Did he try getting you to do drugs or something?"

"No. There were no drugs."

"Then tell me what happened."

"He told me that he invited some people over to his place for an after-party. I didn't know where you or Vivi were. I was drunk. We both were. We took a cab together to his apartment."

Clark squinted, not quite piecing together what was to come but sensing it was worse than he'd imagined.

"We got to his place and he told me that nobody else was coming, that everyone had bailed. I guess I should have left then, but I didn't think I was in any danger. We were just drinking and talking when all of a sudden we were kissing. I didn't know what to do. I didn't dislike it, but I also knew it was wrong. One thing led to another and he started to take off my pants. That's when I stopped him. I told him that I had to go. I reminded him about his wife and his daughters. Then he hit me."

Clark remained still and silent as he listened, hugging his chest with his arms. I could feel my body quivering as I spoke.

"I tried to get away. I pushed him off me and ran toward the door. He grabbed me. He was so strong. Then he — forced — himself on me."

I drank from my glass until it was empty and waited for Clark to speak. Finally he said, "What are you saying? Are you saying that he forced you to have sex with him?"

I nodded.

"So you're saying he raped you? Am I understanding this correctly? That you were raped?" His voice was louder.

I nodded again, my face burning with shame.

"I need you to speak, Coen!" he shouted.

"Yes. He raped me."

He exhaled loudly and rubbed his temples with the palms of his hands. As incredible as the story might have seemed, he knew I wouldn't have made it up. He took a deep breath and looked at me, his green eyes searching mine. "You kissed him willingly, right?"

My face felt warmer. "Yes, but why does that matter?"

"What you are saying could be very dangerous. It could be damaging to all of us. I'm just trying to get the facts straight."

The pricking of the needles began, soft yet undeniable. I focused on drawing one breath at a time, inhaling then exhaling.

Clark looked down at the table as he clenched and unclenched his fists. After a minute or two of silence, he turned to me. "What do you want me to do about this?"

"I don't know," I said. "Nothing. I just thought you should know."

That was a lie. I wanted him to scream. I wanted him to be furious. I wanted him to hold me. I wanted him to beat Adam's face until it was unrecognizable. Instead, he listened to me. He did nothing.

I watched Clark cradle his forehead in his hands. After what seemed like a long silence, he said, "You're not going to go to the police, are you?"

"I don't know. Should I?"

"They'll never believe you. These types of charges are almost impossible to prove. Plus, this happened over a month ago. It would be his word against yours."

"So you think I should just keep quiet."

He cracked his knuckles before he continued. "I'm saying that pressing charges would likely make the situation worse. He's a successful thirty-five-year-old man with a wife and children. I doubt he even has a speeding ticket on his record."

I nodded. "You're right. I should just keep quiet and let him victimize someone else. That's what I should do, right?"

"Coen, listen to me. Do you really want to put yourself through that? You'd be interrogated by the police. You'd probably have to go to court. Your entire personal life would be on display to the public. Think about what that would do to you. Think about what that would do to Mom and Dad."

It was harder to breathe, but I forced the voice out my mouth. "You only care about yourself, Clark. Don't try to pretend like you worry about what would happen to me. You know you'd probably lose your job. You know this would be a blow to your reputation."

"That's bullshit. I'm trying to look out for you."

I laughed so loudly and abruptly that Clark backed away from me in his seat. "I wish I could believe that."

"You don't make this easy," he said. "You know that, right? Being your brother can be such a struggle. I'm sure being your father and mother is even harder. We have gone through so much for you. You don't give us any gratitude. All we get is your resentment, your bitterness. I can understand that it's not easy being you, but you're going to learn one day that we are not the enemy."

"You don't know anything," I said. It came out like a whisper. I didn't recognize the voice.

"I know that you got drunk. I know that you got into a cab with a man you barely knew."

"Stop it."

"I know you found that man attractive. You went to his home. You kissed him. Then things went too far."

"Shut up."

"I don't doubt that what he did was against your will. But it wouldn't have happened if you hadn't put yourself in that situation. Now what are we supposed to do about it?"

"I just want you to leave," I said.

The only thing worse than the shadow is its chamber. Over the previous few weeks, it had pulled me into the darkness despite my resistance. Sometimes the door would be left ajar. Usually I would be able to emerge for some time before falling back in. It was after my meeting with Clark when I was pulled so deeply inside that I didn't know if I would make it out again. I was so tired of fighting.

The chamber isn't really a pit of darkness. The world around me looks the same except it's clouded with smoke. The colours are duller. The light is softer. The sounds are either hushed or deafening. I could be in a room filled with laughing people and still be utterly alone — both physically there and mentally elsewhere, isolated from the warmth of the sun.

Nothing matters in the chamber. I stopped cleaning my apartment obsessively. Towers of dishes grew high in the sink while layers of dust slowly caked the countertops. I stopped responding to messages and invitations.

The dangerous thing about the chamber is that it's not an entirely uncomfortable place to be. The pain is steady and numbing, making it easier to endure than living in constant fear of the shadow. There are no expectations to meet. No surprises. It strips away the costumes that I wear like armour. It allows me to weaken my resistance. I can stop fighting.

I forced myself to attend my mother's birthday celebration at the house in Deep Cove. Before leaving for the event, I looked at my reflection in the bedroom mirror and was impressed with the person staring back at me. Besides the bags under his eyes, this person could pass for normal.

It took every ounce of energy within me, but I spent the evening being as charming as I have ever been. I smiled as I greeted the guests. I laughed at their jokes. I listened to their stories. By their approving expressions, I could tell I had them fooled. None of them — my aunt Sheila, my cousin Taylor, Mom, Dad — would have known I couldn't pull myself out of bed most days.

Despite the show, I wanted them to notice. I wanted someone to see through me, to pull me aside and ask me what was wrong. I would have told them everything.

At one point in the night, Clark and I found ourselves alone on the deck overlooking the inlet. "How are you doing?" he asked with a glint of concern in his eyes. He kept his voice low, as if we were sharing a secret.

"I'm doing well," I responded, smiling broadly to prove it.

It was a lie. I felt trapped.

"Seriously," he said. "Coen, how are you doing? Our last conversation did not go well. I'm sorry for what I said."

"Really, I'm fine. You were right."

"You seem like you're doing okay, but I can never really tell with you."

"I decided to put that in the past. I'm moving on."

Clark knew me better than this. I had never felt so empty. He must have been able to see there was something wrong with me. I suppose it was easier for him to believe the act. Could I blame him?

"Good," he said. "I think that's probably the right thing to do. You'll let me know if anything changes, right? Just be strong."

"Of course. I'll be strong."

Vivi was the only person who wasn't fooled. She knew what I was like when trapped in the chamber. She had seen it before. She still visited almost every day, but she seemed slightly less troubled each time as though coming to terms with this new reality. She would still lecture me as she washed my dishes and dusted my shelves, but I learned to tell her what she wanted to hear. Yes, I would talk to my parents. Yes, I would think about meeting with Dr. Dana again. I knew she didn't believe me, but what else was she supposed to do?

If it were not for two events, my life might have gone on like this forever. First, I discovered that Clark had been fired. "If you say anything to anyone, I will ruin you" was the last thing Adam had said to me. "I will ruin Clark. You would regret it."

Two days later, Decker coaxed me out from hiding to have lunch at a restaurant near the beach. It was a rare occurrence during this time. I avoided straying from a five-block radius around home.

Decker and I sat on the patio. Spring had finally arrived, and the city was alive. Everyone was out basking in the sunshine. The cherry blossoms had fallen weeks ago, but every other living thing was crackling with colour. Even through the smoke of the chamber, it was blinding. We went for a walk through the neighbourhood after lunch and passed a playground tucked inside a grove of leafy trees. That was when I saw him.

He laughed as he pushed his two daughters on the swings. The girls squealed with delight as they flew through the air, hair blowing in the wind. They swung in alternating directions — one would go up while the other would go down, forward and backward, as their father kept them swinging with a single hand on each little back. Beside him stood his lovely wife, holding a cup of coffee in both hands while laughing along with them. They looked so carefree. So untouchably happy.

I made a decision then. I wouldn't suffer alone. If I was going to be made aware of how easily happiness can crumble into dust, I would not let these people escape. If that meant destroying this portrait of perfection, waking them all from this dream, so be it.

The following day was Sunday. The sun shone brightly as I made my way to the handsome brick building where Adam lived. I waited by the locked entrance until an elderly couple emerged from inside. As they opened the door, I held it for them with a pleasant smile. *What a nice young man*, I imagined them thinking as I slipped inside the building's lobby.

The elevator seemed to ascend even more slowly than I remembered. As it climbed to the sixth floor, I realized I didn't have a plan. I suppose I was going to confront him. If he was alone, I would threaten him until he agreed to confess. If his wife was there with him, I would tell her everything. My hammer sat in the backpack slung over my shoulders. I still don't know what I intended to do with it, but it gave me strength.

I finally reached the sixth floor and walked down the carpeted hall toward the big wooden door, just like I had done months ago. I don't know how long I stood on that black welcome mat, hands by my sides. All I had to do was raise a fist and knock on the door, and it would all be set in motion. Everything would play out the way it was meant to.

But I just stood there. I couldn't raise my fist. I couldn't knock on that door. Again, I was powerless. Perhaps this is why my first instinct was to swing at the figure that approached me many years later, as though it took that much time for me to find the courage to raise my fist.

Eventually it dawned on me. This was how things were meant to be. Adam was supposed to carry on happy and unburdened by the damage he left behind. I was supposed to remain trapped in this violent cycle, failed by my brother and everyone else in the world. This had existed long before Adam entered my life. He came to me to serve a purpose — to remind me that no matter how much I pretended, no matter how much I let myself be fooled, I would always be one misstep from falling to the bottom again.

The chamber would always be there to catch me. The shadow would always be there to reel me in.

I turned away from the door and climbed the stairs to the rooftop.

. . . . .

I could tell I was in Vancouver without opening my eyes. The scent was undeniable — damp and wild. The air was steeped in cedar and sweat and ocean, then carried by the breeze to purify the grit of the city. This was home.

My eyelids fluttered open. Below me was a courtyard filled with magnolia trees. It was surrounded by tall brick walls painted white, each of them with six rows of shuttered windows stacked on top of one another. I stood on the edge of the rooftop, gazing down at the cloud of muted pink petals below. I knew the magnolias blossomed for only a handful of weeks every year. I was lucky to see them in full bloom.

At that moment, there was a noise from behind. I turned around to see a man emerge from the doorway with such command that it startled me. There was a noble quality in the way he carried himself. His eyes were as dark as his hair, but they reflected the light like two satellites in a starless sky.

I could tell by his face that he was surprised to see me standing there. He froze, his black eyes locked on mine.

"What are you doing on the roof?" I asked curiously.

"I live in the building," he responded. "I come up here to read."

I glanced at the book in his hands. The pages were worn and the cover was faded, but I could still make out the title. *Peter Pan.*

"Nice choice," I said.

"What are *you* doing on the roof?"

"I'm going to fly," I answered. "Just like Peter."

That was when I jumped.

Part Three

The Virgin
or the Skull

I know I'm in the chamber as soon as my eyes open. The dullness of my senses and the smoke in my mind aren't strangers. The shadow has been trying to pull me inside since the day I learned about the crash, but I fought. I resisted because I'd almost forgotten how futile it was. I had myself fooled so well.

Now I am so tired of resisting. I have let go.

I sit up in the king-sized bed with my back against the headboard and wait for my vision to adjust to the cloudy darkness of the room. There's a person asleep on the couch wrapped in a blanket. I can tell by the angular helmet of straight black hair it is Vivi. On the floor is a makeshift mattress of cushions and sheets. There lies Decker, limbs sprawled in all directions.

Elias's altar remains on the windowsill. The marigolds are dead now. The candles burned out days ago.

The pain inside my chest announces itself, throbbing so severely I can feel it in my lungs. Without my hammer, I've been using the glass cylinder of the candle from the altar — the one with the angel that Maria had given to me. It has helped me find relief over the past few days from the pain inside. I look into the angel's peaceful eyes as I pound it against my chest. I want to reach for the candle now, but I won't do that with Vivi and Decker asleep in the room.

I lie back in bed and pull the sheets over my head. My legs and back sting with pain, something I've lived with for the past eight years that I doubt will ever leave me.

There is clarity inside the chamber. I no longer need to pretend — about who I am, about the day I met Elias, about how happy we were, about the crash. All of these costumes we wear and stories we tell no longer matter. I've been telling them for so long that I believed them myself. In here, they mean nothing.

Life is trivial. The rules we place on ourselves. The trials we choose to go through. The deadlines we set and the promises we make, then break. For what? For whom?

Life is nothing more than an elaborate house. It starts out small, a simple shelter. Then we build upon it, room by room, believing in the necessity of every expansion, every renovation. By the time we realize it is no longer shelter but a tomb, it's too late.

This is all clear from the inside.

I think about the life I once hoped to build with Elias. Photographs of us laughing, hung on the walls. Untouchably happy. More a Coca-Cola advertisement than a life. Isn't that what I used to think?

This was Adam's life I had come to want. I've been trying to emulate the man who sickens me most in the world. This is how sick I've become.

Soon Vivi and Decker wake up and lie beside me in my bed. I see something in their eyes that was once so common — the look of helplessness. It is more complicated than sadness. It is more severe than concern. It is tenderness and love and anger and fear. They see me and know there is nothing they can do to help me. They haven't looked at me like that in such a long time.

The waves were powerful when I ran into the sea. I didn't get far before I was carried out of the water by arms that felt stronger than the ocean's current.

I don't recall much of what happened after that. I do remember lying on the beach with the vast night sky spread out above me, stars shooting in all directions as they redrew the constellations. The sky was the colour of Clark's suit. Then I saw a face hovering above me. His long black hair was wet. His skin was speckled with sand. The stars danced above him.

"Gabriel was the first one to reach you," Vivi confirms. "He sprinted so quickly and dove right in after you. He pulled you out of the ocean by himself."

Vivi and Decker lie on either side of me as they recount the events of the previous night. I was conscious but despondent as I lay on the beach. Maria called the hotel's doctor, and they brought me back to my room. The doctor's opinion was that I needed sleep. I was unconscious as soon as my head hit the pillow. Everyone left except for Vivi and Decker, who insisted on spending the night with me. They undressed me and dried me off. Vivi cried when she saw my chest.

"What about Clark?" I ask, fearing the answer.

"He's fine," Decker says. "I mean, you messed up his face. He's not so pretty anymore, but you don't have to worry about him." He forces a strained smile.

The only visitors I allow that day are my parents. They are also the only people who attempt to visit. They cringe when they see what I've become — a ghost. They've seen this before, but they were fooled just like I was. They thought this was behind us all, that it could be buried in the past and forgotten.

They ask questions I can't answer. They tell me I must come home with them. I sit in my bed and watch as they demand and then plead. Unlike Vivi and Decker, they haven't learned that it's useless. They think they can still help me.

"I'm not stepping foot on a plane," I say calmly.

"We'll send a boat then," says my mother.

I laugh. "You're going to whisk me away on a grand voyage? Will I be sailing through the Arctic or the Straits of Magellan? Because I don't think they're going to let me through the Panama Canal."

"We'll go over land then. We'll hire a car. We just want to bring you home. It doesn't matter how. Just tell us what you want, and we will arrange it."

"I'm not going anywhere. I'm sorry. I'm not ready to leave." *This is my home now.*

The next two days stretch out in slow motion like time is taffy being pulled. I don't leave my room. As always, the curtains remain closed. Slivers of light escape from the edges during the day, illuminating the dust that floats through the air.

Vivi and Decker spend most of their time alongside me. At least one of them is present in my room at all times. A few days ago, I would have been offended by the notion that I couldn't be trusted to be alone. Today, I understand this is true. I can't be trusted.

Sometimes we talk; other times we stay silent. I welcome their company. It doesn't really matter when I'm in the chamber. They may be by my side, but I'm alone on a different plane. We leave the television on during the silent times. I think the constant noise brings them comfort. The steady stream of voices, so mundane and ordinary.

The television plays on in the background as something catches our attention. Somehow it always finds its way back to the same dreaded news station, as though it follows me.

"News Cloud has uncovered disturbing details about Elias Santos, the Mexican-born pilot of flight XI260." The face of the unholy messenger can switch from grim to gleeful in as little time as it takes to transition from one story to the next. The softness of her blush-coloured blouse hides the hardness underneath.

"The investigation remains ongoing with little new evidence for what might have caused this tragic event. Days ago, authorities released a cryptic radio transmission that was delivered from the flight deck of the doomed jetliner. The voice heard in the recording is believed to belong to First Officer Elias Santos, stating 'pronto dios,' the Spanish words for 'soon god,' mere seconds before impact."

Her voice is both serious and upbeat with just a hint of salaciousness, as though she derives pleasure from sharing such scandal. The authoritative English accent lends her unearned credibility.

"There has been much speculation about whether Elias Santos might have orchestrated the crash deliberately, killing all three hundred and fourteen passengers on board, including himself. We do know that he had been living in Canada for the past thirteen years. He was granted his commercial pilot licence four years ago and had maintained a spotless record, including the routine medical and psychological examinations that all pilots undergo.

"Although much of his early life remains a mystery, News Cloud has uncovered new details that place Elias Santos in Mexico City prior to relocating to Canada. Sources tell us he was employed at the Black Box, a former bar in the district of Condesa. The Black Box closed fourteen years ago shortly after the death of its owner, Jonathan Wagner, a fifty-four-year-old Canadian expatriate living in Mexico City. Wagner previously resided in Vancouver, working as a commercial airline pilot."

An image of a cheerful-looking man appears on the screen. He is smiling broadly, and his cheeks are rosy. Tufts of white hair poke out from underneath the cap on his head.

"Elias Santos was the sole witness to Jonathan Wagner's death fourteen years ago. According to his statement to the police, the two men were in the process of closing one night when two masked intruders entered the bar carrying handguns. Wagner was killed by a single gunshot to the chest. The bar's safe was emptied of the cash that was stored inside."

The footage cuts to a crime scene. Police cars are parked outside a brick building, their flashing lights illuminating the street as they spin like a carousel. Patio chairs sit empty on the sidewalk along a wall that's painted black. The second-floor windows are dark except for one, which appears to be lit by a single light bulb.

"Initially considered a suspect in the shooting death, Elias Santos was released due to lack of evidence. The shooter was never found. Gloria Hernandez was also a bartender at the Black Box during this time. Here is what she had to say."

The screen reveals a woman who appears tough, her skin creased like aged leather. Her silver-streaked hair is pulled into an untidy bun, and there are dark circles under her eyes. She sits inside a barren room with nothing on the walls except for a single wooden cross. She speaks emphatically in Spanish, but her frenzied speech is dubbed over by a translator's calm and emotionless voice.

"I don't remember how long we worked together. It was many years ago. I do remember Elias though. I will never forget that boy. He was a strange one, very quiet, very serious. He was always trying to gain favour with John. I saw through his lies. I never trusted him. He had the blackest eyes. Elias killed John and took the money. I know he did. It doesn't surprise me that he also crashed that plane with all those poor people." She performs the sign of the cross, hands darting across her thin frame, before the camera returns to the messenger.

"As previously reported, Elias Santos was supposed to be married two days ago to his fiancé, Coen Caraway, the son of —"

The screen goes dark. Decker has the remote control in his hand. "I think we've had enough," he says solemnly.

Later that night, I know what to name the pain in my chest. Eight years ago it was shame. Nine days ago I called it guilt. Now I understand what it is — doubt. The chamber might have revealed the truth about many things, but it hasn't taught me what happened to Elias.

I quietly creep toward the windowsill while Vivi and Decker sleep. With stealthy, measured movements, I retrieve the tall candle in its glass pillar and return to my bed. The relief is immediate. It floods my body, numbing me inside.

I almost died on the day I met Elias eight years ago. His face was the last thing I saw before I fell backward into the courtyard, arms spread outward like wings. As I lay at the bottom seconds later, near death, his face was the first thing I saw when I regained consciousness. He looked like an angel despite the panic on his face. The light that filtered through the tree branches created a halo around him. Above him hovered a cloud of pink. I watched as little pieces broke away and floated around us. Beyond that was the sky, endless and blue.

He spoke to me as I lay there. I didn't want that moment to end.

The following few months were spent in the sterile confines of the hospital. I had broken several bones. My pelvis was smashed to pieces. The doctors didn't know if I would ever walk again. They told me to be thankful. I should have been dead. They said the magnolia trees must have broken the fall.

I was thankful. I did as they told me. Whenever it became difficult, I would close my eyes and transport myself back to that magnolia-covered courtyard. I would gaze at the shining satellites in his eyes as the petals rained down on us. I forgot about everything else. I forgot about the past. Nothing else existed but his eyes and the magnolias and the endless sky.

On that very first day, he had insisted on staying in the hospital's waiting room until the doctors confirmed I would survive. My parents had to grant him permission since he wasn't family. The first thing I asked when I woke up was "Where is he?"

He looked uncertain when he stepped into the room. I learned that his name was Elias. I made him promise that he would visit soon.

He kept his promise.

Now, as I lie here in this foreign bed, chest burning with doubt, I close my eyes and remember his face looking down on me in that courtyard. I remember his voice as he read to me beside the hospital bed. I'm ready to give up on myself, but I'm not ready to give up on Elias. Still, the dull pain in my chest throbs worse than ever.

Morning comes and sleep has been elusive. Decker heads out for a swim while Vivi and I order room service. I'm not hungry, but she insists that I eat.

There's a knock on the door, and I can tell by its rhythm that it's not the hotel's staff. Vivi disappears around the corner to answer it. I hear her step into the corridor, closing the door partially behind her. There are hushed voices, but I can't make out the words.

Two minutes pass before she returns.

"It's Clark. He wants to speak to you, alone. Can I let him in?"

My body stiffens. After a moment's hesitation, my head nods.

She leaves the room and closes the door behind her. A few seconds later, Clark appears from the hall.

"Good morning," he says. He walks tentatively across the room before taking a seat in the armchair nearest the bed.

I cringe when I see him. The skin around his right eye is various shades of purple and yellow, radiating outward as though his eye were diseased. His lower lip is swollen twice its normal size. Even from here, I can see the stitches.

"Good morning," I respond, not knowing what else to say.

"You've become nocturnal," he says with a nervous laugh, looking around the dark room. He hesitates. "How are you feeling?"

"Never better."

"Seriously. I want to know how you feel."

I consider my answer and decide there is no longer use in pretending, to him or myself. "It hurts."

He nods, breathing heavily.

"I'm sorry," I say. "Your face …"

"No, Coen." His voice is forceful as it interrupts me. "I'm the one who should be sorry." He takes a few seconds to compose himself before going on. "I failed you. I am your brother, and I did nothing. Just like you said the other night, I stood and watched and did nothing our entire lives. You were right. I will never forgive myself for that."

I study his battered face as he speaks. He is far from his usual cool and collected self. The protective facade has cracked to reveal he is as confused and vulnerable as the rest of us.

"Why did you never try to help me?" I ask. The words come out so effortlessly, even though I've never before had the courage to say them.

He pauses. "Because I was stubborn. I was ignorant. I used to think you were weak. I couldn't understand why you weren't able to just face it, to overcome it. Then I realized I was the weak one. I couldn't handle having a brother who was in so much pain, knowing there was nothing I could do to help him."

"Sometimes I forget that people can't relate to what it's like to be me."

"I hated myself for not being able to understand what you were going through. You scared me, and I hated myself for that too. It was easier for me to just believe you whenever you told me you were fine."

"I can be pretty convincing."

"And I can be pretty stupid," he says.

We both laugh. It hurts my chest.

Clark's face becomes serious again. He leans forward, gripping the arms of the chair so hard it looks like his fingers will pierce the fabric. "I need you to know that I tried this time. It wasn't enough. I know that. But I came to this island determined to be there for you. I wanted to understand what you were going through. I tried my best to help you, to talk to you, to be honest with you. I failed."

"I don't think there's anything anyone could do to help me."

His swollen lips press together in defiance. "I refuse to believe that. I am here for you. Vivi and Decker, Mom and Dad — they're all here too. Together, we'll get through this. You are not alone."

I try to force a smile, but I know Clark won't believe it anymore.

"Remember how you felt eight years ago?" he asks, choosing his words more carefully now. "There were days when I could barely recognize you. It was bad, but you survived it. You were stronger than I could ever be. Elias didn't save you. You saved yourself."

Clark's face lights up as he speaks, and his voice is fortified by a note of intensity. The sound of it clears the smoke ever so slightly.

"But Elias was the catalyst. He gave you strength when the rest of us failed you. We weren't exactly close, but I'll always be grateful for him. He was there for you when I couldn't be." His eyes dart away from mine as he exhales a silent whistle, as though ashamed for what he's admitting.

"Elias wouldn't want to see you like this," he continues. "He may be gone, but this isn't over. There's still something you need to do, for Elias and for yourself."

Clark pulls the chair closer to me and retrieves something from his pocket. He holds it in front of my face.

It is an old photograph of a boy. He wears tattered brown shorts and a wrinkled green shirt. No shoes. His hair is thick and wild. He looks at the camera with a curious expression, his arms hanging at his sides.

"Vivi showed this to me the other day. She said you asked her to bring it to you." He looks at me with such power in his eyes and something stirs inside me. "Coen, you are going to find his family — and I am coming with you."

CUEVA DE LA SANTA MUERTE
Eleven days after the crash

The smoke doesn't seem quite as heavy the following morning. I wake up in the same bed with the same pain inside, but something is different today. I don't feel quite as sedated. I'm not completely untethered.

Vivi once asked how it felt inside the chamber. I told her to imagine a thousand alarm clocks ringing at once, but they're covered by a heavy blanket to dull the sound. The blanket helps quiet the noise to a bearable level, but it also blocks you from being able to turn the alarms off. It's like feeling everything and nothing at all, just a steady pain that's both piercing and numb.

Today, the alarms are quieter.

Clark was right. The story of Elias can't end here. There is more to tell. I just have to find the beginning.

I climb out of bed and sneak past Decker, an unconscious heap of muscle on his makeshift mattress. The shower washes over me, and I can feel every drop as it collides with my skin. The smoke transforms to steam. I can breathe again for the first time in days.

After getting dressed, I look at myself in the mirror and the man staring back at me is not yet a complete stranger. There is still time.

Inhaling deeply, I open the door. I have a journey to begin, and it starts here. But first there is someone I need to see.

· · · · ·

The Terrace Bar is almost empty when I step inside. The sunlight filters through the curtained windows, and it reminds me of my room.

I expect to see my black-clad friend behind the bar, arms flexing as he wipes the counter or mixes a cocktail. A ripple of concern passes through me when I see that Franco, another one of the hotel's bartenders, is there instead.

"Señor," he says. "Would you like a drink? Or do you seek Gabriel?" He flashes me a knowing look.

"As a matter of fact, I am looking for Gabriel. Do you know where I could find him?"

"He is on a pilgrimage." He chuckles as though sharing an inside joke with himself. Seeing the confused look on my face, he says, "You might still catch up with him if you hurry. He heads west along the beach."

I thank Franco as I push open the heavy doors that lead to the terrace. The brightness of the sun is blinding. Once my eyes adjust, I see that the courtyard below has returned to its peaceful state. There are no overturned chairs. No flickering lights. No pyramid of white. No shattered glass. It's as if the other night were only a dream.

The only thing that has changed since the first time I stepped onto this terrace is the sight of the magnolia trees. What were once gloriously alive are now succumbing to the cold embrace of death, their petals wilted away to reveal the bones underneath.

I pull myself away from the view and run down the stairs, across the mosaic of the moon, beneath the trees, and through the far gate toward the sea. I pull off my shoes, and the hot sand sears the skin on my feet as I veer westward. The wind whips my hair about my face. I breathe in the salt in the air. My lungs heave as I run, and the pain in my chest becomes fainter.

I sprint along the beach past lounge chairs and umbrellas, sunbathers and servers carrying trays of elaborate beverages. The farther I go, the emptier the beach becomes until it is just me and the wind and the salty air.

My legs are beginning to ache when I see a figure cloaked in black in the distance.

"Gabriel!" I shout, panting.

The figure turns around and walks toward me. Every contour of his face is illuminated. This is my first time seeing him in the sunlight.

"Coen, what are you doing here?"

"I came to find you. Franco told me which direction you went."

"Well, you have found me." He smiles as he squints from the brightness of the sun. Even so, I detect what might be one of his subtle winks.

"I want to thank you for what you did the other night. I'm sorry you had to witness that. I haven't been myself."

He looks at me for a moment without saying a word as the wind streams through our hair. "You do not need to thank me. You certainly do not need to apologize." He pauses. "Walk with me. I want to show you something."

We continue along the beach. The waves wash up against our feet, spraying salt water onto our clothes. There is something calming about the rhythm of the ocean.

"You are in pain," Gabriel goes on. "What happened that night was an expression of your pain. It was necessary. It is nothing to be ashamed of."

"That's kind of you to say, but I am ashamed." I want to say more, but I can't find the words.

"Sometimes we try to control so much of ourselves that we are bound to become undone. Our emotions and instincts are not designed to be controlled. It is okay to not hold on so tightly."

I sink into his words, and I know he is right.

"How did you come to be so wise?" I ask.

He laughs. "I am not wise."

"I haven't seen you be anything but steady and strong. You are a rock."

"I am a man," he says, looking at me through the corners of his eyes. "Like all men, I am flawed. Trust me when I tell you that I am no stronger than you."

"I can't do that," I say. "I just don't believe it."

"I have made many mistakes in my life, Coen. I have many regrets. I have suffered, and it has always been by my own hand. When you endure as much loss as I have, you learn much about yourself." His face clouds over despite the sunshine that makes his eyes shimmer like carbon.

"Tell me," I say. "What happened to you?"

He pauses before turning to me. "I will tell you my story, one day."

I understand, but I look away. The wind becomes stronger as we resume our journey across the sand.

"Have you ever been to Mexico City?" I ask. "I guess you would probably call it DF."

Gabriel nods and flashes me a curious glance.

"Elias lived there before he left Mexico," I go on. "That was many years ago. He worked at a bar where a man was killed.

Now the reporters are trying to pin the blame on him. As though the crash weren't enough, they want him to be guilty for that man's death. Where does it end?"

"What you believe matters more than what they say."

"That's the thing," I confess. "I don't know what I believe anymore."

Something not too far in the distance catches my eye. As we get closer, I see it's a little wooden house tucked into the trees overlooking the beach. The house is square with a triangular roof. Several wooden stilts keep it from being flooded when the tide comes in. A ramp leads from the beach to the front balcony, which spans the facade with a single door and window. It's the colour of this quaint discovery that sparks my memory. The entire house is painted bright yellow, like the sun.

"The English prince and princess," I say. "That must be the house they lived in when they first came to the island, before their estate was built."

Gabriel lets out a laugh. "You have been listening to the mythology of the island."

"Maria told me the story a long time ago. It was only a few days ago in actuality, but it feels much longer."

"You are right. That is the house."

"It looks so new."

"It is much loved by the islanders. They give it a fresh coat of paint at least once a year. It has looked the same since the day I arrived. I suspect it will look the same generations from now. They let the garden die as a reminder of love's fragility, but they keep this house alive as a reminder of love's strength."

"What do you think happened to the prince and princess?"

A thoughtful look passes through his eyes, then he shrugs. "Everyone has their own theory. For me, I think the same thing happened to them as happens to the rest of us. They grew old.

They fell out of love. They came to this island to escape their demons. They wanted to begin again. Then they realized there is no escape. Your demons follow you."

I stare at the little yellow house as we walk by, imagining the prince and princess standing on the balcony so many years ago, holding each other closely as they gazed out to sea.

We continue along the beach until the sand gives way to a stretch of boulders that wrap around a rocky promontory. The surface is slick with salt water as the waves collide around us.

"We are almost there," Gabriel tells me as we clamber over the boulders, making our way to his secret destination. Once we turn the corner of the outcrop's jagged edge, the beach is no longer visible. We are in a cove sheltered by the high walls of the cliffs above. The waves are more forceful here as they crash against the rocks, spraying in all directions.

Staying close to the cliff walls, I follow behind Gabriel and concentrate on my footing. My legs are soaked up to the thighs. Gabriel turns around with an excited grin as he says, "Give me your hand." I do as he says, and he leads me around a corner.

We find ourselves in a small cave hidden within the cliff. The sounds of the ocean are muted in here, and the light is dim. I'm relieved to see that the ground is dry.

Gabriel walks farther into the darkness of the cave. I can see his silhouette crouch down before individual flames begin to appear around him. One by one they burst alive, illuminating the cave with a flickering glow.

Taking a few steps forward, I see that Gabriel is lighting candles that have been placed along the ledges of the far wall. There are dozens of them. Some are red, others are gold, and there is a lonely one in black. Many are encased in glass pillars like the candle Maria gave me, except instead of angels and virgins, there are skulls and bones.

Scattered among the candles are seemingly random artifacts. There are several flowers in varying stages of death, including the marigolds I would have expected to find in a scene such as this. I see coins, partially rotted fruit, and a few bottles of liquor that are mostly full. It seems strange to me that someone would abandon so much drinkable liquor. Several cigarettes have been placed throughout, many of which had been lit and allowed to burn, leaving telltale trails of ash.

I begin to understand as my eyes ascend. These objects serve a purpose — they are offerings, arranged around a central figure. Her flowing white robes and holy pose suggest a sacred woman, but she is no virgin. The robes part just below the collarbone to reveal the skeleton underneath. Her ribs are outlined against the cloak, and her delicate neck displays each little vertebra. Instead of the demure, angelic face I've become accustomed to seeing, there is a skull. Her eye sockets are empty yet strangely expressive. The curve of her jawbone forms an eerie smile. The hood of her cloak covers her skull like a mane of hair.

The candles flash around her, reminding me of the flickering lights in the courtyard the other night.

"What is this place?" I ask.

Gabriel lights one last candle before standing to face me. "You asked me once what I believe in. This is the answer. I believe in her." He gestures to the statue of the cloaked skeleton.

"Who is she?"

"She goes by many names. La Flaca. La Huesuda. Like most, I call her Santa Muerte — the Saint of Death. She has many followers throughout Mexico and beyond, but her devotees on the island come to this cave to pray to her."

Her bony hands hold two objects. In one hand is a long scythe, like the one belonging to the Grim Reaper. The other hand holds a globe mounted on a small pedestal.

"Nobody knows for certain where she comes from," Gabriel continues. "The Aztecs believed in a queen who ruled the underworld. She protected the bones of the dead. For me, Santa Muerte is this queen."

"The Aztec underworld — Mictlan," I say, conjuring images of blood-covered jaguars.

"You know your mythology." Gabriel smiles at me, looking impressed.

"It's been on my mind."

"The Aztecs revered death. It was the one thing connecting us all to each other and to the universe, more so than life. They understood the power of death. They respected it."

"Death perpetuates creation," I say. "Without death, there would be no life."

"Precisely!" Gabriel beams at me. "Then the Spaniards arrived in Mexico, and everything changed. They brought with them war. They also brought fairy tales of virgins and angels. They promised redemption and eternal life, spitting on the sanctity of death. You could live forever, they said, as long as you sacrificed yourself to a life of confession and shame.

"As Mexico evolved, so did its spirituality. Today, you will find shrines of Our Lady of Guadalupe everywhere from bus station toilets to fast food restaurants. She may be Mexico's Virgin, one who Mexicans can be proud of, but she is still a remnant of conquest."

The flames cast a glow along the lines of his face, illuminating some corners while darkening others. "The past is not so easily erased, however," he continues. "The queen of the underworld hid away, but she never abandoned us. She lives on."

"I'm not a religious man, but I can understand why someone would want to believe in god," I say. "It gives people hope. It gives their lives meaning. Worshipping death seems rather defeatist, doesn't it?"

"Quite the contrary," Gabriel responds passionately. "Santa Muerte gives hope to those who cannot find it in the judgmental god of the Catholics. Santa Muerte does not give a shit about how you live your life, or what you do to survive, or who you choose to love. She provides protection for the abandoned and the condemned.

"Santa Muerte first came to me during a dark time in my life. She accepted me when nobody else would. Life is fleeting, and she allows me to live it on my terms. After all, death is the great equalizer. Rich or poor, virgin or whore, we become the same in the end — ash and dust."

I watch as the candlelight dances across her hollow face. Her smile seems wider than it was earlier, but she is less menacing now. Her empty eyes invite me in.

"Life is fleeting," I repeat, turning toward Gabriel. His eyes are a welcome contrast to those of the statue. They are alive with electricity. "It can end any day."

"This is true," he says, looking back at me. "You must make every moment count. Regret nothing."

With that, his lips are on mine. We kiss tentatively at first, waiting for the other to grant permission to proceed. Then we begin to melt into one another, inhaling and exhaling the heat of each other's breath. I can feel the pulse of his body as it presses against mine.

I want nothing more than for Gabriel to strip away the layers until I'm more naked than I've ever been. I want him to cure me with his touch, to purge my pain. Then I look into his face, illuminated by the flickering flames, and for a passing moment I see Elias's eyes like the starless sky.

My body stiffens, and I put my hands gently against Gabriel's chest. "I'm sorry."

I know he understands. There's tenderness in his eyes, though he exhibits no shame. "You can come to me whenever you need to," he says quietly. "Whatever you need from me, I will give to you."

"I know you will."

Gabriel crouches in front of the shrine and picks up a red candle encased in a pillar of glass. "Take this," he says. "It represents love. It will bring healing to your heart."

I take the candle from his outstretched hand. An image of Santa Muerte is emblazoned around it. She wears a cloak of red, and her skull is bowed. In the centre of her chest is a heart surrounded by flames.

"Isn't it wrong to steal someone else's offering?"

"It would be," he says, "but that offering was mine. I brought it to Santa Muerte because of you."

. . . . .

The midafternoon sun beats down as I return to the hotel to find the corridors quiet. My legs have begun to ache. I'm looking forward to lying in bed and replaying the events of the day in my mind.

I step into suite 319. Vivi and Decker are nowhere to be found. Glancing down, I see a large envelope under my foot that must have been slipped beneath the door. I pick it up to find my name handwritten on the front in elegant, looping letters.

Inside the envelope is a thin stack of papers held together by a metal clip. The front page is a handwritten note on Ōmeyōcān Hotel stationery.

Dearest Coen,

I'm sorry to say I have a confession to make. I am not who I claimed to be. Do not think that I was entirely deceitful. Much of what I told you is true. I broke off my engagement mere weeks ago. I came here to this gorgeous island to celebrate my honeymoon alone.

However, you probably didn't realize that I knew who you were the first time we met. When you had to pick me up off the lobby floor? I truly am such a clumsy giraffe, but I knew then you were the poor soul engaged to the pilot of that ill-fated airplane. It was an incredible coincidence that I would find myself staying in the same hotel as you. I told myself it was fate. It was meant to be.

You see, I uncover and report news for a living. I'm grateful you never asked me what I do for work. I didn't want to have to lie to you about that. It's a boring question anyway.

I wanted to share your story with the world. Well, with our viewers and readers, at least. People would want to learn what it is like to lose a fiancé so soon before what should have been the happiest day. People would want to hear your side of the story, what you have to say about the accusations.

It became more complicated, as you know. Looking back, I regret not telling you the truth and giving you the option to share your story the way you would want it to be shared.

My intention is not to harm you or to cast further doubt on Elias. Here is the story that will be published in the coming days. I hope you find it honest and sympathetic, with a few thoughtful omissions.

I leave for London today. Take care of yourself, Coen Caraway. You are a strong and special soul. You will survive this.

xo
Raina

I stare at the papers in my hand before dropping them in the wastebasket. Perhaps Maria was right that afternoon in the English Garden. You can never truly know anyone other than yourself. Even so, I don't feel anger. I am immune to the sting of deception. I have a purpose now, and it's the only thing I care about.

The room is silent as I remove my shoes, but Vivi or Decker must have forgotten to switch off the television. It projects a ghostly sheen on everything in the otherwise dark room. The walls are dully iridescent, blue like an electric sea.

I'm not the least bit surprised to see the familiar face of the messenger, the texture of her skin seeming more plastic than before, her eyebrows too symmetrical to be human. Despite my resistance, my hand picks up the remote control and my thumb presses a button. Her voice purrs through the air.

"... despite these disturbing new details about his fiancé, there is still little known about Elias Santos himself. Authorities in Mexico have been contacted in an effort to locate his family and to uncover clues to the many questions that remain unanswered. Who was Elias Santos? Was the plane taken down intentionally and, if so, what would have driven him to commit such an unthinkable crime? And perhaps the most curious question of all, what is the meaning behind his final message, those mysterious words, pronto dios?"

"Don't you fear," I say to the messenger. Her eyes connect with mine, and I swear she can see me. "I'm going to find out."

CASA PARAÍSO
Twelve days after the crash

"I wish you didn't have to do this," says my mother, holding my face in her hands. Her hair is tossed around by the wind as we stand on the pier. The sky has begun to cloud over, and the gentle island breeze that once seemed omnipresent has grown steadily rougher.

"This is important to me," I say. "There's no reason for you to worry. Think of it as a harmless road trip. Besides, it's not like I'll be alone."

She strains a smile and turns to Clark, who stands beside me. "Look after your brother. Stay close and be careful. There are dangerous people out there."

"I will guard him with my life," he says, the delivery dramatic and a little patronizing.

Her focus shifts to Vivi, who stands on my other side. "Vivian, I'm going to need you to make sure my boys stay out of trouble. If they try to do anything stupid, I want you to stop them. Do you hear me?"

"Don't worry, Claire," Vivi assures her. "I know a thing or two about keeping these boys in line."

"Good," says my mother, taking a step back to size us up one last time. "We'll be here when you return."

"You and Dad should go home," I say. "Everyone else has already left the island. I appreciate you cancelling your flight to stay with me, but I won't even be here. Go home and let things get back to normal. We'll keep in touch."

"Just stay safe," she responds. "There's a storm coming."

The ferry arrives and we say our farewells. My father, who has been silent for most of the day, pulls me in for an embrace. I get the sense that he doesn't want to let me go. As the ferry pulls away from the concrete pier, I stand on the top deck with Vivi and Clark. My mother and father continue waving until we can barely see them.

Wrapping a sweater around myself, I watch as we sail away from this island that has served as the setting for the most tragic chapter of my life. It was my sanctuary and my fortress. It protected me from the cruelty outside. I was doubtful I would ever find the courage to leave. Clark is right though. There is something that needs to be done, and it has to happen away from this place.

Soon the island is merely a heap of rocks and trees floating in the distance. The pier and my parents are no longer visible. The clouds that appeared from the east earlier today are more sinister now, impenetrably thick and charcoal coloured, like smoke. The boat begins to rock along with the waves.

"Woooo!" Clark screams with his fists in the air. The wind whips his wavy hair and blows his jacket out behind him like a parachute. I laugh as his designer sunglasses fly off his face and into the ocean below. His blackened eye is revealed.

"That's not funny!" he shouts. "Those were my favourite pair." He runs to the railing to confirm that the sunglasses are forever lost. I imagine him jumping in after them.

"Don't do it. They're not worth it!" Vivi screams comically, clearly imagining the same ridiculous scenario.

He turns around, his face grim, before bursting into laughter.

I was skeptical about taking this trip with Clark. I suppose I still am. His words moved me two days ago, but I don't forget so easily. His neglect has shaped me more profoundly than I would ever admit to him.

I wish I could accept him and all that comes with it — his assumption of superiority, his overt need to commandeer every situation to serve himself, his inability to understand anything outside his own realm of experience — but I've failed every time I've tried. He was adamant about embarking on this mission together though, and I couldn't help but believe he may actually care about the outcome. I doubt this will heal a lifetime of ambivalence between us, but it could be a start.

"Give him a chance," Decker said yesterday evening before checking out of the hotel to begin his long journey home. "He's your brother. It sounds like he's trying to make things better, so let him."

"You're right," I said, "as always. I've learned to prepare myself for the worst whenever it comes to Clark. That way the disappointment is never a surprise."

"Maybe he'll surprise you still," Decker said. I responded with a doubtful look, and he laughed. "You're probably right." He paused before looking at me apologetically. "I really wish I could come along."

"I wish you could too, but you need to go home. You have a pregnant wife who has been patiently waiting for you. I won't keep you away from her any longer than I already have."

He wrapped his arms around me, and we stood there for a long moment. "I hope you find what you're looking for," he said.

What am I looking for? I've been struggling to find an answer. I don't have a plan. I don't know what I'm going to say to Elias's parents, if we're even able to locate them. I don't know what I expect to gain. Peace? Closure?

All I know is that it can't end here. There is more to this story, and I'm going to see it through to its end.

I pull the photograph out of my pocket, being careful not to lose it to the wind. Behind young Elias stand the concrete blocks and corrugated metal that formed his childhood home. Beyond that, two large buildings loom ominously in the distance. They are painted a sad shade of red.

"I think this terrible place produced nuclear energy," Elias had told me once, long ago. "I grew up looking at it every day from my bed, a reminder of how trapped we were between the beautiful and the ugly."

It hadn't taken me long to find the place where Elias must have come from. I located it years ago, the night of Decker's Christmas party, when Elias had found the evidence of my search. I still don't know what possessed me to dig up the past that Elias tried so hard to bury, but I felt a thrill when I came across images online of this lonely place that he had only once described to me.

I couldn't find images of his house or his father's shop, but the red rectangles of the power plant were unmistakable. There aren't many of these complexes in the state of Veracruz, let alone those that produce nuclear energy. They matched the buildings behind young Elias in the photograph. Finding this secretive place he used to see from his window every day gave me a new sense of connection to him, despite having to hide the discovery.

As it turns out, our destination is only a two-hour drive from the dock that we're sailing toward. The road will take us along the coast, through the city of Veracruz, past the little towns and rolling fields of the countryside, and straight to his old home. His past has never been more within reach.

A rumble of thunder echoes across the smoky sky before the clouds unleash curtains of rain. Soon it feels as though there is as much water above as there is below. We retreat to the lower deck for cover as the boat lists from side to side.

An elderly man mutters indecipherably to me as we walk past. He's wearing a thick wool sweater fit for a fisherman.

"Pardon me?"

"The gods must be angry!" he says loudly, enunciating each syllable with care. He grins to reveal a mouth of teeth that are either crooked or missing.

I smile back at him politely and hurry away. "What did that man say?" Vivi asks, looking back at him.

"Nothing."

We huddle together on a bench, holding on to one another as we slide from one side to the other in rhythm with the rocking of the boat. Clark and I grew up being on the water during countless family sailing trips, but I can tell Vivi is struggling. I see she is not alone as I look around at the other passengers.

Finally, a voice blares over the intercom speaking Spanish in between bursts of static. "Thank god," Vivi says. "We're approaching the dock." I'm hoping that Vivi's Spanish skills come in handy. She spent a year studying abroad in Seville where she learned the language, more so from several local romances than in the classroom.

It takes longer than usual for the boat to secure itself to the dock. Once we are able to disembark, we rush out onto the pier and are whipped from all sides by the lashing rain. I run toward the welcoming doors of the terminal building with my jacket held above my head.

The stark fluorescent lights greet us as we find refuge inside. It doesn't take long for the yellow-tiled floor to be covered in muddy footprints.

The curved walls of the building are lined with booths representing bus companies and car rental agencies. We follow Clark as he finds the company that he reserved our car through. The sign hanging above the counter is a string of bright green letters.

"Hola," Clark says to the smiling woman behind the counter. "Do you speak English?" The woman's smile widens as she shakes her head. "I have a reservation," he goes on.

"She just told you she doesn't speak English," I say.

"Well, what am I supposed to do then?" he asks, flustered.

"Let me handle this." Vivi pushes him aside. Her Spanish is stilted and uncertain, but the agent seems to understand what she's saying. After a brief exchange and a few taps on the keyboard by the agent's manicured fingernails, Vivi turns to us and says, "They can't find your reservation."

"What? That's absurd," Clark responds. He turns to the agent. "Listen, I made a reservation through the Ōmeyōcān Hotel. They confirmed there would be a car here."

"Clark, she doesn't understand you," I say, trying to stay composed.

Vivi elbows him out of the way and resumes her conversation with the agent. After another crossfire of words, she turns to us and says, "They have something."

We're taken through a back door to a covered lot where the agent reveals a sporty black convertible with a retractable roof.

"Not bad," Clark says, pleased. "Not bad at all." He takes the keys and within minutes we're speeding away from the terminal. Clark is in the driver's seat beside me, and Vivi is perched in the middle behind us. The vinyl interior emits a faint odour of cigarettes and bleach.

"You'll have to guide me, little bro," Clark says. "Where are we going?"

"We're in a town called Antón Lizardo," I say, studying the fold-out road map that I bought from the hotel's gift shop. "We're going to take Highway 150 to Veracruz, which is probably about twenty minutes away. It looks like we'll need to cut through the city before turning onto Highway 180. That should take us straight to Elias's home."

Saying those words out loud doesn't make this feel any less surreal.

"Next stop: home of young Elias Santos," Clark says, flashing me a reassuring glance.

The storm doesn't weaken as we glide through the streets. The windshield wipers are on full speed, swishing back and forth with an aggressive sense of purpose. The ceiling of clouds above darkens as dusk begins to fall.

Clark switches on the radio and finds a station playing what sounds like new-wave Latin disco. "Cha cha cha!" he sings with a laugh. The upbeat energy of the music can't combat the gloom outside. I gaze out the window at the wind terrorizing the trees and the sheets of rain battering the pavement.

We enter Veracruz and even the lights of the city are smothered by the storm. The streets are deserted. The entire cityscape is grey and featureless. It's certainly not the colourful place I passed through thirteen days ago.

Before long, the city is behind us and the surrounding scenery is dark except for the occasional flash of lightning in the distance.

"So we probably should have talked about this earlier," Clark says, breaking the silence, "but what are we going to do when we get there?"

"Good question," I say. "I have no clue."

"What do you mean you have no clue?"

"I don't know. I thought we'd figure it out when the time comes."

"It's getting kind of late to show up at their door unannounced, don't you think?" The pitch of his voice heightens when he's irritated. "Especially when you don't even know what you're going to say."

"He has a point," Vivi interjects, sticking her head between us.

"Of course," I say. "We could just scope things out tonight. Let's find somewhere to sleep in town and then make our move in the morning."

"Are you sure there's going to be a hotel there? I thought this place is supposed to be pretty desolate."

"I don't know, Clark. We could just —"

I'm interrupted by a loud thud as a bundle of palm fronds hits the windshield with force. The leaves get tangled in the wipers, obscuring the road in front of us.

"Pull over!" Vivi screams.

"Calm down!" Clark shouts. With a jerk of his arm, he veers to the side of the road and brings the car to a halt. "I'll be back."

We watch him climb out and remove the fronds from the wipers with little grace. The headlights illuminate the agitated look on his face as he's pelted with rain. Once the windshield is cleared, he clambers back inside and dampens everything that touches his rain-soaked body.

"Bloody hell," he mutters. "I left Vancouver to get away from the rain." He turns a knob and looks at the windshield. Nothing happens. He turns the knob again before shouting an incomprehensible string of curses.

"What's wrong?" Vivi asks from the back seat, poking her head forward.

He opens the door and climbs out again without answering. We watch as he fiddles with the wipers before returning even wetter than before. He turns the same knob with a hopeful look on his face. Then he closes his eyes and leans back in his seat, defeated. "The wipers are broken."

"You're kidding," I say helplessly. Even Clark wouldn't conceive of such an ill-timed joke.

"Those stupid branches must have done something when they got tangled in the wipers."

"Or maybe you broke them when you ripped out the fronds," Vivi shoots back. "You were too rough!"

"Vivian Lo, don't you dare try to blame this on me," he says.

"Be quiet, both of you!" I shout. They go silent. "None of this matters. We just need to figure out what to do."

"How?" Vivi asks, distressed. "We can't drive in this rain without wipers."

"Look up ahead." I point through the windshield at a colourful blur in the distance. "Those lights don't seem too far. It could be a gas station. The road is quiet. I think we can make it."

"I'm not going to drive blind and risk our lives," Clark says.

A few minutes later, we are slowly cruising down the highway with our hazard lights blinking behind us. All of the windows are rolled down, and the seats are instantly soaked. Vivi and I act as Clark's eyes. The upper half of my body leans out of my passenger-side window while Vivi surveys her side of the road from behind.

"A little to the right, Clark!" Vivi screams over the noise of the storm. "You're almost crossing into the opposite lane!"

My hand shields my eyes as the rain stings the rest of my face. We are close enough to the lights to see they belong to a gargantuan sign mounted to the side of a building. I can almost hear the buzz of the neon lights that sear through the darkness, blinding with colour. They outline a green palm tree sprouting from perfectly scalloped blue waves. The name of this place burns brightly in the night, bold and pink: Casa Paraíso.

"I think it's a hotel," I say excitedly, pulling myself back into the car. "Turn right toward the lights, carefully."

Clark drives slowly into the lot and brings the car to a park almost directly beneath the lights. "It's a sign," he says, looking up at the neon above. "We were meant to stay here tonight." He flashes us an idiotic grin.

Vivi and I exchange glances. Neither of us can think of a reason to object.

We jump out of the car and run toward the front doors. The hotel's sign casts an electric glow on the wet concrete below, and I notice only a handful of other vehicles parked in the lot.

A bell announces our arrival as we emerge through the doors and into the lobby. We're instantly transported to a Palm Springs motel circa 1962. The faded wallpaper that covers the room is a pale shade of blue with an undulating pattern of white starbursts. The midcentury furniture is upholstered in avocado-green fabric and teal vinyl with cracks along the edges, foam spilling out from within. Puddles of rainwater begin to form on the pastel pink carpet underneath our feet.

A middle-aged woman with a kind face stands behind the front desk. There are circular stains on the Formica surface left by years of morning coffees. The wall behind her features a painted mural of a beach scene complete with swaying palms and glistening surf. A copper clock in the shape of the sun hangs in the mural's sky directly above the woman's head.

"Buenas noches," she says with a smile.

Vivi's Spanish sounds more confident now. Clark and I stand in the middle of the lobby to avoid making the room any damper than necessary. I look around and see a knee-high statue of Our Lady of Guadalupe standing modestly in a corner. She is surrounded by flowers.

Vivi returns with two keys, each attached by a metal ring to an acrylic diamond with the hotel's name inscribed in pink letters.

"They only have two rooms," she says.

"That can't be right," Clark says. "There are hardly any cars out front."

She shrugs. "Coen and I can share a room. We wouldn't want to impede on your privacy, Clark."

"No," he says. "I'll bunk up with Coen. You're the lady. You should have your own room."

"Save your patronizing macho bullshit for another lady." Vivi glares at him with a face full of contempt.

"I'm just trying to be a gentleman." Clark throws his hands in the air with an incredulous laugh. The woman shoots us a curious glance from the front desk.

"You two need to simmer down," I say. "Vivi, you take the private room. Clark and I will be fine."

We run out to the car to retrieve our bags. Unbelievably, the rain is coming down even more heavily than before. The thunder rumbles more frequently. Once we're back inside the dry lobby, the receptionist points down a hall that leads to a glass door.

The two-level hotel consists of three long wings that wrap around an oblong swimming pool. The outdoor pool is enclosed on all sides but one, which opens out to the darkness beyond. There's probably a beach in the distance, but tonight there is nothing but wind and rain.

The corridors along the wings of the hotel are exposed to the elements. They face the pool on one side and are lined with doors and windows on the other. We climb the stairs to the second level and find our rooms.

"We'll come get you in thirty minutes," I say to Vivi. "Then we can grab something to eat downstairs in the restaurant."

"Sounds good," she says as she pushes her door open. "I'm starving."

After a bit of fiddling to unlock our door, we step into our room. Clark switches on the lights, and we're greeted by a similar midcentury motel motif as in the lobby. Two single beds lie side by side with a wicker nightstand between them. The blankets on the bed are intensely floral, depicting tropical flowers of all colours. Most of the furniture appears to be made of wicker. The large vanity mirror above the dresser is lined with round, bare light bulbs. I flick the switch beside it, and the bulbs burst alive.

"Ugh, turn that off," Clark says, shielding his eyes.

"What do you think?" I swing my arms open as though revealing the grand prize on a game show.

"It's no Ōmeyōcān, but it has its charm," he says, setting his bags on a chair beside the closet. He pokes his head into the bathroom. "I don't see any roaches, so it gets bonus points for that."

We hang our wet clothes in the closet and take turns showering. For a minute, I worry the cold water won't heat up, but soon the bathroom is filled with steam. I wash the storm off me.

It feels good to pull on dry clothes, especially as the thunder rumbles outside.

"Remember that family trip when we drove to Jasper?" Clark asks, carefully styling his hair in front of the mirror.

"You mean when our car broke down and we had to spend the night in the Little Hunting Lodge of Horrors?" I smile at the memory.

Clark laughs, and it doesn't sound quite as ugly as usual. "I thought Mom was going to have a conniption."

"Can you blame her? Every piece of furniture was made from an animal. There was a stuffed beaver in our room."

"And an elk's head over Mom and Dad's bed!"

"They're the ones who wanted the premium suite."

"That was a fun trip." His voice softens as he turns to face me. "I think that might have been the last road trip we took together."

"I think you're right," I say, slipping on my shoes. "That is, until today."

A clap of thunder resounds so loudly throughout the room that it seems to come from directly above us. The lights flicker rapidly, bringing me back to the courtyard of the Ōmeyōcān five days earlier, before shutting off completely.

We stand there in the darkness, unsure of what to do. "The gods must be playing a joke on us," Clark says. Looking out the window, I see that everything has been cast into darkness. The hallway lamps are out. The swimming pool is no longer lit up like a giant blue amoeba.

"It's a blackout," I say, expecting Clark to point out the uselessness of stating the obvious. He remains quiet.

My words are punctuated a few seconds later by three loud thumps on our door. Someone bursts into the room. I can't see who it is, but I know the voice. "The power is out," Vivi says.

"Really? We hadn't noticed." Clark's sarcasm was just delayed.

"You're lucky I can't see you or the stupid look on your face right now," she says. "You guys don't have a flashlight, do you?"

I think of something. "Give me a second," I say, feeling around for my backpack in the dark. Once I find it, my hands rummage through the contents until they wrap around a familiar cylinder, cold and firm. I locate the book of matches buried at the bottom of the bag. A single flame bursts to life a second later, the light casting an ominous red glow on the skeletal face of Santa Muerte. I place the candle on the dresser in front of the mirror. It's the candle of love given to me by Gabriel.

"Do you always carry around creepy-ass candles?" Clark asks. The light illuminates the contours of his face except for his one bruised eye. It looks like a shining emerald floating in a pool of black tar.

"You'd be surprised about some of the things I find myself doing these days."

"What are we going to do for food?" Vivi asks. "I guess it's safe to say the kitchen will be closed."

Clark's eyes light up. "I have something you may be interested in," he says in a mysterious voice. He places his overstuffed duffel bag on the bed before unzipping it slowly for dramatic effect. He then pulls out a plastic sack with theatrical flair and empties the contents onto the floral bedspread. There are several different boxes of crackers and prepackaged pastries, as well as three sandwiches in plastic containers.

Vivi squeals with glee. "Clark, you are my hero."

"I never hit the road without the proper provisions," he says, beaming. "Buon appetito!"

"You mean 'buen provecho,'" Vivi corrects him. "You just spoke Italian, not Spanish."

"Whatever."

We crowd onto the bed and tear into the food, sampling a bit of everything. The candlelight flickers nearby while the storm rages on outside. I eat ravenously, my appetite returning slightly to what it used to be.

"These crackers are basically bread and sugar," Vivi says in between chews. "Ingenious."

Before long, our stash of food is reduced to a heap of plastic containers and paper wrappers. The bedspread is covered in crumbs.

"I've got one more surprise in store for you two," Clark says with a devilish grin. He reaches into his duffel bag and pulls out a large bottle of tequila the colour of gasoline.

"No, you did not!" Vivi says, laughing. "I admire how prepared you are, but did you think this trip was going to be a Contiki tour?"

"Of course not," he says. "But we are stranded in this so-called paradise motel while caught in the middle of a storm that may very well drown us all. Plus, we've known each other most of our lives, and I can't think of any other instance when we spent this much time together, just the three of us. We are on an epic mission together. If that is not cause for tequila, I don't know what is."

Vivi looks at me. "The man has a point."

"I can't dispute that logic," I say.

There are two ceramic mugs beside the coffee maker and one glass by the bathroom sink. Clark pours generously, and we hold up our cups ceremoniously.

"To Elias," he says.

"To Elias," Vivi and I echo as we clink our cups together. I wince as the liquid burns its way down my throat before warming me from the inside.

"That is potent," Vivi says, exhaling dramatically. "I approve."

"Only the best for the two of you," Clark says.

"Remember when we used to hang out in your parents' basement together?" Vivi asks with a nostalgic look on her face. "We would watch cheesy horror movies and play Truth or Dare."

"We were such ambitious teenagers," I say with a laugh.

"I thought the two of you had a thing going on back then," Clark says, his eyes darting between me and Vivi.

"You were dating that awful girl," Vivi says to him. "What was her name?"

"Becca," I answer instantly with more disdain than I intend.

"What was wrong with Becca?" Clark asks in disbelief. "She was super sweet."

"She was a nasty cow," Vivi says. "As much as I hate using terms like that to describe my fellow women, I'll make an exception for her. She was horrible to everyone, except perhaps to you."

Clark looks pensive for a moment before responding. "No, you're right. She was pretty awful to me too." We laugh and take another sip of tequila.

"Let's play," Vivi says, looking at us eagerly. She reads the confusion on our faces. "Truth or Dare. Let's play for old times' sake."

I shake my head. "We're not sixteen anymore."

"What else are we going to do?"

"I'm in," Clark says. "Come on, Coen. Let loose a little. Let's get crazy."

I watch the candlelight flicker across their faces. "Fine. I'll play, but only if I get to go first."

"You've got yourself a deal," Vivi says with a triumphant smile.

I take another draw from my glass as I consider my options. "I choose Vivi."

"What a surprise," she responds. "Dare me."

"Ooh," Clark says in a low voice. "We're off to an intense start."

"I dare you to strip down to your underwear and run around the pool, not once, not twice, but three times."

"Piece of cake," she says, standing up. "Clark, will you be able to handle such indecency?"

"First of all, you're pretty much my sister," he says. "Second, contrary to popular belief, I have in fact seen women in their skivvies before. I think I'll be okay."

Vivi wastes no time disrobing until she's standing in the middle of the room in nothing but strips of black satin.

"Can I wear a hat?" she asks.

"Sorry. That was not stipulated in the terms of the dare."

She flashes me a vicious look before taking a deep breath and darting out the door. Clark and I huddle by the window. We watch as she gingerly descends the staircase and begins her first lap around the pool. The only light comes from candles that can be seen through the windows that line the halls, as well as a few electric lanterns the hotel staff must have placed throughout the grounds. We can barely see her except for the occasional flash of movement as the light reflects off her slick skin.

Her footsteps are heavy against the hallway floor when she returns a few minutes later. We applaud as she slams the door shut behind her. Her skin is red and raw from the rain. Clark gathers the spare towels from the bathroom and wraps them around her shivering body.

"Holy shit!" she says. "It is a dark, cold, wet, scary mess out there."

"Well done," I say. "I'm impressed you didn't bail down the stairs."

She takes a minute to dry off, then pulls on a pair of sweatpants and a hooded sweatshirt that Clark offers. She returns to her position on the bed and instantly resumes the game. "I choose Clark."

"Well, I'm going to look pathetic if I don't choose dare after that spectacle," he says, "so give it to me, Lo."

"Clark Caraway, I dare you to summon Bloody Mary in that mirror over there."

"Wow," he says. "We are really getting juvenile now. How do I do that again?"

"If you say 'Bloody Mary' three times in front of a dark mirror, she appears to you. It's terrifying."

"Bring her on." He downs a shot of tequila before walking over to the mirror. His reflection looks sinister above the flicker of the flame.

"I'll take that," Vivi says, grabbing the candle. We stand on either side of him. He begins.

"Bloody Mary."

He whispers the name slowly, then pauses. His reflection stares into his eyes from the other side of the mirror.

"Bloody Mary."

His voice is louder as he draws out the sound. The corners of his lips curl up wickedly before they open to say the name one final time.

"Bloody Mary."

The room is plunged into darkness as the flame disappears. I hear Clark scream beside me. I imagine his reflection transforming into Bloody Mary. She looks exactly like Santa Muerte. Her hands reach through the glass and grab Clark by the arms, her bony fingers like talons piercing his skin. Clark screams as he's pulled through the mirror and into the other side — her realm of the underworld, what the Aztecs called Mictlan.

I fall onto the bed, my hands held protectively in front of me, when an evil cackle resounds around the room.

"What is wrong with you?" Clark's voice is unsteady. "Let go of me."

"Admit it," Vivi says between fits of giggles. "I got you."

"Just light the candle again, please."

"Follow my voice," I say, breathing heavily. "I have matches."

A moment later the room is bathed in the warm glow of the candle's flame. "Here's your Bloody Mary," Vivi says, holding the candle in front of Clark's face. Santa Muerte smiles at him with her bleached-white bones.

"You are twisted," he says, looking unamused as he takes a gulp from his mug.

"You know it."

We take our seats on the bed. Clark's eyes turn to me. "Truth or dare, little brother."

"I think we've had enough daring for the time being. Truth."

His green eyes don't leave mine as he pauses, pondering what to ask. Finally he says, "Describe me in three words."

Vivi looks at me with anticipation. I take a sip from my glass and roll the question around in my head. There are so many words flooding my mind, most of which probably shouldn't be said aloud. They flow through my consciousness like a river.

Narcissistic.

Self-obsessed.

"Egocentric."

Brash.

Audacious.

"Bold."

Arrogant.

Ignorant.

"Proud."

I can see by the expression on his face that he doesn't know what to make of these words. He seems neither pleased nor displeased.

"Okay," he says, his mood less cheerful than it was earlier. "Your turn."

"I choose you, Clark. Truth or dare?"

"Considering I'm still traumatized from my last dare, let's go with truth."

There is one question that has been on my mind lately, but I hesitate, not knowing how it'd be received if I were to ask it.

After a pause, I decide to forge ahead. "We built a fort in the woods together when we were kids. Do you remember that?"

He nods, waiting to hear where this is going.

"We spent weeks building that thing. Then when it was complete, you kicked me out and let your friends take over. Why did you do that?"

He remains silent and motionless, not knowing if I'm being serious. When he realizes that I am, he shakes his head.

"Why? Because we were kids, Coen! Kids do cruel and awful things. Please don't tell me you've been holding on to this for that many years."

I notice Vivi look down at her hands, and my face goes flush with embarrassment. I don't answer him, but he goes on. "Do you want me to tell you how terrible I was as a brother? Is that what you want to hear? Fine. I was the worst fucking brother. In fact, I still am. I am just an awful, egocentric, poor excuse for a human being who doesn't give a shit about anything but himself."

"Do you at least regret it?" I shoot back. The hum begins in my ears. It's faint, but it's there.

Clark's face softens. "Of course I regret it," he says, his tone gentler. "I regret a lot of things, Coen. How many times do I need to apologize to prove that to you?"

I don't answer him. The room is silent except for the rumble of the storm outside. "Your turn," I manage to say.

"Coen, truth or dare?" he responds immediately.

"Truth."

His eyes try to penetrate mine. He has a question he wants to ask, I can tell, but he's debating whether or not to ask it. I know him well enough to know he will go for it in the end.

"Do you blame me for what happened eight years ago?" His tone is steady and resolute.

"What do you mean?"

I know exactly what he means.

"For what happened with Adam and everything that followed — do you blame me?"

I feel the shadow run its fingertips along my arms. It awakens every cell in my body.

I can't speak, but I look into Clark's eyes. He already knows the answer.

"This isn't necessary," Vivi says. "Let's move on."

"This is necessary," he protests. "Coen, you have punished me for the past eight years. I've just been taking it — the constant abuse, the coldness. I don't know how much longer I can stand it."

"So you're the victim here?" My voice is sharp. The needles dance freely throughout my body now.

"I'm not the only one who did nothing," he says, his tone louder and bolder. There is no going back now. "Everybody else saw what was happening to you, and nobody did a thing. Yet I am the one who is made to suffer still for that mistake we all made. I want to know why."

It sounds like the storm is inside my head now. It screams through my ears. The patterned wallpaper in this tiny candlelit room begins to close in on me. I need to get out.

"Where are you going?" I hear Vivi say over the shrieking of the storm. Pulling on my jacket, I march out the door and into the night. I don't know where I will go or what I will do, but I need to get away.

I take one of the electric lanterns that line the halls and run down the stairs. The shock of the rain as it strikes my face and the force of the wind bring relief. My nerves are both numb and on fire. The storm permeates my body inside and out.

I walk toward the expanse of darkness beyond the hotel. As I approach the swimming pool, a hand grabs me firmly by the arm from behind. I spin around to see Clark, his sweatshirt and shorts already drenched.

"Coen, stop it!" he screams over the noise of the rain as it pounds our bodies and the tiles below us. "What the hell do you think you're doing?"

"You want to know if I blame you for what happened eight years ago?" I shout. "Yes. I do blame you. I blame you for leaving me alone with Adam that night. I blame you for making me feel like it was my fault. I blame you for doing nothing to help me." The words spill from my mouth so forcefully that my body trembles.

"Why me?" he screams, rainwater rolling down his face like so many tears. "We were all to blame. Nobody did anything. Why am I still being punished?"

"You are my brother. You're supposed to protect me. More than anyone else in my life, you had the power to help me. From the time we were young, you could have made me stronger." I pause, breathing heavily. "Instead, you just made me feel more defective. More damaged."

The storm rages around us. I've never seen him look so helpless as when he says, "I don't know what you want me to do."

"I don't know if there's anything you can do."

"I can't change the past, but I won't give up on you again. You can push me away, but I'm not going anywhere. Do you hear me?"

Suddenly the sky above cracks open as a streak of lightning explodes toward us. Its veins splinter overhead, illuminating the darkness with brilliant white light. We cower to the ground, guarding our faces with our hands, reminded of how small and perishable we are.

I prepare myself for the worst as the jagged bolt dances in the sky before connecting with the earth. A deafening sound crackles through the air, and sparks erupt from where the lightning has struck. From our vantage point by the swimming pool, we can see only the top portion of the bolt's victim: the neon sign of Casa Paraíso.

Clark and I seize this moment of safety to run for cover. We slip and slide along the wet tiles before finding refuge in the nearest covered hallway. Eyes wide and chests heaving, we huddle inside a stairwell and lean against the wall to regain composure.

We look at one another with a renewed sense of mortality, and there is nothing to do but laugh. We burst into fits of hysterics, wrapping our arms around each other while we shake and shiver.

"We're invincible!" Clark screams at the sky.

There is a sudden crashing noise so loud and near it could only be the hotel's neon sign colliding with the pavement below. Clark's eyes meet mine. "The car!" we scream in unison.

I hold the electric lantern in front of us as we run down the hall, across the pink carpeted floor of the hotel lobby, and out the front door. What was once a beacon of fluorescent nostalgia is now a charred pile of metal and glass. The outlines of the palm tree and waves are twisted into abstract shapes. The individual letters have managed to remain mostly intact, now scattered across the parking lot. The O lies at our feet. Smoke drifts toward the sky from the heap of debris.

Clark and I walk carefully along the wall of the hotel, stepping over fragments of the damage. Once we get to the car, we see that it remains untouched. The sign landed directly beside it, but there doesn't seem to be a scratch on the car's shiny black exterior. We look at each other, and for the second time tonight there is nothing to do but laugh.

"Maybe the gods were on our side all along," he says.

SANTOS SERVICIO AUTOMOTRIZ
Thirteen days after the crash

I awake in the morning to stillness. The sounds of rain and thunder no longer scream from outside our room or inside my head. The curtained windows are orange with warmth. The sun has returned.

I roll over to see that Clark's bed is empty. Even the sheets and blankets have been stripped off. Sitting up and rubbing my eyes, I'm surprised to find the missing bedding stretched across pieces of furniture. The sheets hang from the top of the vanity mirror and fan outward to four wicker chairs arranged around the dresser. Blankets are draped across the chairs, creating thin walls of a makeshift tent.

"Clark? Are you in there?"

He appears all of a sudden, his head poking out from the small opening in the middle of the tent. "Good morning, sunshine."

"What the heck are you doing?"

"I built a fort," he says as though it should be obvious. "It's not quite as elaborate as the one we built as kids, but I think it's pretty decent under the circumstances."

I shake my head at how ridiculous he looks crouching through the doorway of his blanket fort. "Clark, this is stupid."

"Just shut up and come inside," he says before disappearing.

I groan, unsure of what to do, before throwing my hands up in surrender. I lower myself to the floor and crawl inside on my hands and knees. The interior of the fort is lined with pillows and lit by the flame of the Santa Muerte candle. Clark is seated on a cushion with his back against the dresser. He offers a box of biscuits that I happily accept.

"You're right," I say, taking a seat beside him. "It doesn't quite have the same craftsmanship as our forest fort, but there is a certain cozy charm."

"I went for a wicker-and-floral motif," he says, "to confuse the enemy."

"Smart."

His smile slowly vanishes, and his face becomes serious. "I know this doesn't make up for how terrible I was to you when we were kids, but I hope it's a start."

"You didn't have to do any of this," I say. "You were right. We were just kids. I need to let go of the past."

"There's something broken between us. I want to fix it."

I don't know what to say. I just nod.

"Last night, you said that I made you feel more damaged. What did I do to make you feel that way?"

I lean back against the dresser with a silent sigh. "I always felt like there was something wrong with me. You just had a way of reminding me of it. It wasn't always your fault. You just being yourself was enough. You were always stronger and cooler and more confident. I suppose I wanted you to give me some of what you had, even just a fraction of it."

"Growing up, I thought you despised me," he says. "It seemed like everything about me was the opposite of what you wanted to be. I never thought you would have wanted, or needed, my help with anything."

"It would have helped if I knew how to talk to you then."

"At least we're talking now."

I look down at my hands.

"If it's any consolation, I was never as cool or confident as I tried to appear," he says.

"That may be true, but at least you were strong."

His laughter fills the tent. "You should know better than to believe I am anything but a helpless child, scared that he'll never be a real man. I'm damaged too, just like everybody else."

"You? Damaged? Since when?"

"Always, little brother."

My eyebrows crinkle with skepticism. "I can believe you're not quite as perfect as you want everyone to think you are, but you're still a modern-day prince in most people's eyes."

"Did you know that I still get nervous when I'm around Dad? He terrifies me."

"Seriously?"

"My palms start sweating and my ears go red whenever I'm around him. I can't help it. I guess it's because I know what he thinks whenever he looks at me — I'm not good enough."

"Why do you care so much about what he thinks?"

"I honestly don't know. I just care, and I always have. I'm a thirty-three-year-old man and the most important thing in my life is trying to prove to my father that I'm not a disappointment."

"That is pretty pathetic."

"Isn't it?" he says with a laugh. "It's not just Dad. I'm generally afraid I'm never going to be good enough for anybody. Every relationship I've ever had has failed. I wouldn't trust most of my friends with a houseplant. I certainly don't have friends like Vivi or Decker. When I think about the future, I picture myself alone."

"That's awful, Clark," I say, looking at his solemn face. "It does make me feel a little better about myself though."

His face brightens as he laughs, and he looks like the carefree boy he was before he became conscious of what people thought of him.

"See?" he says. "Everyone is damaged in one way or another. We are all hopelessly and spectacularly flawed."

"Amen, brother."

He hesitates before going on. "I've never felt more helpless than I did eight years ago, after what happened with you and Adam. I look back at it now and hate myself for how I handled the situation. What you said last night was true. I misplaced the blame on you. I saw what it was doing to you, and I did nothing. There is no justification for that. The truth is I just didn't know what else to do. I didn't know how to help you."

"It was a long time ago," I say, as though the healing is complete.

"It weighed on my conscience every day. But one day I cracked," he continues. "I never told you that I confronted Adam about what happened. I told him I knew everything. I threatened to tell Theresa unless he turned himself in. I could see in his face that everything you told me was true. Then I quit my job."

My heart pounds like a sledgehammer against a steel beam as I picture the scene Clark describes. "I heard you were fired."

"That's what I told everyone. It would have raised too many questions if Mom and Dad knew I quit. I couldn't bear being around him or seeing his face every day. I worried that one day I wouldn't be able to stop myself from beating the shit out of him. A part of me wishes I had. I also knew he'd have leverage as long as I worked for him. The only option left was to quit."

"Did you follow through with telling Theresa?" My throat tightens, holding my breath inside.

"No," he says, casting down his eyes. "I was planning to tell her. A few days later, I found out you were in the hospital. It seemed less important then."

Silence hovers between us as the light of the candle's flame flickers against the bedsheets.

"Why didn't you tell me about this before?"

"I don't know," he confesses. "You became really closed off to me after that. I didn't know how to bring it up. I guess I didn't know how to talk to you either."

"I'm sorry." It's my turn to confess. "I was so angry. I couldn't help but direct all that anger toward you. It wasn't fair. You weren't the one who raped me. You didn't make me jump off that rooftop." I wince as these words pass my lips. It's the first time I've stated what happened to me so plainly. No euphemisms, no fairy tales. I was raped. I tried to end my life. That is what happened to me.

I can tell Clark finds this difficult to hear as well. "I'm the one who is sorry," he says. "I should have been there for you. I'll regret it for the rest of my life. I can't change that, but it's not too late to change the way things are now. I can be better." He looks at me with his emerald eyes, and I notice the bruising is beginning to heal. "Let me prove that I can be better."

We sit there on the floor, two grown men in a fort made of bedsheets, and for the first time in a long time I feel protected.

• • • • •

The sun blazes above from a cloudless sky as Vivi and I make our way along the rear of the hotel to the restaurant for breakfast. Except for the debris that covers the ground, mostly empty cans and lifeless foliage, one would never have known that a storm had ravaged the site such a short time ago. It's already just a memory.

The restaurant is located at the far end of one of the hotel's three wings. We see what lies beyond the swimming pool for the first time. Last night, it was a vortex of darkness. Today, it is nothing but a peaceful stretch of alabaster sand framed by the infinite blue of the sea and sky.

We slide onto the vinyl cushions of a booth and feast on chilaquiles drenched in green salsa and cream. I watch as seagulls soar overhead and dive for the garbage that scatters the ground. Two of the birds fight over a piece of bread, squawking at one another with their wings beating the air.

"Today is the day," Vivi says, holding a steaming mug of coffee close to her body. "Have you thought about what you're going to say when we get there?"

"I'll probably just vomit my emotions all over them. Or maybe I won't be able to say anything at all. I really can't predict what's going to happen."

"Clark and I will be by your side the entire time." She reaches for my hand across the faux-wood tabletop.

"I know. Don't let me make a fool of myself."

"That's a promise I can't make," she says with a sly smile. She pauses, staring thoughtfully into her coffee, before going on. "What if they haven't heard the news about Elias? Are you prepared to break it to them?"

I nod resolutely, hoping I appear more confident than I feel. "They should know what happened. I can do it if I have to."

She squeezes my hand and gives me an encouraging look. "Yes. You can."

After breakfast, we take a walk around the hotel grounds to survey the damage from the storm, carefully stepping over mysterious fragments from unidentifiable objects. We hear voices as we round the corner and find Clark with five other men. He's wearing a pair of old gloves and helping one of the men carry a large piece of the neon sign — what's left of the palm tree — to the edge of the parking lot.

"Hey, kids," he grunts, struggling to carry the weight of the awkwardly shaped load, sweat running down his face. "We're just clearing the wreckage away from the entrance."

"I thought you were going for a swim," I say.

"This is more important," he grunts back. "These guys need our help. Don't just stand there. Pick up a piece."

One of the men hands us gloves and we clear the debris from the parking lot, gingerly transporting the sign piece by piece. I'm surprised by the weight of each fragment as I carry it toward the heap of jagged metal at the side of the building.

Once all the larger pieces have been cleared away, Clark and I begin picking up the smaller shards while Vivi goes inside to find a broom. The sun travels across the sky until there is nothing left of the shattered sign. The only things that remain are the charred blotch on the concrete and the empty support beams that jut out where the sign was once mounted.

The five men smile at us and shake our hands, speaking exuberantly in Spanish. We're exhausted and coated in a mixture of sweat and soot, but we smile back and wish them luck. "I sure as hell hope they've got good insurance," Clark says as we return to our room.

After showering, changing into a fresh set of clothes, packing our bags, and scouring the wicker-and-floral-covered room for anything we might have left behind, we take one last look inside before closing the door behind us.

"We survived the storm," Clark says as we throw our bags into the car. "That can only mean one thing." He looks at me and Vivi with an air of suspense. "It's top-down time."

We help him retract the convertible roof and fasten it behind the back seat. Clark gets behind the wheel. Vivi joins him up front. I stretch out in the back, breathing in the fresh ocean air that surrounds us.

"¡Adios, Paraíso!" Clark shouts, revving the engine before peeling out of the parking lot. I twist around in my seat to get one final look at the lonely building behind us, now nameless.

The wind blows through my hair as we speed down the highway across the countryside. Verdant mountains tower in the west while the ocean glistens to the east. It's how Elias had described it once — an endless seam of ochre and blue, though today there's no mist in the mountains.

We pass stalls overflowing with fruit and roadside shops with bright signs, solitary houses surrounded by sapodilla trees and clusters of buildings painted in all the shades of the sky. Every now and then the road curves around the calm surface of a lagoon or over the rush of a stream. I sit back and soak in the simplicity of the beauty around us.

I don't know how long we've been driving when Vivi turns around from her seat to face me, snapping me out of my trance. She takes the sunglasses off her face and says, "I think that's it."

Following her pointed finger, I see that she's right. The pale red boxes are unmistakable. They loom in the distance like a joyless mirage. After so many attempts at putting myself in Elias's shoes, picturing this view every day and every night, it feels anticlimactic to finally be here. There is nothing extraordinary about this place — no sizzling neon sign, no magnolia-covered courtyard, no candlelit cave, no forgotten house of glass. It is as Elias had described it.

Our eyes are fixed on this industrial temple as we drive closer. My heart beats forcefully in my chest, but the ache is even fainter today. As we approach, we see that the complex is protected by a tall fence lining the perimeter. There are several trucks and smaller buildings enclosed within, all uniformly white and angular. Electrical lines dangle overhead from giants made of beams and bolts.

Soon the temple is behind us, and there is no sign of a road-side repair shop. "Do you think we passed it?" Vivi shouts over the noise of the wind.

I pull the photograph from my pocket and compare the configuration of buildings with the view that is now behind me. "No," I shout. "Keep going. It should be up ahead."

The road winds around a small lake before continuing up a gradual hill. As we clear the top of the hill, Vivi looks at me and doesn't need to say a word. I see it too.

Up ahead, tucked a short distance away from the side of the road, sits a little building. Its walls are made of concrete blocks surrounded by trees with broad green leaves. The roof is a sloping sheet of corrugated metal, rusted red over time.

A larger version of this building stands beside it. Painted across the front wall in bold orange letters are three words: Santos Servicio Automotriz.

"What's the plan, little brother?" Clark asks as he slows the speed down to a crawl. "Do we roll up to the front like the pride parade?"

"Yes," I say, trying to steady my breathing, timing each inhale and exhale to every four beats of the heart. "The front door."

He turns onto the unpaved driveway that leads to the little house. The wheels send up a cloud of dust around us. He pulls the car to a stop, and we are so close to the front door. Clark and Vivi turn around to face me in the back seat.

"You can do this," Vivi says with a reassuring smile.

Clark pats me on the cheek. "It's now or never."

We climb out of the car and walk slowly toward the door, the dirt crunching underneath our feet. The pale red boxes of the power plant can be seen beyond the house, and I realize this is the spot where young Elias stood in the photograph. For the first time, I see this view framed by the endless sky.

The wooden door is white with flowers painted across it in colourful swirls. I study the flowers for a minute, buying time as I maintain control of the air in my lungs and the pounding of my heart. My fists are clenched. Vivi and Clark stand on either side of me, but they don't move. This moment is mine, not theirs.

For a second, I fear I'll be unable to lift my hand and knock, like that day in the white brick building with the magnolia courtyard so many years ago. Then, without warning, my fist rises and delivers three sharp thumps against the painted door.

I hold my breath. There is silence. I am about to knock again when the door swings open.

Standing there in the entryway is a woman. Her face has been moulded by time, motherly and kind. There are wrinkles around the eyes from years of laughing or crying. Her wavy hair is streaked with silver and tied together by a blue ribbon. She wears a simple cotton dress, brilliantly white with blue and orange flowers embroidered along the neckline. I know right away that she is Elias's mother. Her eyes are as dark as a starless sky, but the satellites sparkle with life.

She looks at the three of us curiously before smiling. "Good afternoon," she says.

"Buenas tardes," I respond. "I mean, good afternoon. You speak English?"

She lets out a good-natured laugh. "It is not very good English, but I am still learning. I can see you are not Mexican."

"You're right. We're not." I glance at Vivi and Clark. They flash me looks of encouragement. After a brief hesitation, I say, "Are you Señora Santos?"

She nods.

"My name is Coen. This is my brother, Clark, and my friend, Vivi. We're from Canada. We came here to find you." She listens patiently with a calm expression on her face. None of this seems out of the ordinary to her. I take a deep breath before going on. "Do you have a son? A son named Elias?"

Her face glows as she smiles, the slightest hint of tears forming in her eyes. She takes a step toward me and places her hands on my face. She looks at me with such warmth and understanding. "You are his love."

My mouth hangs open, unable to speak, and my eyelids blink erratically like they're transmitting a message in Morse code.

"Come in," she offers, stepping aside to let us through the door.

The air is cool, and the walls are awash in the lazy sunlight bleeding through the windows. It's a cozy space with embroidered rugs under our feet and wooden furniture covered in knitted blankets.

One feature of the room catches my attention. On the far wall sits a wooden cabinet, the kind used to display china. Every surface is covered in candles, their flames flickering gently as they cast a glow throughout the room. A garland of fresh orange marigolds is strung along the highest shelf. Vases filled with flowers surround the base.

At the centre of one shelf is Elias. His unsmiling face looks noble. My breath catches in my throat as I see how handsome he is in his pilot's uniform. It's the photograph that has appeared in every newspaper over the past two weeks. I can tell by the faint colours that the image is made of newsprint, now displayed in a simple wooden frame.

"I knew it was my Elias as soon as I saw his picture on the news," she says. "Those eyes."

"I'm so sorry for your loss," I say. "We weren't sure if you would have heard about what happened."

"I lost him long ago," she responds, the lines in her face softening. There's a wistful look in her eyes that I understand all too well. She wraps her arms around herself and I know how she feels, torn between the past and the present. Despite the tragic end, I imagine her pride at seeing this magnificent man that was once her young son.

She returns to reality seconds later and faces me. "I am sorry for *your* loss."

We sit at a table covered by a yellow cloth. In the centre stands a thin glass vase with a single purple dahlia. Señora Santos places a plate of biscuits on the table and hands each of us a glass bottle of fizzy soda before taking a seat.

"You have travelled a long way from home," she says. "I am thankful for your visit. You are all so young." Her face lights up, though her eyes wander past us with a rueful gaze. "Tell me. What brings you here?"

"Elias never said much about his past," I begin uncertainly. "It was important to me to see this place and to meet you. Otherwise, how could I say that I truly knew him?"

She smiles and nods with understanding. "It is a blessing you are here," she says. "Otherwise, how could I say that I truly knew him either?"

"I'm happy you feel that way," I respond, the relief showing itself on my face through a nervous grin. "I didn't know what to expect would happen."

"How did you find this place?" she asks.

I reach into my pocket and pull out the faded photograph. "I found this picture of Elias as a young boy," I say, handing it to her. "We pieced together a few clues and figured out where your house would be."

She's been holding back tears since we arrived, each eye the glassy surface of a well, and now they spill over the edges as she looks at the photograph in her hand. She smiles in the way people do when remembering the past, a mixture of happiness and regret.

"It has been so long ..." she says, the sentence forming, then fading. Her chin trembles as her head nods in silent agreement to the thoughts in her mind. "This brings me much happiness. But this boy is not Elias."

Vivi and Clark glance at me from across the table, their expressions reflecting my confusion. "What do you mean?" I ask.

"This is not Elias," she says again. "It is his brother."

"He had a brother?" I manage to stammer.

"Yes," she says. "He had a brother. Pedro was his name."

"Elias never told me about Pedro. Why would that be?"

"Guilt," she says simply.

. . . . .

Elias was always different. He was not like the other children in our town. He dreamed of more than we, or this town, could give him.

"I will live in the city one day," he would say to me. "My life will be extraordinary." We tried to convince him that he belonged here with us, but I knew we would lose him one day.

The only thing that brought him joy was his brother. Pedro was younger than Elias by five years, but they were the closest friends. They would laugh at jokes only they understood. They lived in their own little world, those two.

Pedro and Elias were very different boys. There was always a smile on Pedro's face. He was filled with curiosity, but he was also happy with this simple life of ours. This family, this house, this town — it was enough for him.

I would bring my two sons to church. I felt so proud with them by my side, dressed in their finest clothes. Neither of them believed in god the same way I did. I accept this now. I raised them to be devout, but they were too headstrong to be told what to believe.

To them, everything was a joke. They would even taunt god. They shared one joke they would laugh at whenever we prayed. They would scream it to the sky, then laugh until they fell off their chairs. It used to anger me. Now, I would do anything to hear their laughter one last time.

The years went by and Elias grew into a man, strong and proud like a mighty tree. He also became restless. His roots refused to settle for the ground from which they grew. Our time with him was coming to an end.

I could not have predicted that everything would happen so quickly.

We hired a boy to help with repairs in the shop. He and Elias became close. They would spend hours watching the sky. Elias would tell me about the stars. His father and I found their hobbies strange, but we were glad he had found a friend.

It was the day after his seventeenth birthday when we found the two boys kissing. They were inside a car that was being repaired in the shop. Elias's father did not mean to surprise them. He only wanted to see if they would like something to drink.

I stepped into the garage to find the boy on the floor. "Do not touch him!" Elias screamed at his father. The light was dim, but I could see the furious look on my husband's face. The boy got to his feet and ran away.

I convinced Elias and his father to come into the house. I tried to calm them down, but there was so much anger.

"I love him," Elias said to us. "I do not care that he is a man. Can you not let me love him?"

We said hurtful things. I regret this now. Two men in love was not something we understood.

Pedro was still so young, but he came to his brother's defence. "Why is it wrong to love a man?" he asked. "Because your god tells you so?"

It was too much for me to bear. I ordered Pedro to go to his room and close the door. Then I looked at my eldest son. He waited for me to speak, to hear what I had to say.

"I feel shame for you."

Of all the things I could have said to my son, these are the words I chose to speak. He was shaking with fear. I could have held him in my arms. I could have told him I loved him. Instead, I let shame overcome love.

He looked at me with such sadness in his beautiful eyes, and I knew he was lost to me then. He did not say a word. He turned around and walked out the door.

I regretted what I had said as soon as the words passed my lips. I tried to run after him, but his father stopped me. "Let him go," he said.

We did not know what Elias was going to do. We did not realize that Pedro was no longer in his room. We did not know something was terribly wrong until we heard the screams.

You see, Elias had climbed into the car that was sitting in the shop — the same car his father had found him in with the other boy. Elias did not know that Pedro had run after him as he was driving away from the house.

We went outside to follow the sound of the screams. Elias was crouched on the ground in front of the car. The engine was still running. He looked like an angel, illuminated in the headlights. There was something held in his arms, something precious. As we came closer, we could see it was his brother.

Pedro was covered in dirt and blood. He was still alive, but he must have known he did not have much time. Before he died in Elias's arms, he looked at his brother and smiled. They shared one last joke together — the same joke they had created to taunt god.

"Pronto dios," Pedro said as he laughed.

· · · · ·

Clark's eyes catch mine, and I know that everything he has said these past three days is true. The regret, the guilt, the pain, and, most of all, the hope — I see it all in his emerald eyes.

We wait for Señora Santos to continue, but she looks down at her hands placed neatly in her lap and the silence hangs above us all. The tears have dried on her cheeks, leaving trails of salt she doesn't bother to wipe away.

Finally, her head tilts upward. She sits straight in her chair, proud and resolute, and places her hands on the table. The longing in her eyes has transformed into something more present.

"It was painful," she says, looking at us with a piercing directness that reminds me of Elias. "But the joy they brought me is more powerful than the pain."

"What does it mean?" I ask. "Soon god?"

Señora Santos laughs unexpectedly, diluting the sorrow in the room with a substance that's vital and alive. "It does not mean 'soon god.' My sons said it in a way that means 'quickly, god.' They would say that joke whenever we prayed — 'Pronto dios!' — as though impatiently asking for a miracle. 'Hurry up, god!' is what they were saying. 'Grant us a miracle!' It is supposed to be funny."

Clark looks around the table with disbelief on his face. A laugh escapes him, and soon we are all laughing. The sound cuts through the sorrow like a jet through a cloud. Tears stream down our faces as we laugh at a joke from so many years ago that is now misunderstood around the world.

"So you think that Elias was speaking to his brother when he said those words on the plane?" Vivi asks.

"I know he was," Señora Santos responds. "His brother brought him comfort in those final moments. Pedro gave him peace. I also like to think he wanted his father and me to hear his voice one last time."

I look around the peaceful room and imagine the emotional scene that fateful night. I see Elias crouched on the ground in front of the house, his silhouette radiant in the beams of the car's headlights, his brother cradled in his arms. That moment would haunt him for the rest of his life. Many years later, in the cockpit of a plane, he would leave one final message — not for me, not for the world, but for the brother he lost, the parents he abandoned, and the past that was buried but never forgotten.

"The people on the news doubt that the plane crash was an accident," she goes on. "My son had a gentle soul. When he was a young boy, he found a little bird who had been hit by a passing car. Elias nursed this bird back to health until it could fly again. The people on the news do not see this. If they knew my son like I did, they would never believe he would cause such harm to so many people."

She turns to look into my eyes, and I know these next words are for me. "Guilt might have followed Elias, but it would not have driven him to hurt people. It would have compelled him to save them."

My breath lingers in my throat. I hear my own mother's voice drift through the room. *Because he saved you.*

"What happened next?" I whisper.

"A few days later, Elias was gone. He left a note on this table. He told us he could no longer face us. He chose to flee. I blamed myself for a long time," she continues. "His father and I made terrible mistakes. Because of this, we lost everything.

"I turned to god during this time, but he brought me little comfort. The priest told me Elias was an abomination, that this was his punishment. I could not accept that. I loved my son. I wanted him to love whomever he chose. I realized, too late, that he deserved that right. So I chose a different god, one that would accept Elias and me for all our flaws."

She turns to face the altar, and I notice for the first time that the images wrapped around the flickering candles are not of virgins and saints. They are skeletons.

"Where is Elias's father now?" I ask, afraid of the answer.

"He is no longer with us," she says. "His heart stopped one day."

"You live here on your own?" Vivi asks. "Who runs the repair shop?"

"I do," she says with a satisfied smile. "I learned many things from my husband. I considered closing the shop after he died, but then I realized a woman could repair cars just as well as any man. I decided to keep it open. Now I have two men from town who work for me."

Vivi beams at her, impressed.

"Losing everything gave me a new life," she says. "I was once only a mother and a wife. My purpose for living was to serve my sons, my husband, and my god. There was no time left for myself. Even though I would do anything to have them back, their deaths allowed me to live again."

"How did you get through it?" I ask, almost pleading. I need to know how she survived.

"I suffered for a long time. The guilt and the regret haunted me." She takes a deep breath, reliving the pain she describes. "At one point, it became too much. I knew I would have to make a decision. I could be held prisoner by the pain of the past, or I could move forward. I chose to persist." She reaches across the table and takes me by the hand. "You too must choose."

We sit at that table for hours as the candles burn nearby. She shares tales of Elias as a boy, while we share tales of Elias as a man. Together, we laugh and cry at these memories that we bring to life through the stories we tell.

"Would you like to see Elias's bedroom?" Señora Santos asks once the sunlight has become fainter.

The invitation catches me off guard, and I don't know how to respond. Vivi and Clark give me silent looks of encouragement. I nod.

"Elias and Pedro shared everything, including a room," she says as I follow her to a wooden door on the far wall. "I have learned how to live in the present, but that does not mean I must erase the past."

She opens the door. I look at her, unsure. "Go be with him," she says, her hand ushering me inside.

The door is closed quietly behind me. The room is plain. One wall displays pictures of cars that have been snipped neatly from magazines. They're arranged in straight rows, and the colours have faded over time. In a less tidy fashion, another wall is covered in pictures of wildlife. Alligators yawn, grizzly bears swat at red-cheeked salmon leaping over rapids, antelope sprint across the savannah.

Against the wall of beasts is a little wooden bed. The carved headboard is smooth and weathered from time. There's a splash of colour in the centre, oddly vibrant given its age. The strokes of paint depict a figure with a brown face, white eyes, a green suit, and a pointed hat sitting crookedly on his head. His arms and legs extend in whimsical angles around him. The identity of the figure is undeniable. Peter Pan.

The other bed is no larger, its frame constructed with the same smooth, knotted wood. Above this bed is a window with no glass. I open the shutters. The pale red boxes of the power plant sit lifelessly in the distance, casting long shadows across the bottom of the hill. I imagine Elias waking up to this daily reminder of how trapped he was between the beautiful and the ugly. I feel now what he felt then — an aching need to be free.

His bed is covered in a knitted blanket that's soft and orange. I lie on top of it, my stomach against the sheets and my face buried in the pillow, hoping to detect his scent. It smells like nothing but dust.

"I needed to do this," I whisper. "I needed to find your beginning." My eyes close, and I feel the softness of the pillow against my face.

I hear no answer except for my heart beating like a gavel in my chest. I feel no pain. The throbbing inside has left me for now. There's only my heart, its forceful rhythm evidence that I am not broken. It's the only evidence I need.

"You could have told me everything," I say, my face deeper in the pillow, "about Pedro, about the guilt. I wouldn't have blamed you." My breath escapes like ripples in a stream until my lungs feel hollow. I stay there for a moment, breathless and still, before my chest expands. "I understand though. Speaking it makes it real again. It's easier to pretend to be strong. But I wish you'd let me help you."

I picture Clark sitting beside me in our candlelit fort. I see Vivi's face struggling to make sense of the bruises on my chest. It's not too late to let them help me.

I turn onto my back and stars look down on me from the ceiling. Their paper edges are wilted and their points are no longer sharp, but the constellations hover over the room like a private sky.

I can almost hear Pedro's laughter from across the room, filling the air with innocent music. Elias is laughing as well. Two brothers in their beds, staring at a sky of paper stars, taunting god.

Hurry up, god.

Grant us a miracle.

Pronto dios.

The sunlight is a fiery shade of orange when we decide to depart. Señora Santos offers her home to us for the night, but we decline. I got what I came here for. Now it is time to go.

There is one last thing I need to do before we leave. Reaching into my backpack, I pull out the glass pillar of the Santa Muerte candle. The red wax has burned away slowly throughout the trip. I set a match to the wick before placing it beside the photograph of Elias on the cabinet. The light flickers across his face. His eyes are alive.

Señora Santos waves at us from her doorway as we drive away from the little house. Waving back at her from the front passenger seat, I see a man standing in front of the concrete wall of the repair shop. He looks to be about Elias's age. His hair is as black as a raven. One hand shields his eyes from the sun as he watches us drive away, while his other hand is buried in the pocket of his pants. He turns and disappears through the door of the shop, his white T-shirt streaked with black.

We don't say much as we speed down the highway. Clark grips the wheel from his seat beside me, uncharacteristically quiet as his eyes stay fixed on the road. The sun dips behind the mountains in the distance, and the sky above us is the colour of burning sand. A song we all know plays on the radio. Clark turns up the volume and the three of us sing along as loudly as we can, the wind streaking through our hair and carrying our voices through the air.

Without warning, mid-verse, I begin to cry. I don't feel it coming until I'm blinded by the tears. I can hear Vivi and Clark singing as my body shakes. I can't see a thing when I feel Clark's arm wrap around my shoulders. He pulls me toward him and holds me closely. I sob against his chest until his shirt is wet and my eyes are dry.

DEPARTURE

It has been fifteen days since you crashed into the frigid waters of the Arctic, and the investigation is nearly complete. The likely conclusion on the cause of the crash: undetermined. There was no real evidence pointing to your guilt. The black box was never found, and neither was your body.

I suppose the world will never know what happened in that airplane. People will tell the stories they want until you're no longer a person but a character. I suppose it's not their fault. All they can do is try to make sense of what is in front of them. To be human is to be limited — to be hopelessly, desperately small.

What they don't know is how alive you made me feel. You helped me save myself. You made me stronger when nobody else could. This is the Elias I will remember. The story I will tell is of your life, not your death.

What is life anyway if not merely a collection of stories we tell ourselves? The memories we embellish and the things we choose to forget. These illusions protect us. They help us survive.

A garden built by a prince for his princess.

A cloud of magnolias above a handsome stranger.

An underworld guarded by jaguars.

A gunshot in a black room.

A forgotten joke told in the cockpit of a plane.

A kiss in a candlelit cave.

A single flame in a lightning storm.

A boy who never got to grow up.

A deathly saint granting refuge to the abandoned.

The healing of a bruised eye.

The line between fantasy and reality is easily blurred, but you can't bury the truth. It will always find a way to surface. A story has a beginning and an end. The truth goes on.

The shadow will be with me always. I accept this. Where there is a shadow, there is light. The truth can be painful, but I don't need to face it alone.

Elias, I want you to know that I loved you. Despite your flaws. Despite your secrets. I feel closer to you than ever, now that you're finally free.

I know you're not going to answer. That's okay. I will never forget you, but I won't be held prisoner by the past. I have to move forward, one day at a time. I choose to persist.

• • • • •

"Last call for boarding," Clark says, turning to face me. "We don't have to do this today if you're not ready."

I stand motionless in the middle of the crowded terminal. My grip tightens on the handle of my suitcase as people hurry around me. Every one of them has a different story. They have their fears and their flaws, their triumphs and their tragedies.

"I can do it," I say. "Let's go home."

ACKNOWLEDGEMENTS

I once believed writing to be a solitary pursuit. I'm humbled by and grateful for how wrong I was. This novel was made possible by the support, enthusiasm, and expertise of the following remarkable people.

My lion-hearted agent, Jessica Faust, who believed in my story and never gave up on it.

Rachel Spence, Allison Hirst, Jenny McWha, Crissy Calhoun, Laura Boyle, Sophie Paas-Lang, Stephanie Ellis, Elham Ali, and the rest of the extended Dundurn team, who gave my debut novel a passionate and collaborative home.

Andrea Wesley and Vanessa Butler, my fabulous friends who gave me gentle yet honest feedback on early versions of the manuscript in exchange for wine.

Julio Castellanos-Lopez, Catalina Ramírez-Aponte, Pam Hernandez, and Janette Tobon, for refining my poor Spanish.

Adam Kemp, for taking the time to educate me on the intricacies of aviation despite my morbid questions.

Amanda Mandzij Li, Jamie Chapman, Patrick Tambogon, Sean Wesley, and Sara Wright, for offering their perspectives so freely on random things throughout the process.

Those who shared their struggles with mental health, who continue to shine light on the darker corners of the human experience.

My father and mother, who filled my childhood with books and acted as my very first editors when I became old enough to pick up a pencil.

Boozy, for keeping me inspired, curious, and calm during countless hours of writing. You deserve all the Timbits.

All my friends and family, who bring such colour to my world.

And above all, I am nothing without the love and support of Thomas — my biggest fan, most honest critic, and partner in this adventure called life. Anything is possible with you by my side.

Photo Credit: Amalie Tan

Eddy Boudel Tan's second novel, *The Rebellious Tide*, is slated for release in 2021. His work depicts a world much like our own — the heroes are flawed, truth is distorted, and there is as much hope as there is heartbreak. Besides having professional experience in communications strategy and brand design, he serves home-cooked meals to the homeless as cofounder of a community initiative called the Sidewalk Supper Project. He lives with his husband in Vancouver.